CW01429566

THE Triple THREAT

LOVE IN Dayton Valley SERIES BOOK 1

NIKKI ASHTON

Copyright © Nikki Ashton 2020 All Rights Reserved ©

The Triple Threat

Published by Bubble Books Ltd

The right of Nikki Ashton to be identified as the author of this work has been asserted by the author in accordance with the Copyright, Designs and Patents Act 1988.

All rights reserved. No part of this publication may be reproduced, stored in a retrieval system, or transmitted, in any form or by any means, without prior written permission of the publisher, nor be otherwise circulated in any form or binding or cover other than that in which it is published and without a similar condition being imposed on the subsequent purchaser. A reviewer may quote brief passages for review purposes only

This book may not be resold or given away to other people for resale. Please purchase this book from a recognised retailer. Thank you for respecting the hard work of this author.

The Triple Threat

First published September 2020 All Rights Reserved ©

Cover design – LJ Stock of LJ Designs

Edited by – Anna Bloom

Formatted by – Lou Stock of LJDesigns

This book is a work of fiction. Names, characters, places and events are products of the author's imagination and are used fictitiously. Any resemblance to actual events, places or persons living or dead, is entirely coincidental.

THE *Triple* THREAT

WARNING

This book contains scenes of a hot man in
grey sweats and no underwear
Please think twice about reading in public

DEDICATION

For my beautiful niece, Ellie May Casewell
May all your dreams come true

ACKNOWLEDGMENTS

I know these aren't usually at the front, but hey, it's been a strange year!

Goodness, I've had fun writing this book. Mainly because I got to look at pictures of some seriously hot cowboys for days on end. So, thanks to all those photographers out there who supply stock photo sites – I salute you and the pain you must suffer for your art.

Mr. A thank you as usual for making sure I sleep and sometimes move my big fat ass from the chair. Obviously, you didn't need to encourage me to eat, that's something I'd never forget to do, hence why the ass is big and fat.

I'd also like to give the hugest thanks to my wonderful little team of ladies. They're the ones who read it first and then tell me that maybe I'm not as funny as I think I am. Donna Wright, Lynn Newman and Sarah Dale, you've been *amazing*. Not only did you read the words, but you helped massively with the concept and the nitty gritty of creating the wonderful people and community of Dayton Valley. Also, I know helping me to pick my muses was a chore for all of us. The hours of pain it took for us to decide Jorge Del Rio Romero was our Hunter! (Yeah right, like looking at men for hours at a time was difficult!)

Thank you too, Kimberley Newman and Leanne Johnson for reading the final manuscript. The messages that you sent to me every day because you knew I was panicking made me smile, a lot. I love you both dearly.

Praise in abundance to Mr. Scott Eastwood. Thank you for your beautiful face and how well you fill those jeans in *The Longest Ride*. You will never know or see this, but in the words of the band Chicago, 'you're my inspiration'. Love you, Scott. Keep up the good work.

Finally, and by no means least, thank you to you for reading The Triple Threat. I hope that it brightens your day in what has been an awful year. If I make you smile just once in Ellie and Hunter's story, then I've done my job. And, if I did make you smile, and you enjoyed it a review would be much appreciated. If you didn't smile and thought it was a whole load of pants then I apologize, but a review would still be welcome.

Anyway, take care everyone, be safe and here's to a better year in 2021.

CHAPTER 1

Hunter

The girl looking over at me was damn cute. The huge rack just made her all the more delectable. Her tight jeans looked as though they'd been sprayed on, and those tits of hers were pouring out of a low-cut top.

As she looked over at me and licked her lips, I couldn't help but imagine what my dick resting between those two globes of sheer joy would feel like. Heaven I bet. Carter, my best buddy, nudged me with his elbow and growled from the back of his throat.

"She wants you man, so damn much."

"Yep," I replied, unable to take my eyes from her. "She's got a girlfriend with her too."

"I know and *she's* got the ass of a damn angel. Sheeeit, will you look at that."

I stared over at the blonde who was bent over the pool table and while it was a pretty spectacular ass, my attention was fully on her friend's tits.

"We going over there?" Carter asked, puffing out his chest.

"Yep."

"I get the bedroom."

"You had it last time," I complained, my eyes still on the prize.

"It's my fucking apartment. If you want a bed take her back to your house."

"Like that's going to happen," I scoffed. "My pop and my aunts are having a card night."

Carter chuckled beside me. "You really need to get your own place. Get your pop to build something on all that fucking space you've got."

"And what do you propose we do with all the heifers and steers?"

"There's plenty of land."

"Yeah, right next to my pop's place so what would be the point of that because you know Janice-Ann and Lynn-Ann will have their telescope aimed permanently at my bedroom window to check who is going in and out."

Carter poked me in the shoulder bringing my gaze to his. "So, what you're saying is you're going to stay living with them and your pop and not getting any, just in case they spy on you?"

"I get plenty." I said and poked him right back.

"Well, if you're happy getting it on my sofa or in the bed of your truck then..." He shrugged and turned back to the view at the pool table.

I knew what he was saying but I didn't see the point of having a house built or buying an apartment in town, particularly as the main house would be mine one day. Pop reckoned once he met someone he wanted to settle down with, he'd retire from the ranch and move into town and set my aunts up in a nice little place of their own. And yeah, you heard me right, when he found someone he wanted to settle down with – you see my pop was a good-looking bastard who was desperate to find me a stepmom and had been for the last three years. My mom had passed away seven before, when I was nineteen. It had taken Pop four years before he could even think about another woman and by then his balls were so blue, he decided it was time to screw his way around three counties to find the next Mrs. Delaney.

As I wondered where I'd fuck the brunette if she didn't like the idea of Carter's sofa, I didn't notice the person who'd joined us until I heard her.

"Oh dear, oh dear, oh dear," she said, standing close to my side. "You boys really are slumming it tonight aren't you."

"Fuck off, Ellie," Carter said.

"Just looking out for you both," she replied and folded her arms across her chest—which had to be said was one of THE best in the whole of Texas; but hey she was my best friend's little sister and a pain in the ass. Ellie Maples' tits were kinda like having a cold beer locked in a glass box on a roasting hot day—the idea of it was fantastic, but you just couldn't touch it.

"We're fine." Carter growled. "Now go home to Mom and Dad."

Ellie let out a deep belly laugh and stamped her foot hard on the wooden floor of the Stars & Stripes bar.

"Oh boys, how can you say you're fine?" she asked, turning to stand in front of us and placing a hand on each of our shoulders. "When clearly you're not thinking straight."

"How so?" I asked as I looked around her and noticed Jimmy Foster, our fire chief, had moved in on the girls at the pool table with his best friend Dusty Chalmers, owner of the town auto repair shop.

Ellie moved to block my view and smiled, her brows almost up in her hairline.

"If you were thinking straight, Hunter Delaney you wouldn't be willing to put yourselves at risk now, would you?"

"What risk?" I asked and frowned as Dusty began to talk to my brunette.

"Ellie, just go." Carter groaned and began moving away from us, his gaze on the prize. "Hunt we need to step in there quick."

Ellie reached behind her, her eyes still on me, and snagged her brother's arm and with some strength yanked him back in front of her.

"Listen," she said and leaned in close. "I know for certain you boys don't want to mess around with those girls."

Carter tried to free himself from Ellie's grip, but she held on tight. "Just cut the bullshit and leave us alone. Just because you kicked Dominic to the curb doesn't mean you can cockblock us."

Carter normally had a lot of patience, after all he needed it as a veterinarian faced with all manner of hysterical pet owners, but he rarely had any where his little sister was concerned, particularly if she was on a mission to stop him from hooking up with a hot girl. It had to be said, Ellie's favorite pastime was to try and stop us from getting our rocks off, and it had been from the first time she realized that we were no longer virgins who jerked off over pictures of the school cheer squad.

"Me cockblocking you has nothing to do with me ending things with that douchebag," Ellie whispered leaning in close. "Me cockblocking you has everything to do with the fact that Audrey Wilson has an itchy pussy."

"I didn't know she had a cat." Carter frowned. "She's never brought one to the surgery."

Ellie rolled her eyes. "Not that sort of pussy, you idiot." She pointed in the area of her crotch. "That one."

I leaned back in surprise "Woah, are you supposed to tell us that? Don't you have to follow some sort of oath that you don't tell anyone about your patient's ailments?"

Ellie rolled her eyes. "I'm a nurse on the kid's ward, Hunter, not the Sexual Health Clinic. In any case, Missy told me, and Amber told her."

"Okay." Carter sighed. "How the fuck does Audrey Wilson having an STI affect us and the two girls playing pool, who incidentally are currently being hit on by Dusty and Jimmy?"

Ellie shook her head and tapped Carter's cheek. "Because, my dear brother, she got that STI from Pauly Jansen."

"And?" I was frustrated, particularly as Dusty was leaned over the top of the brunette while she took a shot. This meant I was about ready to push Ellie on her ass so I could get past.

She glanced over her shoulder. "Pauly Jansen is known for his threesomes is he not?" she asked, turning back to us.

"Yeah, and I repeat, and?"

Carter groaned and ran a hand through his dark auburn hair. "Pauly Jansen has been there before us, hasn't he?"

"Finally." Ellie slapped her thigh and grinned at us. "Okay boys, my work here is done."

She winked at me, leaned closer and pushed her tits against my chest. I had to admit they felt pretty good, soft and comfy, a bit like a feather pillow.

"Oh, and Hunter, next time you want to look at my girls, don't make it so obvious and keep the drool from your chin."

Then she was gone with a swing to her hips as she drew the eye of every red-blooded male in the bar – except mine, of course, because Ellie Maples was one great big pain in the ass.

CHAPTER 2

Ellie

"**Y**ou want him so bad." Bronte giggled as I made my way back to her side and a welcoming bottle of beer.

I waved her away and grabbed my drink from the battered bar top. If you looked carefully at it, it still bore the indentation of my ex-boyfriend's head. I knew Penny had sanded it down and re-varnished since that night, but I think she'd only done that particular section half-heartedly, wanting to leave it as a warning for all other men.

"You might as well admit it, honey." Bronte purred and adjusted her boobs as Jason Miller the deputy sheriff walked past with her a lingering glance. "You want Hunter Delaney and that tight, tattooed bod of his. You want him to throw you over his shoulder, take you to his barn, and then fuck you until you scream so loud you wake up the cows."

As I shuddered, Bronte giggled and slapped my arm. The little bitch knew how much I hated cows. In actual fact, she knew how much they scared the living daylights out of me and she never tired of yanking my chain about it. As much as I had an irrational fear of bovines, I had a whole lot of love for my best friend, despite her not so funny jokes.

With her pretty face and waist-length blonde hair, Bronte Jackson looked sweet as sugar pie, but she was all sorts of crazy. In senior year she'd persuaded me to empty trash over Belinda Jennings car because Belinda had called me fat ass. When we were sixteen, Bronte had also been the one to convince me that we could easily jump a train to Dallas without any money. We managed it but only because when the conductor caught us, she had screamed that he'd touched her inappropriately. She was also the one who, when we were thirteen, had sneaked us into Stars & Stripes as the women of Dayton Valley enjoyed a ladies' night; that being a troupe of male strippers who weren't ashamed to slap their schlongs around. Nope, Bronte held little similarity to the sweet English lady her mom had named her after; but she was my best friend and I loved her.

"Don't," I snapped, shuddering at the thought of cows. "Ugh."

"I have no idea what your problem is with them," she replied with a roll of her eyes. "They're real cute with those long lashes and big pink tongues."

That almost made me retch.

"You've missed some fun times down on the ranch because of those animals," she added as she gave me a wistful smile.

"If you're talking about Hunter's wild birthday parties then I really don't want to know."

I had no idea where my fear had come from, but cows scared me to the point that when Hunter had his birthday party every year, I always made sure I'd been scheduled on at work. Just the thought of being within a few feet of the beasts made my skin crawl and set my nerves on edge. So, while the rest of the town's eighteen to thirty-year-old population were running riot on the Big D Ranch, I spent my time looking after sick kids.

My dad said it started when I saw a cow on the Delaney ranch when I was coming up for four years of age. Apparently, I screamed bloody murder until it was out of sight, and that was that. My mom and dad had never made a big thing of it though, probably thinking it was something I'd grow out of, but I hadn't. I'd avoided Hunter's birthday bash for years, because it was *always* in the summer and *always* outside – so *always* a chance I'd bump into a cow. They were parties which over the years had turned into wild, debauched nights where there was plenty of drink, dance, sex and skinny dipping in the huge pond at the back of his dad's house. Mr. Delaney always took his elder sisters away for the night so that Hunter and his friends could have free rein over the property, so as long as they cleared up before he got home the next day, he was pretty cool about it.

I knew I'd missed some great nights because not only Bronte, but my brother too, loved to give me every detail. Bronte usually because she wanted me to know who'd been there, what the girls had worn and what shit the guys had shot, and Carter, well Carter couldn't wait to tell me all about who he and Hunter had hooked up with, and on a couple of occasions, of the threesome they'd shared.

"Not just his parties," Bronte replied. "His aunts are pretty wild too. And as for that hot piece of ass dad of his."

I shook my head and gave my best friend a look that said I'd labelled her as sick. Jefferson Delaney was indeed a good-looking man, but the thought of Bronte riding him while wearing her favorite cowboy boots was not an image I relished. He was forty-eight and literally old enough to be her father; he was our parents' best friend for God's sake. Recently though, Bronte had insisted on telling me her fantasies whenever we bumped into him, ergo she wanted to ride him while wearing her favorite cowboy boots.

"You do know I caught him in a medical equipment closet at the hospital fucking Miss. Watkins from behind. I mean do you want to go where our most hated teacher from high school has been?"

Bronte thought about it for a few seconds and then shrugged as she took a swig of her beer. "Probably not, but it's great material for when I'm feeling horny."

She smiled and tapped her temple. I couldn't help but laugh. She was crazy but I loved her like a sister – shit, I'd swap her for my brother as a sibling anytime, he was such a dick.

"Just one question."

"Yeah," I replied.

"How come Miss. Watkins was being fucked in a hospital store cupboard?"

"She was in having a tonsillectomy."

"Ah okay," Bronte said with a nod as she looked out over the busy bar. "That'll explain why she wasn't sucking his dick, because I've got to tell you, Ellie if it were me, I'd be all over that. I bet he's built and real smooth."

As she grabbed her crotch and thrust her hips, I almost spat my beer out.

"You're disgusting," I groaned and wiped the alcohol from my chin, unable to stop the smile from breaking free.

"Yeah, but you love me. Okay," she sighed, "tell me how hot Hunter looks tonight and how does he smell? Woodsy and sexy?"

"None of the above." I turned my back to her and took a sneaky look over at the pool table where Dusty and Jimmy were now firmly wrapped around the two girls.

"Whatever," she scoffed. "Like I believe that you didn't get a lady boner when you were over there messing with him."

"I have no idea where you get this idea from that I think Hunter Delaney is hot. I don't even like him."

Bronte's eyes went as wide as saucers as she let out a loud burst of laughter. "Oh, Ellie honey, you really are dumb if you think I believe that. Anyway, what did you say to him and your brother to make them look like you'd pissed in their porridge?"

I grinned and pushed my shoulders back with pride. "Told them the two girls at the pool table had been with Pauly Jansen and probably caught his STI."

"No shit. Who told you that and who are they?"

I chewed on my bottom lip for a second as I studied my brother and his best friend. They had their backs to me, their heads close together as they laughed and joked, occasionally looking over at the pool table.

"Well?" Bronte urged.

"No one told me. I heard they're tourists from Portland passing through."

Bronte chinked her bottle with mine, winked at me and then laughed her cute little ass off.

CHAPTER 3

Hunter

"**O**h, Hunter honey," my aunt Janice-Ann called in that sweet voice of hers that I knew meant trouble. "We need you."

With one foot on the bottom stair, I let my head drop back and looked up to the huge vaulted ceiling.

"What is it Auntie J?" I called, muttering a couple of fucks under my breath.

"You'll see," Lynn-Ann, her identical twin sister added.

"Shit." When they were both together there was no getting away from them. They were like a pair of Black Widow spiders waiting to pounce. "Coming."

I strode across the hall to the den where they usually set up camp for the day, wondering what crap they were going to get me to do for them now;

move some furniture around maybe, do some gardening for them, or more than likely run into town and get them something or other that would be highly embarrassing. Last week's errand had been for hemorrhoid cream, for their eyes and not their asses, apparently.

I loved my pop's eldest sisters I truly did, but they were each as crazy as bed bugs. The fact they were identical twins only added to the craziness, they even dressed exactly the same—more often than not like they lived in the 1940's. You see their favorite film was The Notebook and they just loved how Ali dressed. What they failed to understand was that they were almost sixty-five and Rachel McAdams had only been twenty-five when she played the part. They couldn't quite pull it off. That being said, they didn't give a shit and it wasn't unusual to see them at church wearing pillbox hats, faux leopard print swing coats and satin gloves.

The rumor in the family was that they weren't actually my grandpa's kids, but that Grandma had them out of wedlock when she was only sixteen years of age, which was why there was a twelve-year gap between them and my uncle Miller. Then came my pop followed three years later by my Aunt Sherilyn. Pop said no one ever dared ask Grandma though and that Grandpa doted on them much more than the rest of his kids, so they never ever found out if it was true or not. They sure were different to the rest of the Delaney clan though, so I thought it was probably gospel. The crazy old sweets now lived with me and Pop.

A few years back they lost all the money that Grandpa had left them to a fucking crooked real estate guy. He'd persuaded them to invest in some big housing complex that didn't actually exist. They were devastated mentally and financially, so Uncle Miller offered to take them in. I think he felt it was his duty as the next oldest child, plus he had a huge six- bedroom house on a horse ranch over in New Mexico which he ran with my cousins, Turner, Mackenzie and Anderson. Thing was, my pop had always been the twins' favorite, so when Mom passed away of a heart attack at just thirty-nine, the sisters procrastinated no further about New Mexico. They told Pop they were moving in to look after us. Truth be told I think Uncle Miller and his wife, my aunt Debra, heaved a sigh of relief, but at least they had them to stay for three weeks every summer. As for Aunt Sherilyn, well she and Uncle

Brad moved to Australia a little over three years ago with their twelve and ten-year-old girls Aurelia and Aurora. That meant for forty-nine weeks of the year Pop and I were the ones who had to cope with the crazy, which was why I wasn't particularly surprised to see Pop in the den holding his arms out to his sides and being measured by Lynn-Ann.

"What's going on?" I asked, forcing a smile and acting like I didn't know that we were being measured for Christmas sweaters, just like they did every year exactly a month before Thanksgiving.

"It's a surprise," Janice-Ann chimed. "We can't tell, can we, Lynn-Ann?"

"No, we can't, you'll have to wait and see."

I looked over at Pop as he smiled down at his sisters as if they'd hung him the damn moon. He really did indulge them too much at times.

"You're going to love it." Janice-Ann clapped her hands together.

I doubted it very much. Each year was worse than the last and seeing as last year's sweater had displayed a naked Santa except for his hat, dread rushed up to me and slapped me across the face. Pop and I had laughed at the time, but when Santa's penis was all we could see when we looked at each other, it kind of spoiled our appetite for pigs in blankets when dinner was served.

"Arms out."

I held my arms to the sides and smiled at my aunt as she began to measure and then write down the numbers down in a notepad.

"When you going to get yourself a nice young girl, honey?" Lynn-Ann asked as she held the tape against Pop's arm.

"You talking to me or Pop, Auntie L?'

She giggled and smacked at my pop's arm indicating for him to lower it. "You Hunter, we all know he's never going to get another girl to take his heart like your momma did."

"There was that nice girl, Kitty," Auntie J offered. "You were real smitten with her."

Pop sighed. "I was fifteen and she moved to Florida with her folks. Broke my heart though, gotta be said."

"That's not the point," Auntie J replied as she wrote down one of my measurements. "The point is all the girls you've met recently are far from nice."

"Hey, what about Wendy?" Pop looked affronted. "She made you a chocolate cake."

"Hmm which tasted like she'd scraped it from the cow shed," Lynn-Ann muttered.

"I didn't like hearing her making all that noise either. We couldn't get to sleep could we, Lynnie?"

"No, Janice, we could not." She poked Pop in the chest. "I have no notion of what you were doing to that girl, Jefferson, but whatever it was she felt God could help her in some way."

Pop's face drained of color as he looked down at his sister as she wrapped the tape measure around his waist. I grinned at Auntie J who was giggling quietly to herself.

"She was better than the other girl though," Auntie L announced.

"Which one?" Pop asked gruffly, dragging a hand through his silver hair that was swept back like he was some damn hipster popstar—the good-looking bastard.

"Now, what was her name?" she mused. "You know Hunter, the one with the…" She rolled her hands in front of her chest to indicate what I assumed was big boobs.

"Oh, Carrie," Pop said with a sly grin. "What was wrong with her? She never even stayed the night."

"She didn't need to." Auntie J moved around to my back, stretching her tape. "She got what she needed in the barn."

"How the fu-hell do you know that?" Pop's beard quivered as he glanced between his two sisters, looking a little afraid.

"They know everything, Pop."

"He's right, we do but if you don't want us to know you're servicing your lady friend like a bull serves a cow, then shut the damn barn door."

"Reverend Roberts was here for afternoon tea," Auntie J explained to me. "And when he heard her shouting for Jesus, the Lord Above and Mother Mary he asked us if we had someone who needed guidance in our midst."

I bust out a laugh and leaned over to slap Pop's back. "All three of the almighty's, Pop, that's some going."

"Shit, you never told me the Reverend was here, I wouldn't have taken the opportunity if I'd known."

To be fair to him, Jefferson Maxwell Delaney did look a little upset, even if it proved him to be a damn stud. Pop was a legend and I hoped I was like him when I reached forty-eight.

"Didn't think we needed to tell you. You were supposed to be watching the bulls sire the cows!" Auntie J replied. "Not siring your own heifer."

I roared with laughter as Pop's eyes went huge.

"Janice-Ann," he scolded. "Watch that dirty little mouth of yours."

"Well, you watch where you pull your Johnson out of your pants in future, Jefferson, and I'll repeat, shut the damn barn door next time."

"Yes," Auntie L added. "Apart from anything else I do not want to see your little peach. When you were five years old was one thing, but not now it's a little hairier, and a lot less pert. Now stand still so I can measure your girth."

As she pulled the measure around Pop's waist, the laughter built from deep within my gut and I started to shake.

"You stand still too," Auntie J said with a wink. "I need to see if you've grown since last year."

She had all our measurements from every year in the same notebook, so she didn't really need to bother, unless I'd been working my muscles harder and eaten more. I knew I hadn't because the last time my measurements had been any different, I'd been nineteen. It was the year I'd had a growth spurt and I was pretty much as tall and muscular as Pop through helping out with the cows. It had also been the year Mom had passed away. She'd only been gone a couple of months when it came time to measure us and by then the twins had moved in. All I'd wanted to do was go to my room and not come out until Thanksgiving and Christmas were done. That year, as Lynn-Ann measured Pop and Janice-Ann measured me, as was tradition, I watched Pop watch them. We both knew how excited they were and how hard they were trying to make things better for us, so I stood there and held in the tears and the anger that my mom wasn't there. She wasn't going to watch the usual fussing that went on and to bring us all hot chocolate when they'd finished, but I smiled at my aunts and told them I couldn't wait for my surprise. When

I went to bed that night, I heard Pop cry and beg for Mom to come back to him. It was then that I became determined to enjoy my life and cherish all those I loved—which was why, right now, when Janice-Ann dropped her knitting bag on the floor, I didn't flinch or say a word when I spotted a picture of a sweater with two penguins having sex.

**

"You okay to check the herd," Pop asked as he yawned and stretched his arms over his head, cracking his spine, after dinner.

I nodded, more than happy to oblige. He looked tired and I actually loved the stillness and quiet of the cooler night air when I did my last checks of the day. My aunts always went to bed fairly early as they liked to get up with us at five-thirty and make us breakfast, so last thing at night was pretty much my only quiet time. I was more than happy to do the last checks for Pop.

We didn't have a huge herd – just ten sires and forty-five cows, but presently we also had twenty calves, a mixture of bulls and cows, which were almost ready to go to sale. Seeing as Beefmaster, our breed, were good for milk *and* beef they were pretty valuable. It wasn't unknown for rustlers to decide they wanted a slice of the action. That was why we housed our herd every night. Our land wasn't huge, but big enough that we needed horses to get around which meant plenty of places for rustlers to hide out and take our stock. Experience had also made Pop extra vigilant; when he was kid pretty much the whole of Grandpa's herd had been taken one time.

"How come you're so tired anyway?" I asked as I got up from the table.

Pop gave me a knowing look.

"Shit, Pop, do you really have to act like you're sixteen and just discovered your dick?"

I grimaced and picked up the plates to take to the kitchen.

"Hey, I'm in my prime. I have needs. You're mom and I—"

"Nope!" I exclaimed. "I do not want to know what you and Mom got up to."

Pop's eyes shone, and even though he still had a smile on his face I knew happiness was the last thing he felt. Emotion would be stuck like a huge, brittle ball of whicker in his throat. I knew this because it's how I felt every time I thought of my beautiful momma who had a heart disease that was discovered just before her and Pop married. The doctors advised her not to have a baby, but Pop said she was stubborn and determined. Apparently, they both cried when I arrived, weighing just over 9 pounds and screaming like a banshee. That was also why I was an only child. The way my aunts tell it is that Pop put his foot down when Mom wanted another baby and refused to go near her until he'd been and had a vasectomy. Mom was so mad she didn't speak to him for three weeks, but Pop eventually used his charm to bring her around and by the sounds of the stories I'd heard earlier, it must have been a come to Jesus *and* God moment for my mom.

"You don't mind, do you?" Pop asked tentatively which roused me from my thoughts. "That I see women."

"God no." Why would he even think that? He'd mourned his wife for four years when he was still a fairly young man, now he deserved some happy times. I remained grateful I didn't have to hear them too often.

"It's just no one will ever come close to how I felt about her, you know that, right?"

As I passed by his chair, I slapped a hand on his shoulder. "Yeah, Pop, I do know."

"I do have a favor though," he called after me as I walked through to the kitchen.

"Yeah, what?" I put the dishes on the counter and went to stand in the doorway that joined the kitchen to the dining room.

"Jim and Darcy Jackson have invited us over for dinner tomorrow night, with Henry and Melinda."

"Who, me and you?"

"No, you idiot. Me and Jojo, the lady I'm seeing. I was wondering if you'd drive us over there so that I can kick back and have a drink. I don't want to be worrying whether Sheriff Bennion or one of his goons is lurking in the bushes trying to catch someone out."

I groaned inwardly. I knew it would take me almost two hours to do a round trip out to the Jackson's place, but he was my dad and he'd done enough for me in the past.

"Yeah sure, no problem. Just let me know what time."

"Thanks, son," he said and got up from his chair. "I'm gonna go up, don't forget to lock up when you come back in."

"Will do. Night, Pop."

"Night son, love you."

"Love you too."

I waited to hear his tread on the stairs and smiled thinking about the conversation we'd had earlier with my two aunts. As much as I missed Mom and knew that he did too, I didn't want him to be lonely—yeah, he had a few hook-ups, but not one of the women seemed to have given him what he needed. I was worried that my mom was the only woman who would ever do that for him. That thought pulled me up short. They were married with me by the time that they were my age, yet I'd never met anyone I was remotely interested in settling down with. What if I was like Pop at forty-eight but had never experienced what he had with Mom? It was a sobering fucking thought as I remembered them laughing and joking in this very kitchen and Pop bending Mom backward over the table to kiss the breath out of her lungs.

Could I even imagine myself doing that; share my life, this home with one woman for the rest of my life?

I thought about it and looked through the window into the dark, and when the face of Ellie Maples popped into my head, I dropped one of Mom's favorite plates.

CHAPTER 4

Ellie

I looked in the rear-view mirror at my folks sitting on the backseat of my 1982 Oldsmobile Omega. Okay so it was damn ugly and the color of baby poop, but it was reliable, and my parents were currently making out on the large back seat.

"Really?" I cried and looked back to the road as Dad gave Mom's left tit a squeeze. "Child on board."

"Oh honey, don't be a spoilsport." Mom giggled, already tight from the two large glasses of wine she'd had while she'd waited for Dad to get ready after he got home late from work.

"I'm not, but I don't really want to see Dad getting to second base, thank you very much."

"Well, I'm kinda hoping for a home run later," Dad muttered, not particularly quietly.

Mom fluttered her eyelashes at him and snuggled closer to the big, broad, ex-cornerback who also happened to be her college sweetheart. According to Dad it was love at first sight when Mom walked into the gym wearing her tiny running shorts and tight tank. Mom however was only concerned with making the cross-country squad and didn't give two hoots that Dad had the best burst of any cornerback in the college game. She finally gave in and went on a date with him after a whole week of him sending her a bouquet of flowers every day.

They'd been inseparable ever since and loved each other deeply. Although they liked to argue too, mainly because they were both bull-headed. Tonight's kissing and petting in my car wasn't unusual; they liked to make up *and* make out a hella lot.

Dad's promising football career ended with an ACL injury in his last year at college. Mom had been the one who brought him back from the deep dark depths of depression. Apparently, she slapped him around the head with her sneaker as a last resort when he wouldn't look away from the TV. Dad eventually got over the life changing disappointment and now ran his own insurance company, while Mom worked part-time in the town library. All in all I had a happy family life—well if you didn't count Carter in that; he was the only fly in my bonhomie.

Thankfully, as Dad's face disappeared into Mom's neck, we pulled up outside the beautiful grey brick house. On a quiet tree-lined street, on the edge of Valley Park, which ran along almost the whole west side of town, Bronte and her folks had moved here over ten years before when they'd left the house next door to ours on the east side of town. Both Bronte and I had cried buckets even though we were going to see each other at school the very next week. Being a car ride away from each other seemed like the end of the world when we were fourteen years old.

"We're here," I announced, raising my voice to be heard over the giggling and kissing noises.

Mom extricated herself from Dad and pulled up the top of her dress to put her girls safely back inside.

"You not coming in to see Bronte, honey," she asked as she leaned between the two front seats.

"Yeah, come in and see her," Dad added. "I bet Jim and Darcy would like to see you too."

I looked down at the black yoga pants and baggy white tee which I wore and sighed. I wasn't really dressed to visit with people, especially as I had a huge stain right over my left boob. I'd dropped my chocolate ice cream as I tried to eat while I lay on my back on the sofa and watched TV. My hair was also a messy bird's nest on top of my head, and at least a day past needing a wash – okay I was a slob, but I was on day two of my three off duty days.

"Oh, come on," Mom urged. "You'll get to see Jefferson's new lady-friend when they arrive."

"Another new lady-friend?" I blew out my cheeks. "Geez that man has some stamina for his age."

Mom poked my shoulder, hard. "Eleanor Mary Maples, don't be so disrespectful about your elders."

She said the words, but I could see the smile which twitched at her red lips and her eyes sparkled with mischief. God, my mom was beautiful, no wonder Dad fell in love with her straight away. Of Native American extract, Mom had inherited the gorgeous dark hair, deep brown eyes and olive skin of her ancestors. She was tall and curvy, the muscular frame of her college running years long gone with the arrival of Carter and me. She also owned the dirtiest laugh I'd ever heard. Dad often said he kept himself in shape to make sure Mom didn't go off him and run away with someone better looking, but I doubted that there was any chance of that. Apart from my dad being blond, handsome, tall and broad, he was also kind and sweet and when he wasn't bickering with the love of his life, he treated her like a damn queen. She knew well enough that she'd found her king.

"I think the little blue pill must help," Dad said and laughed loudly as he opened the car door.

"Henry," Mom cried. "You can't say that." She scooted across the seat to follow him out of the car.

"He's one of my best friends," Dad replied as he opened my door. "Of course, I can. Come on, Ellie Belly, let's go."

I groaned. "Dad, I look a mess."

He glanced over my outfit and he grimaced slightly as he noticed the chocolate ice cream stain, but then plastered a smile on his face. "You always look beautiful and besides it's only Bronte and her folks. They've seen you looking a whole lot worse."

He was right, they had, only six weeks ago Jim, Bronte's dad, had had to come and pick us up from Stars & Stripes because Penny had refused to serve us any more drink because we were too drunk and too rowdy. It was the night that I'd slammed my ex's head on the bar, and I'd needed bourbon, the problem was that while it was nectar going in, it was poison coming back out—all over the back seat of Jim's car. The smell had also made Bronte sick to her stomach, and she puked too. To be fair to him he didn't shout, but he did wake us both up at six the next morning with a bucket of hot water and two of the smallest cleaning cloths I ever did see.

With a sigh, I swung my legs out of the car and followed my parents up the drive toward the huge dark-grey front door. We didn't even need to knock before it was swung open and we were faced with Bronte's mom, Darcy, looking perky in her skin-tight jeans and tight denim shirt, that just about covered her latest present from Jim – her new boobs. Mom and I stared at them quite openly even though we'd both seen them before. They were pretty spectacular, and it would have been rude not to give them another look. Dad to his credit barely glanced at them as he brushed a kiss to Darcy's cheek and pushed past her shouting something about catching the repeat of last night's game before dinner started.

"Hi, Ellie," Darcy said as she pulled me against her cushiony chest. "How are you, honey?"

"I'm good thanks, how are you?"

She let me go and gave me a sweet smile before she patted her blonde curls. "I'm great, loving life," she said with a singsong in her voice.

For all she sounded happy, I knew from Bronte that Darcy was worried about her mom who had Alzheimer's. She was declining pretty rapidly, so much so that Darcy had recently entered her into a nursing facility.

"Bronte home?" I asked, with half a hope that she wasn't so I could hop back into my car and get back to feast on more chocolate ice cream and Netflix.

"In her room, honey. Now, Melinda," she said as she turned to my mom, "how long do we think this latest lady of Jefferson's will last?"

As the two women started to gossip, I walked down the long hall to Bronte's room. The sound of Brett Young's *'In Case You Didn't Know'* blasted through the closed door and almost burst my eardrums when I opened it and pushed inside. Bronte, seemingly oblivious to how loud it was, or maybe had already been turned deaf by it, was on her stomach as she looked at something on her laptop. She had her legs kicked up behind her and a pair of pink fluffy slippers hung off both her feet, precariously close to Roderick the family's cat, curled up, asleep, on her pillow.

"Hey," I shouted. "You want to turn it down a little."

Bronte's eyes shot to mine and she grinned, tapping quickly on her phone screen. The music immediately went quieter leaving a buzz in my ears.

"I didn't know you were coming."

"I wasn't," I groaned. "I dropped Mom and Dad off and they insisted I come in and see your parents even though our dads are watching last night's game in the den and our mothers are gossiping about Jefferson's new girlfriend. So, even though I only saw you yesterday for lunch, here I am." I held up my hands and waved them around like some nerdy kid in Glee Club.

"I'm hiding in here because I don't want to meet Jefferson's new girlfriend." She sighed and pouted like a six-year-old.

"Seriously you need to get over that." I groaned with a grimace. "It's too weird that you have a crush on him."

"I'd just like to try the goods, that's all. I think he looks like he's packing and has a real good idea what to do with it." Bronte's smile was devilish. I'd seen that smile many times before, and things didn't always end well when it appeared.

"And that my friend is what makes you not only weird but sick too. Anyway, what are you looking at?"

"Oh, just my internet dating profile. I have thirteen messages already and I only set it up this morning."

"Why the hell do you have an internet dating profile. You have men from three counties wanting to take you out on a date. Actually," I said, tilting my head to one side to study her, "you've already dated most of the men from three counties. Maybe you should try and find someone on the internet."

Bronte narrowed her eyes and threw a small heart-shaped cushion at me. "Bitch. Now come and sit next to me. If you really want weird, read some of these messages."

I plopped down beside her as she scooted over and leaned in to read where she was pointing at the screen.

"Oh my God," I cried as I took a closer look. "That's disgusting. 'Can I lick your ass while I jerk off over your back'. Who the fuck writes that sort of shit?"

Bronte laughed and read, "Phil Ewin, apparently."

Laughing at the name, I looked at the next one "'I would smash the shit out of you, can I have your number?' Yep, he's a keeper alright. What picture did you put on here? Please tell me not your real one."

"Oh God no." She laughed. "It was the one of my mom when she was seventeen and had just won Miss Congeniality at the Galveston Beauty Pageant."

"Bronte!"

"What? She won't know and I'm closing the account down in a week."

"Why a week?" I asked as my eyes went back to the screen.

"Because that's when the new season of Outlander starts so I'll be bored until then. What?" she asked when I shook my head. "Jamie is fucking hot."

"He reminds me of Carter."

Bronte shuddered. "Ugh, now who's being sick and weird."

I tsked and went back to reading her messages, smacking down the lid on the laptop when they hit an all-time low with the guy who wanted to slap her ass with pizza dough.

CHAPTER 5

Hunter

When we pulled up at the Jackson's house, the first thing I saw was Ellie's shit colored car. It was parked badly, almost a foot from the curb and with the front end stuck out; pretty much how she always parked it. With a sigh, I pulled up behind it and turned to Pop.

"So, have a great night."

"Gee, thanks sweetie," Jojo, his new girlfriend chirped from the back seat. "We'll see you later."

"You are still okay to pick us up?" Pop asked.

I nodded and cleared my throat as two arms came around his neck and long, red nails scratched through his beard.

"I'm so excited to meet your friends, Jeff."

I frowned.

"Jeff?" I mouthed silently to Pop who gave me a tight smile before he reached into the footwell for the booze he'd brought along. As the two bottles of JD clinked in the bag, Jojo giggled.

"I think it's going to be a good night. You sure the girls will like what I bought with me though?" she asked and held up a box of wine.

Pop had said that she was classy, but in the forty-five minutes I'd known her there wasn't an awful lot of class evident. To start with—and I didn't want to be judgey—but I'd never seen a catsuit quite like it outside of an 80's Cher video, and once she'd tottered down her path in her leopard print shoes, she'd kissed the life out of my pop, in the middle of her street, with tongues. Finally, there was the box of wine which had 'Multiple not to be sold separately' stamped across it. I knew this because she had pretty much pushed it in my face to ask what I thought of it, and that was before Pop had even introduced us.

"You not coming in to say hello?" Pop asked.

I looked at Ellie's car and shook my head. I could do without her and Bronte's snark for one night. It'd been a long day, one of the bull calves had got caught in the barb-wire fence and cut itself badly. I'd had to call Carter in to come and dress the wound to make sure it didn't become infected and we lost money.

"I'm gonna go home to check on the calf and then watch some T.V. Call me when you're ready for a ride back."

"Okay, son, and I promise it won't be late."

"You could stay at mine, Jeff. I could ask my neighbor Brian to come get us. It would save Hunter the journey," Jojo said with a grin.

I held my breath and waited to hear if Pop said yes. If he did it would mean he really liked her. I knew that because he never ever stayed over at a woman's house and had only ever let one woman stay over at ours—Wailing Wendy—and even then, they'd slept in our spare room. He didn't seem to want to have anyone in Mom's bed just yet.

"No honey," he replied, clearing his throat. "We have an early start in the morning, and I couldn't impose on your friend."

Jojo didn't seem worried by it but gave his beard one last scratch before she flung open the truck door and jumped out.

I turned back to check she'd got out okay and caught sight of a red bra and a huge amount of cleavage as she leaned in to retrieve her box of wine.

Anxious that I'd let my eyes linger too long on my pop's girlfriend's assets, I quickly shot my gaze back to Ellie's poop colored car.

"Please come in," Pop growled from beside me. "I'm nervous."

I turned to him and frowned. "They're your oldest friends, why the hell are you nervous?"

He glanced out of the side window to where Jojo was inching her catsuit from the crack of her ass and heaved out a sigh.

"Ten minutes." I groaned. "And then I'm going home."

Pop grinned and clutched my shoulder to give it a squeeze. "Thanks, son, appreciate it."

***

Thirty minutes later and I was still shooting shit with Pop, Jim and Henry while the ladies hung around in the kitchen to keep watch on Darcy's starter.

"You don't think the Cowboys will get to the Superbowl final this year?" Jim asked me incredulously. "You've got to be kidding me."

I nodded and took a swig of the coke which Darcy had given to me, because I was driving, *and* because she still thought I was twelve. "Their defense is shit."

"Yeah, but they have one of the best wide receivers in the NFL," Henry added.

"Hunter is right." Pop slapped between my shoulder blades. "It ain't their year."

When the three men continued to argue, I decided that was my cue to head out and I slipped from the room. I was almost to the kitchen, when I bumped into Ellie who was leaving one of the rooms off the hall.

"Hey," I said and gave her a nod. "You visiting with Bronte?"

"Yes." She sighed. "But she drives me crazy."

Ellie whirled her index fingers around by her ears and crossed her eyes. I couldn't help but laugh at the sight of her.

"What's she done now?" I asked.

"Internet dating," Ellie huffed out and leaned with her back against the wall, her palms flat against it underneath her ass. "She's about to message some weirdo who wants to wear her underwear while he pinches her nipples."

My eyes bugged out and I almost choked on fresh air. "Say what?"

"I know." Ellie let her head drop back and she let out a strangled groan. "Ugh, she needs help."

"She's not going to meet up with him?" I asked, concerned that Bronte was about to land herself in hot water.

"No, I don't think so. She just knows it pisses me off when she does crazy things and thinks it's totally hilarious. God, if it's not your d—" She stopped speaking and slapped a hand over her mouth, her wide, horrified eyes watched me.

I laughed and poked a finger against her shoulder. "I know all about Bronte being hot for my pop, Ellie."

"You do?"

"Yeah, I do. I caught her rifling through our laundry hamper at my birthday party. She was looking for a tee that smelled of him and was going to take it home."

Ellie's face dropped. "Shit, it's worse than I thought. It's so much worse."

She looked real troubled about what I'd said and I wondered if maybe I should have kept quiet. To be honest though, I thought it was pretty funny that a girl a couple of years younger than me was crushing on Pops. If nothing else, it proved how damn hot he was, and I liked to think that I looked like him.

"Ellie," I soothed and took a step closer to her. "It's all good. It's just a crush."

Ellie's eyes snapped to mine. "She stole his clothes, Hunter, just so she could smell him. It's not all good."

I rumbled a low laugh as Ellie began to pace up and down the hallway. After I'd watched her do three passes, I decided to pull her to a stop.

"Hey." I grabbed her hand and wheeled her around to face me. "Cool it, it's not like Pop is going to return any feelings she has, if that's what you're worried about."

She stared at me and I could almost hear her brain whirling. "I know that, but it does mean that she'll do everything in her power to either a, forget him, or b, which is so much worse, make him jealous."

"And?"

"And," she said, tugging her hand from mine. "That means she'll be irresponsible, indiscreet and downright idiotic. You have no idea what she'll come up with. The damn internet dating is only the start of it."

I watched Ellie as real fear sparked in her eyes. I felt kinda bad for telling her about Bronte and the laundry hamper. It was obvious how much she cared for Bronte and how much she evidently had to take care *of* her and stop her from doing anything stupid—which if I knew Bronte, was pretty often.

"You want me to get Pop to talk to her?" I asked.

Ellie glared at me. "God, no. That would only make it a challenge for her. No, we have to think of something else."

She started to pace again, and my head moved from left to right as I watched her until she eventually came to a stop.

"I know what we have to do," she announced and planted herself in front of me, her hands on her hips.

"We?" I asked, my brows almost disappearing into my hairline.

"Yes, we," she answered with more than a hint of exasperation. "You have to help me get her to fall in love with someone else. Otherwise, if you don't the worst thing possible could happen; Bronte could end up as your step-mom."

The idea was ridiculous, but Ellie sure did sound worried. I muttered a curse and looked up to the ceiling. This was not what I wanted to be doing on a Friday night. I should have gone home when I had the chance.

"I'm not sure—"

Ellie didn't even let me finish. "No, Hunter, you have to help me. You have no idea what a handful she can be. I can't do this on my own."

"Ellie, don't you think you're maybe overreacting?"

She shook her head. "Nope. She's been my best friend since pre-K. I know exactly what she's capable of."

I groaned and nodded. "Okay, so who do you recommend we get her to *fall in love* with. The way I see it, most men in this town would love a shot with Bronte, and if I'm reading her right, Bronte would not want a shot with any man who would want a shot with her. So, who do you propose?"

Ellie beamed. "It's obvious."

"To you maybe, but not me," I replied with a shrug.

"Who do you know who can't stand to be around her, who she irritates more than a fly would."

I frowned and tried to think who Ellie could mean. There was no one, except…

"Shit no," I almost shouted. "Not happening. He'd be more likely to kill her, and I do not want that blood on my conscience. Nope, sorry, Ellie but I ain't helping."

"Please." She pouted and crossed her arms over her chest, which meant my eyes were dragged toward it and the dark brown stain above her left tit, which then meant my eyes zeroed in on the actual tit, and my dick woke up.

"Hunter," she snapped, poking a finger in front of my eyes. "How many times do I have to tell you? Look at my face, not the girls, and concentrate. Will you or will you not help me to save our parents' friendships by getting Bronte to fall in love with Carter and vice versa?"

Before I had time to say, 'hell no' Bronte appeared from her room and filled the hallway with laughter.

"Oh my God," she exclaimed. "That guy was the weirdest. I really need to keep messaging him, if only for the laughs."

"Bronte," I groaned and rubbed a hand down my face. "What the hell are you doing?"

"I'm getting a coke and some Cheerios to keep me going while I converse with Mr. Flirty as he calls himself."

"He doesn't mean that," Ellie snapped. "He means what are you doing by internet dating in the first place, and what are you doing by messaging those douchebags?"

"Ah chill," she said and flapped a hand at us. "It's fun. I have nothing or no one else to amuse me."

I saw the way she smirked at Ellie. When the sound of my pop's laugh unexpectedly rang from the den, I also saw how Bronte's eyes went wider and she pushed her tits out. Fuck, she really did have it bad for my old man.

"Okay." I breathed out. "I'm in."

Ellie's head turned in my direction and she glared at me.

"In what?" Bronte asked, as she began to walk toward the kitchen.

"Hunter offered to help me with the hospital fundraiser," Ellie answered quickly.

I was glad that she'd thought on her feet, but I also realized that she would finally get me to do what I'd always said I wouldn't. Now she'd said it to Bronte, I'd have to agree and actually take part in the damn calendar. She had me. When I looked over to her, the sneaky little witch was grinning like a Cheshire cat and I knew I was right.

"Oh my God, Hunter." Bronte stopped in her tracks. "You always say no."

"Yeah," I muttered. "I know."

"Ellie, what did you do to make him finally agree?"

Ellie shrugged. "Nothing, he just agreed."

I looked at Ellie with narrow eyes, warning her that something would definitely be coming up that would mean I'd regretfully have to pull out.

"Hey, what's going on?" a voice half-way between boyhood and manhood croaked behind us.

We all turned to see Bronte's youngest brother, Austen, sloping out of his room with a pair of huge earphones hanging around his neck. He was thirteen and tall for his age, and by the sound of his voice, his balls were about ready to break free from the confines of his abdomen.

Bronte squealed with excitement and clapped her hands. "Hunter has agreed to help Ellie with the hospital fundraiser."

"And that's exciting, why?" Austen asked, blinking through his blond bangs.

"Because he always says no," Ellie replied as she gave me a sneaky wink.

Austen shrugged. "I'll help."

The way he looked at Ellie I had a feeling we had another little crush going on.

"You're too young buddy," Ellie said, roughing his hair.

"If Shaw was home, you'd ask him," Austen grumbled, evidently a little pissed off that his elder brother was probably everything he himself wanted to be.

Shaw was nineteen and currently at Harvard Law no less. Not only did he have brains, but he was a good-looking bastard too; a smarter version of Jax Teller with his buzz cut was how I'd heard him described by more than one of the Dayton Valley ladies when he came home during his college breaks. He was also Austen's hero. The poor kid had cried for almost a week when Shaw had first gone off to school.

"When you're eighteen," Ellie said softly. "You'll be the first person I ask."

Austen's pout slowly disappeared, and he stared at Ellie, silently swearing her to promise.

"Hey," Bronte shrieked and slapped a hand against her leg. "I have an idea."

"No," I replied and wagged a finger at her. "I'm not doing it naked."

"No stupid," she said and rolled her eyes. "Why don't we get your dad to do it with you. Two Delaney's for the price of one."

Ellie's quiet groan sounded pained as she clutched at her stomach.

"Oh God, yes. Hunter and Jefferson Delaney, Mr. January and Mr. February respectively in the 'Hunks of Dayton Valley' calendar. And," she said with a gleam in her eye. "Both of you naked for December. It'll be epic."

I knew then that I'd get Carter and Bronte together if it was the last thing I did. If I remembered correctly, I had two months to do it until the calendar started shooting

CHAPTER 6

Ellie

I t had been a week since Hunter had agreed to help me with the Bronte situation and I hadn't seen neither hide nor hair of the stupid cowboy. It was pissing me off.

He'd promised to help get Bronte and Carter together but staying up at the ranch and not even calling my brother was not helping. I knew he hadn't spoken to Carter because I'd called at my brother's apartment twice over the last week to 'hang out' and find out what I needed to know. When I'd asked Carter the first time if he'd heard from Hunter, he'd looked at me suspiciously and then accused me – *yes me* – of crushing on his best friend.

Ugh. As if.

On my second visit I'd been a little more subtle and grabbed his cell and taken it to the bathroom with me to check his calls. Thank goodness my brother was an imbecile and used the same passcode for everything – Blake Lively's birthday; he was obsessed.

While I peed, I scrolled and found nothing recent from Hunter. Although I did find a text from a few months before where he'd told Carter he was worried about me being with my douche of an ex. It seemed I looked permanently sad. My loving brother's response was: 'did I lend you my red button down?'. Yeah, I definitely won big time on the brother stakes.

I managed to drop his cell back down the side of his favorite gaming chair and then made myself scarce. The smell of farts, sweaty socks and unwashed bodies being too much to handle any longer than necessary.

The one thing I hadn't done and wished I had, was to take down Hunter's number because then I could have called him myself. Problem was, I'd been too busy wondering why he'd felt it necessary to tell my brother that I looked sad, and also thinking about my need to buy new panties as I looked down at the once white and now greyish ones around my ankles.

Hunter and I had never been close enough that I needed his digits, but they really would have been useful the last week. Especially as Bronte had mentioned with glee that Jefferson and his lady friend, Jojo, had argued at her parents' house at Friday night's dinner. It had resulted in Jojo storming into the yard and sitting out there for over twenty minutes until Jefferson finally went out to talk to her.

"Can you go and help out in the ER?" A breathless voice roused me from my thoughts. I whirled around on my seat at the nurse's station to see Mimi, our hospital administrator, breathing heavily and clutching at her side.

"Sorry, hon, I ran up here. I'm trying to get some weight off my tush and I kind of underestimated how long three flights of stairs actually are."

When I noticed her glasses had begun to steam up, and her blouse was pulled from the waistband of her skirt, I couldn't help but smile. Mimi was a little like a comfy sofa; all soft and squishy and coming apart at the seams.

"What's the deal with ER?" I asked as I got up from my chair and moved around the desk.

We were a hospital that served three small towns, the closest being Dayton Valley, but even so we weren't often short staffed for the number of patients we had. The kid's ward which I worked on rarely had above ten patients on it, which was why I worked on a small rotation of six staff members.

"There's been a stomach flu epidemic down there." Mimi groaned, making a face as though she was about to puke herself. "They're down to two nurses and one doctor and seeing as we've just had six people come in who were in a car accident on the Western Lake road, we need your help."

I knew I was an obvious choice. I'd started my career in the hospital on the ER until a place had come on Pediatrics, which was what I'd majored in.

"Okay, let's go," I said and guided Mimi with a hand to her elbow. "But we'll use the elevator."

***

Most of the casualties from the accident had been patched up and sent home or sent for x-rays. Things were finally calm. I'd persuaded the two nurses and a doctor to go and grab a quick break while I held the fort, knowing I could call them back if I needed to.

No one had been in or out of the ER for almost a half hour and Beth, the receptionist, and I were both taking the time to catch up on paperwork, so when the next person to come to the desk was Hunter, I was a little surprised.

"Hey," I said and stood up to greet him. "What brings you here?"

He pulled up his shirt to reveal deep black bruises along his side. "Your brother was checking on a calf and like an idiot, I walked behind it just as Carter injected it with antibiotics."

I leaned over the desk to take a closer look. "Sheesh, looks painful. Does it hurt?"

He shook his head. "Nope, but Pop insisted I get it checked out for broken ribs, so here I am."

"Beth can you check Hunter in, please," I said and pushed my chair back.

"Sure, honey. Hey, Hunter," Beth sighed. "Not seen you for a while." She flashed her blue eyes at him and flicked her long blonde hair back over her shoulder. If she hadn't been Beth, I'm sure Hunter may well have flirted back. Beth was a good-looking woman but not known for being particular about the men she took to her bed. I mean I didn't judge her for it; her fiancé had been killed in Iraq when they were only twenty and three months from getting married. Since then, Beth had enjoyed a lot of attention in the bedroom department and didn't care who knew it.

"Hey Beth, how you doing?"

"Better than you by the looks of it, honey." She gave Hunter her bedroom smile again, but when he turned to watch me walk toward him, she gave up and continued to book him in. I grabbed a clipboard and chart from the desk and ushered Hunter down to one of the examination rooms.

Once I'd pulled the drape I rounded on Hunter.

"Where've you been and why haven't you been trying to get Carter to fall for Bronte?" I whispered.

Hunter took a step back and put his hands to his hips, with a wince I should add.

"I've been busy," he retorted. "I have cows to look after. And who says I haven't been trying?"

"Carter. He said he hadn't heard from you all week, and I checked his phone." I poked my head around the drape to make sure no one was hanging around. The last thing I needed was to get into trouble for not caring for a patient and interrogating him instead. When I saw the coast was clear, I pulled my head back inside. "She's going to do something stupid; I know she is."

Hunter ran a hand down his face. "Ellie, don't you think you're overreacting a little. My pop isn't interested in Bronte."

My eyes widened and I felt the nerve endings of my hair bristle at his stupidity. "Hunter your pop is a dog, in the nicest possible way. My dad does jigsaws for a hobby, your dad does women. So, you really think if a hot twenty-four-year-old comes on to him he isn't going to give it a thought?"

Hunter frowned and shook his head. "He's best friends with her dad. So, no, he isn't."

He had a point, but I knew *my* best friend. "Well, you really don't know Bronte then. She won't care as long as she gets to do the nasty with your dad. That'll be all she cares about. I'm telling you her crush is getting worse."

"And I'm telling you, you're overreacting. Now do you think you could look at my damn ribs some time this century?"

I knew he was right; I had a job to do, but it didn't stop me worrying about Bronte and Jefferson. We would have to continue our chat another time. I pointed to the bed.

"Halle-fucking-lujah," Hunter grumbled.

"Okay," I said once he'd hopped up on the bed, his legs dangling over the side. "Take your shirt off and I'll check it out."

Hunter undid the cuffs and the top few buttons of his flannel and then taking the bottom of it, pulled it up and over his head. He winced as he threw it to one side and while his eyes were closed in a grimace, I risked a quick 'non-medical' look at his abs. Damn he was ripped. I had time to quickly count at least six deep ridges of muscle. There was no doubting he was sexy and hot. Tattoos adorned his chest and biceps, not so many that you couldn't see his smooth, golden brown skin, but enough to make him look like a bad boy who you knew would ruin you in the bedroom. Of course, I had no clue whether he was good in that department, he was my brother's best friend, he was a pain in the ass, and he was a cocky son of a gun at times. The fact that the sight of his naked torso got me a little hot under my scrubs, made me take a step back and shake myself.

I soon got back into nurse mode; felt around Hunter's ribs, asked him to take deep breaths, and then to twist his body from side to side. Despite the black and blue bruising, Hunter said he didn't feel any extra pain when he did all the things I asked, so I was pretty sure the ribs were intact.

"I'm confident they're not broken," I finally said after listening to his breathing. "But I can send you for an x-ray if you want to be sure."

Hunter shook his head. "Nope it's fine. I've had a broken rib once before and this feels nothing like it. I'm good. I only came because Pop insisted."

I wrote on the chart and held it against my chest as Hunter twisted to find his shirt. The muscles in his body were strong and taunt, and all moved in unison which made my damn mouth water. I'd fallen out of nurse mode and had slipped back to 'woman who hadn't had a man induced orgasm for nine weeks. Of course, my eyes fell to the bulge in his jeans. He wore a leather belt and the big brass buckle sat right on top, like some sort of billboard alerting me to the fact that there was a sale on huge dicks. I squirmed but still couldn't take my eyes off Hunter as his shirt slithered down his body and disappointingly covered up his abs and the sexy little trail of hair that disappeared into his jeans down to that huge dick that I'd been imagining and salivating over.

"You okay?" he asked as he lowered himself off the bed. "You seem a bit out of it."

I literally shook myself and cleared my throat. "It's just a little stuffy in here."

"Yeah," he said and wiped his brow. "It kinda is. So, I'm good to go?"

I scribbled something else on the chart and then looked back up at him. "I'm going to ask the doc to prescribe you some pain relief but he's having a quick break. You okay to hang around until he's back?"

"Yeah," Hunter sighed, looking up at the clock on the wall. "Pop was busy with a buyer when I left. I'll have to wait for him to come get me anyway. Don't know why he didn't just let me drive here, but he damn well insisted Carter give me a lift."

"I'm off in a half-hour," I said without thinking. "I can give you a lift."

"No Ellie," he protested. "Going out to the ranch is out of your way."

As he said the words 'going out to the ranch' I realized that meant going to the place where the cows lived. Oh shit, maybe I'd withdraw my offer and agree it was *way* out of my way.

"But if you're happy to," Hunter said before I had a chance to speak. "It'd save Pop coming out."

I smiled tightly and whipped back the drape of the examination room.

"It'd be my pleasure," I replied wondering whether it would be okay to push Hunter out of my moving car because that way, I wouldn't even need to stop

CHAPTER 7

Hunter

As I followed Ellie to her car, I couldn't help but enjoy the view of her ass in her blue scrubs. It had a rhythmic swing which made me want to shout 'boom, boom, boom' in time with its movement. As for her rack in the top with bugs and flowers all over it, which I reckoned was especially for the kids, well, she wore the usually ugly uniform damn well.

The fact that the last couple of times I'd seen her I'd found my eyes attracted to her tits didn't sit well with me; she was Carter's little sister. Yes, she was hot, no doubt about it, but she'd always looked the same, the same mocha colored hair, big chocolate eyes and pretty pink lips. The only thing that changed about her over the years had been her curves, which for some reason I'd only just realized existed.

The human brain sure was weird.

"Thanks for this," I said as I kicked a plastic drink carton out of the way in the footwell of the car.

She reached forward, picked it up and threw it onto the back seat. "No problem. Sorry it's a little messy in here. I've had a busy week pulling double shifts because Cindy is on vacation."

"No problem," I replied glancing through the window to the blue sky outside. "I'd be more worried about the color of the actual car if it were me, not the trash on the inside."

I grinned and didn't look at her until I heard a snort of laughter.

"It's reliable," Ellie said before she poked her tongue out at me. "The color is irrelevant."

"Hmm, if you like a car the same shade as baby poop."

Ellie laughed a little louder and started the car. "That's exactly how I describe it. I think that's why I got such a good deal on it. Dusty said it was in great condition for its age, so it can only be the color that put it at a thousand dollars under the list price."

"I think I'd probably agree and the fact that it is such a good car, I'd suggest you should take better care of it."

Ellie shrugged as she maneuvered out of the parking lot and pulled onto the main road. "Like I said it's been a busy week. I don't normally use it as a four-wheeled trash can."

"Good to know," I replied and glanced at her profile.

Her nose had a little wrinkle in it and there was real concentration on her face.

"Do you need glasses?" I asked.

Ellie took a sharp intake of breath and threw a quick glance at me before she turned back to the road.

"There's nothing to be ashamed of," I said, cranking down the window an inch to let in the breeze and let out the smell of burger and fries.

"I'm not ashamed," she snapped. "I forgot to put them in my purse."

"Should you be driving?" I instinctively reached up for the 'oh shit' handle and held on tight.

"Stop being a pansy." Ellie slapped a hand at my arm. "I'm a perfectly safe driver, with or without my glasses."

I raised my eyebrows and coughed out a laugh. "If you say so, Ellie."

"I do say so, and if you're that scared you can always walk."

As we'd just passed the seven-mile marker to get back into town, I decided to keep my mouth shut and trust her driving ability.

We remained silent for a couple of miles until I heard Ellie take a breath as if she was about to speak but the silence continued for a couple more minutes until she took another, followed by quiet again.

"Spit it out, Ellie," I groaned wincing as we hit a bump in the road which jarred my sore ribs.

"I just… well I just think you should take it seriously about Bronte and your dad."

Shit not again. I was sick of talking about a subject which I thought was totally unnecessary.

"He's dating Jojo, he's forty-eight years of age, and he's her daddy's best friend. Listen carefully to me, Ellie. It. Ain't. Gonna. Happen."

"Hah well there's the problem with your argument." She briefly took her eyes off the road to smirk at me. "Bronte said your pop and Jojo had a bust up during dinner and that Jojo sat in the Jackson's backyard for twenty minutes before he went out to talk to her."

I reeled back a little in my seat. "I didn't know that. They seemed okay when I picked them up. How were they when you got there for your folks?"

Ellie pressed her foot down on the accelerator and her grip tightened on the wheel.

"Loaded," she barked. "All six of them. I had to practically pour my dad into the car and then had to listen to him and my mom whispering sweet nothings to each other all the way home."

I let out a laugh. That pretty much summed up my own journey home. I'd been a little late picking up Pop and Jojo because I'd fallen asleep on the sofa and missed his first two calls, so Ellie's mom and dad had already left.

"Same here," I sighed. "So maybe Bronte got it wrong Pop and Jojo were pretty happy in the back of my truck."

I watched Ellie as she chewed on the inside of her mouth, her eyes narrow as she evidently contemplated what I'd said.

"Hmm maybe." She drummed a beat on the steering wheel for a few seconds and then blew out a breath. "Do you like her? Jojo I mean."

Did I like Jojo? How the fuck did I answer that? At least not without coming across as a rude douchebag who didn't think my pop's latest girlfriend was fit to lick my dead mom's boots.

"She's nice enough." It was the best I could come up with.

"But?" Ellie asked, glancing at me.

There were a whole lot of buts. I felt bad saying them though as Pop seemed to like her. I decided to go with partial honesty.

"But she's not my mom."

As I stared out of the side window, I heard Ellie take a sharp intake of breath, but I couldn't look at her. I didn't want to see the sadness on her face. I had enough of my own to deal with.

"What do you miss most about her?" Ellie asked, her tone tentative.

I considered not answering and accusing her of being too nosey, but the need to talk about Mom was greater than the worry that I might break down in front of Ellie.

"Her smell," I replied with a smile. "She always wore the same fragrance; *Miss Dior* and it smelled flowery and feminine. We have lots of video films of her, you know holidays and birthdays, so I still get to hear her voice and see her, but that smell is gone from the house."

Ellie gave a soft whimper beside me and I turned to see her swipe a hand at her cheek.

"You could buy the fragrance," she offered with her eyes dead ahead.

"Pop doesn't know I know, but he started to about a year after she died. I figured he must have finished Mom's original bottle because I went up to tell him dinner was ready and saw him unwrap it and spray it on his pillow." I sighed as I remembered how the cry of pain had caught in my throat as I watched Pop from the doorway. "I went back downstairs and pretended I hadn't seen it."

"Why?" Ellie asked, her voice gentler than I'd ever heard it before.

"Because it was his private moment. It was him trying to find a way to cope with the death of the love of his life. I didn't want to invade on that."

I turned to look at Ellie who had her eyes focused on me, there was a tremble to her bottom lip.

"I went back up there while he did the last check of the night, but it didn't smell the same." I swallowed hard and turned back to watch the trees blowing in the breeze. "It didn't smell like Mom, and no matter how often I sneak into Pop's room and take that bottle of fragrance out of his drawer and smell it, it still doesn't remind me of her."

Ellie blew out a shaky breath but otherwise remained silent as she concentrated on the road ahead. I looked out too, but from the corner of my eye noticed that she kept glancing at me. I thought about telling her not to worry about me, but I didn't want to bring the subject of Mom up again. I wanted to talk about her, but like every other time I did, it broke my damn heart all over again. Now I'd have to let it heal until the next time I felt the need.

After a few minutes I couldn't stand the silence any longer and reached over to turn on the radio. Sam Hunt's *'Body Like a Back Road'* was playing and Ellie immediately started to sing along. Shit she was bad.

She kept one hand on the wheel while the other swung around in the air, punching in time to the beat while she crowed like a rook about driving with her eyes closed and knowing every curve like the back of her hand. I'd heard about folks being tone deaf but had never experienced it until now. Ellie was making my damn ears bleed.

I turned in my seat to watch her as she bounced around, her voice growing louder and louder and higher and higher, until on the final note I looked over my shoulder to check we weren't being chased by a pack of dogs.

When the next tune slowed things right down, Ellie pulled her shoulders back and gave a big smile like she was real proud of herself.

"What the actual fuck?" I couldn't stop the belly laugh bursting to get out.

Ellie's gaze snapped to mine and if looks could kill, my pop would be burying me tomorrow. "What?" she asked.

"What the hell was that?" I poked a finger into my ear and wiggled it around.

She curled a lip at me and then turned back to watch the road. "I was in the choir."

"Really?" I asked incredulously. "Was it a choir for the deaf?"

"You think you're so funny, don't you? Well, let me tell you, I had a solo in the Thanksgiving festival when Bronte and I were in middle school."

"Seriously, they let you sing on your own? Was it in an empty room or something?"

I let out another burst of laughter and then winced as I felt my ribs complain.

"Serves you right," Ellie grumbled. "And no, I sang in front of the whole school. I'm surprised you don't remember. I was a triumph according to Miss Gruber at the Dayton Valley Press."

I trawled my memory banks to recall Ellie being called a triumph, but I had nothing. To be honest, I failed to see how anyone could call that noise a triumph. She sounded like a bobcat that I once trapped in the barn. In fact, the angry little critter sounded a whole lot better than Ellie did in full voice.

"Wasn't Miss Gruber the one who wore hearing aids? Or hey," I said as I held my aching side. "Was that after she'd heard you sing?"

Ellie actually growled and put an extra swing into the turn she took as she pulled off the main road to the track leading up to the ranch.

"Some people are so damn rude," she muttered under her breath as she reached to turn off the radio. "Next time you can wait for your dad to pick you up."

"No problem," I replied. "He at least can hold a tune."

That was it for Ellie, I'd evidently said too much. She slammed her foot down on the brake which jerked me forward so far in my seat, I almost hit my head on the dash.

"For fuck's sake, Ellie," I groaned. "My ribs."

"Oh no," she mocked, with a flutter of her eyelashes and a hand against her heart. "Did I hurt you? I'm so sorry."

The pain stung like a red-hot poker in my side and I really wanted to punch something. Ellie's dash was looking favorite.

"I could report you for dereliction of duty." I blew out a couple of quick breaths. "That and cruelty to the world with that fucking awful singing voice."

"There's nothing wrong with my singing."

"You think?" I asked, laughing disbelievingly.

I'd never really seen Ellie mad before, but she was now. She actually snarled and slammed her hand against the steering wheel as we jolted to a stop.

"Get out," she growled and leaned across me to grab the handle and open the door. "You can walk the rest of the way."

"*What!*"

"You heard me," she said, folding her arms over her chest. "Get out and walk"

With my eyes as wide as dinner plates, I looked out of the window up the long track that led to the house. It was another mile and a half and while normally that wouldn't bother me, today I had been kicked by a bull calf with a grudge and was in a lot of pain.

"Aww, come on, Ellie. Don't be so stupid."

And that was totally the wrong thing to say. It wasn't enough that she'd already opened my door, she actually unbuckled her belt, got out of the car and stormed around the hood, pulled the door wide open, and invited me to leave her shit-colored vehicle.

"Enjoy your walk," she hissed as she leaned in closer to me. "And don't forget to take your painkillers."

"Seriously?"

Ellie jutted her tiny chin out and tapped a foot. "Yep, seriously, Hunter."

"I was joking, come on, Ellie."

"Goodbye, Hunter," she ground out.

By the way she was breathing heavily through her nostrils I knew she wasn't going to change her mind, so I snatched open the belt and dropped my feet to the dry, dirt ground. The track was bumpy, the sun beating down, and what would normally be a little stroll for me was going to be murder on my aching ribs.

"Well thanks for the help, Ellie," I said as I leaned into her space. "Really appreciate it."

She gave me a smirk of satisfaction and I had a sudden urge to throw her over my knee and smack her ass—I'm pretty sure I would have if I hadn't been in so much pain.

"Sometimes you can be a real bitch, you know that."

She nodded. "I know and sometimes you can be a real dick. I reckon that makes us equal."

As I walked away, I looked over my shoulder wondering whether she might change her mind, but she was already walking back to the driver's side of the car. A couple of things stuck in my head as I watched her, and both made me feel uneasy. First off, her ass looked fucking amazing with the extra swing of anger in it and second, well shit, my dick seemed to agree with my head.

CHAPTER 8

Ellie

I had been wracking my brain for a couple of days on how I could bring Carter and Bronte together, but nothing was forthcoming and the reason – they damn well hated each other. As for Hunter he'd been about as much use as chocolate coffee pot. He'd actually dropped my call twice after I'd called the house and got his cell number from Janice-Ann. I'd told her it was about his pain medication for his ribs, and she seemed to believe me because she spent the next twenty-minutes telling me all about the yellow bruising that was creeping up his side.

I was probably overreacting about Bronte's crush on Jefferson, but I knew her, and she was likely to do something real stupid that would have a devastating effect on all our families.

If for any reason she managed to persuade Jefferson into her bed, there would be no way that all our parents would be able to remain friends. It would cause a huge split in their little group, a group in which most of whom, bar my mom, had been friends since high school; a group who had helped Jefferson through the hardest time in his life.

Mine and Bronte's dad had stayed with Jefferson for two days while he cried and drank bourbon after Sondra's passing: they'd been his rocks. Sondra had also been Mom's closest friend and had been from the minute she'd moved to Dayton Valley to marry Jefferson at twenty years of age. Mom hadn't been here long either, plus they were a similar age. They became firm friends, welcoming Darcy when she started to date Jim a year later. My mom still to this day, cried for her lost friend. They were a real close group; we'd even been on camping trips together when we were kids. To think that Bronte's need to bed Jefferson might ruin all of that was totally unacceptable. I had to stop her.

I would have had more faith in Jefferson to keep her at arm's length if he wasn't such a dog with the ladies, but he seemed to be on a one-man crusade to bed as many women as breaths he took; evidently where Hunter got it from.

The thought of Hunter made me growl. Mom threw me a look.

"What the hell's wrong, baby?" she asked as she put a huge plate of chicken parmesan in the middle of the table. "That face you're pulling is ugly enough to crack a looking glass."

"Gee, thanks, Mom," I muttered, picking up my cell and considered calling Hunter, *again*.

"You know what I mean. Stop splitting hairs with me. So, you going to tell me?"

I looked up at her and pursed my lips as I thought about it. If I told Mom I knew she would help me, and it did look like Hunter was going to be any use at all. I opened my mouth to say something when Dad came into the dining room holding a bottle of wine.

"Hmm, smells good." He slid an arm around Mom's waist and kissed the side of her head. "Thanks, sweetheart."

"Can you go call your brother please, baby." Mom smiled warmly at Dad, her interrogation forgotten as he took his seat at the head of the table and made goo-goo eyes at her.

They were in a damn romantic mood today and that could be even more annoying than their bickering mood or their horny mood. Romantic mood saw them smiling dreamily, giving little kisses and holding hands at any opportunity. At least the horny mood usually saw them disappear to their room for a few hours which meant I didn't have to witness their weirdness.

Glad of a few seconds of respite from the smoochy noises as Mom moved behind Dad to wrap her arms around his waist, I went to the bottom of the stairs and shouted for Carter. He had come over for Thursday night dinner and had been taking a call in his old room for the last ten minutes.

"*Carter*," I yelled for a second time when he didn't appear straight away. "Dinner."

"Okay, okay," he complained as he emerged from his room. "I'm coming." He started to descend the stairs as he pocketed his cell.

"Who was that?" I wondered if it was Hunter and he'd actually started with our plan.

"No one you know," he said as he jumped the last two stairs and ruffled my hair. "A friend."

His grin was lazy and there was a definite gleam in his eye, which could only mean one thing, it was a girl.

Shit.

I hung back and pulled out my own cell and fired off a quick text to Hunter.

Me: Stop ignoring me you douche. We have a plan to put in place and Carter has just called a girl, so we don't have much time. It's Ellie btw.

I looked at the screen for a few seconds to check whether the dancing dots appeared, but there was nothing – Hunter was still ignoring me.

"Ellie, baby," Mom called. "Dinner is getting cold."

"Coming." I glanced at my cell once more and when I was sure Hunter wasn't going to answer I put it back into the pocket of my sweats and joined my family for dinner.

***

"Really, Ellie," Carter groaned. "Could you not have just stayed home with Mom and Dad?"

Carter had actually taken a call from Hunter over dinner asking if he wanted to meet at Stars & Stripes for a beer. I'd seen it as an opportunity. An opportunity to see Hunter and ream his ass out for ignoring me, and then to get him to start the damn plan. What the plan was, I had no idea, but I'd think of something. In the meantime, he could start by bigging up my friend to my brother at any chance he got.

"I have a late shift tomorrow and I feel like a beer. Plus, you did see that Mom had her hands down Dad's pants while he was washing the dishes, didn't you?"

Carter shuddered. "Ugh, they're fucking forty-eight, they need to stop all of that shit, it's gross. What is it with all the old folks around here? They're a bunch of horn dogs."

"I know, although it is quite sweet that they still find each other hot." I looked out of the window and smiled as I thought about our parents, knowing that they'd probably be making the most of their alone time. I knew I should have left home by now, but apart from the fact I was too lazy to look for and move into an apartment, I loved my Mom's cooking too much. Also, I hated being on my own and Bronte had made it pretty clear she wasn't leaving her pink princess bedroom until the right man came along. Getting her as a roommate wasn't going to happen.

"You can't hang with us all night," Carter said as he threw me a glare. "So, unless you call Bronte to come join you, you're gonna be lonely."

"Why can't I stay with you?" I snapped and poked his bicep. "You're so damn mean."

"I'm out with my buddy, I do not want you hanging around and ruining any chance I have of getting some action."

"I didn't realize it was like that with you and Hunter." I grinned.

"Fuck off, you know what I mean."

"Carter, it's a Thursday night. Who the hell do you think is going to be in Stars & Stripes looking for action on Bingo night? Unless of course you have a liking for the Delaney twins."

"You're one sick bitch, Ellie, you know that?" He scowled and gripped the steering wheel tighter.

I laughed and flipped down the visor to take a quick look at my reflection. My hair was pulled into a messy bun and I was wearing hardly any makeup, but my brother hadn't given me much time to get ready. It'd been leave when he said, or not go at all, and I'd needed to see Hunter.

I pinched my cheeks to try and bring a little color to them but sighed when they remained pale and uninteresting. I definitely needed to get out more and sleep a little less when I wasn't working. The trouble was, Dayton Valley was farming and ranch country. There were damn cows everywhere, and I really hated cows. It was a pretty part of the world, all green and lush, but the damn bovines just spoiled it.

While I shuddered in my seat as I thought about *the cows,* Carter pulled into the parking lot of the Stars & Stripes. I was right about it being a bad night for him to get some action. There were at least five motorized scooters parked by the front doors, and the minivan from the Sunny Years Old People's Center was taking up two other spaces. Thursday night was Bingo night and as its usual venue, the Goodwill Hall, was being refurbished, so Penny had told Mr. Parker that he could hold it in the Stars & Stripes until the hall was finished. I had my doubts the old folks would ever want to go back to the hall though; it had no bar and no Penny to serve them grilled cheese sandwiches at the end of the night.

"Shit," Carter muttered. "Bingo night."

"I did tell you." I sighed haughtily. "And I reckon Hunter brought his aunts over, which is why he wanted to meet you here."

"They damn well throw pens at you if you even breathe a tiny bit too loud, and God-for-fucking-bid you actually talk while Mr. Parker is shouting out the numbers."

"We could go over to the café," I offered and nodded across the road to the Café Au Lait.

Carter unbuckled his belt and turned in his seat to look at me. His brows furrowed so much that his eyes were like tiny slits. It was not a good look on him.

"I think I recall saying you couldn't hang with us, so fill your boots, Ellie if you want to go over there. Me and Hunter will take our chances where the beer is sold."

"Okay," I replied and gave him the biggest smile I could muster. "I'm cool with that. It'll be fun watching you both dodge pens thrown by a bunch of senior citizens."

Carter sighed and pinched the bridge of his nose. "Sometimes I really wish Dad had had a vasectomy after they had me. I love you because I have to, but you really piss me off just by being around."

I laughed loudly and slapped Carter's leg. I knew he loved me, and I knew I pissed him off, but it was all part of the fun of being his little sister. Aside from which, if push came to shove, he'd be there for me if I needed him.

"Okay," I said with a huge grin. "Let's go and grab us some beer."

When we got inside the bar, Bingo was in full swing and apart from Mr. Parker calling something about two little ducks, you could have heard a pin drop.

"I'll kill him," Carter whispered into my ear as we moved to the bar.

"We can always go to the café like I said." I gave him a look that clearly expressed the fact I thought he was stupid, but he chose to ignore me.

"I'm not buying you drinks all night, you know that, right?" Carter pulled his wallet from his back pocket and threw it down onto the bar.

"I don't expect you to." I shoved my card under his nose. "Now stop being a dick to me."

Penny approached us and held up two fingers and pointed at the bottled beers evidently too scared to speak in her own bar. When she passed them over to us, I handed her my card and then poked my tongue out at my brother.

"Happy now," I said offering him a tight smile.

Carter mumbled something and without waiting for me, picked up his wallet and turned to go and look for Hunter.

Penny returned with my card and when I reached for it, she took hold of my hand. "Thought you might want to know," she said quietly, her eyes darting toward Mr. Parker. "Dominic is back in town."

My stomach dropped and my hand fell to the bar. "You're joking right?"

Her mouth thinned into a line and she shook her head. "Sorry, honey. He was in here earlier."

Dominic Taylor my douche of an ex was back in town – well shit.

"Was he alone?" I asked and picked at the label on my bottle.

Penny nodded. "Yeah, but he said he may come back in tonight."

"Okay," I whispered. "Thanks."

"No fighting, honey, okay?" Her hand drifted over the bar where I knew there was a dint.

"No fighting, I promise."

As I gave her a smile, someone shouted bingo behind us, and Mr. Parker was no longer the only person speaking. The bar buzzed with conversation and noise as Mrs. Hubert had her card checked. I made my way over to the high table in the back corner of the bar where my brother and Hunter were sitting.

"Ellie," Hunter muttered with the briefest of glances toward me.

"Hi," I replied, a little distracted by the news that Penny had given to me.

"Who pissed in your grits?" Carter asked, nudging me with his shoulder.

I took a deep breath and looked up at him. "Dominic is back in town."

Carter groaned. "You're fucking kidding me?"

"He on his own?" Hunter asked. "Or is she, whoever she is, with him?"

I shrugged. "Penny said he was alone earlier, but he may come back in tonight, so who knows."

"Fuck, I'm sorry, Ellie." Hunter tipped his bottle to mine. "He's a dick. You're better off without him."

I nodded because I knew that for fact. On the night Dominic had said we were coming to the bar because he had something big to tell me, I'd thought he might say he wanted us to move in together. I knew he wasn't going to propose, because who would *tell* someone that? Plus, Dominic knew that 'telling' me we were getting married would not go down well with me. I'd been ready to move in with him though. I really liked him, and we had great sex, so why not – actually, not good reasons. The problem was he didn't want to ask me to move in together, he wanted to tell me that he'd met someone else and would be moving with *her* to damn LA where he'd got a job as a physical therapist in a private clinic.

That was what the fucking dick wanted to *tell* me, and he chose a packed Stars & Stripes to do it. I kept my cool at first because I was not one to beg. If my mom had taught me anything, it was that I should never lower myself to beg a guy for anything, least of all his time and attention. So, I nodded, asked him to leave my few pieces of stuff from his apartment in the break room at work and then went to the bathroom and sent out an SOS to Bronte.

She arrived within twenty minutes and found me sitting in a toilet stall crying. We stayed there for a half hour and drank the bottle of bourbon she'd bought from over the bar. By the time I licked my lips of the final drop I was wasted, we both were, but I was wasted *and* thought I was heartbroken – I realized soon after that it was the booze that made me feel like that, because it was '*Dominic who?*' after three days, max. So, drunk and heartbroken I stormed out of the bathroom intending on dancing the dick out of my head, but when I saw him at the bar laughing and joking with my brother of all people, I lost it. I ran at him screaming like a warrior on the attack, jumped on his back and grabbed his hair.

And that's the story of why there is a dent in Penny's bar the size of Dominic's head.

"Hey, El," Carter said.

"Yeah?"

"You in a fighting mood tonight?" he asked, rubbing a hand over his stubbled chin.

"Nope, not really why?"

He nodded toward the bar and I heard Hunter groan. I swiveled around already knowing what, or who, had caught their attention. I wasn't wrong. Dominic stood at the bar with his arm around the shoulder of a woman as he nuzzled his nose against her neck. At the time I'd had no clue who he'd cheated on me with, he would never say, and when he left no one heard from him, so I was shocked to see who it was.

"Well would you look at that," Carter gasped, his bottle of beer paused in midair.

"You didn't know?" I asked.

"Nope," he replied.

I turned to Hunter who was staring hard at Dominic.

"You?"

Hunter shook his head. "No and I doubt my Pop did either, not that he'd care overly much."

"So why do you look so mad?" I asked and glanced back at Dominic and his woman.

Hunter looked down at me, his brown eyes dark and intense. "Because you're Carter's sister and I've known you since you were a baby," he stabbed his finger in Dominic's direction, "and he hurt you and you deserve better."

Something pricked at my throat and I found it hard to swallow. I took a deep breath and then slowly let it out, my eyes on Hunter the whole time.

"Thank you," I whispered.

"I tell you something," Carter said as he slapped a hand on Hunter's back, startling him. "Miss Watkins ain't improved much since she taught us in high school."

We all turned back to Dominic and our ex-teacher. They kissed and giggled at the bar and we clinked our bottles together. "Here's to being rid of douchebags," I toasted.

"To being rid of douchebags."

We laughed and everything seemed relaxed, so I could only be shocked when Dominic looked over and winked at me with his hand on Miss. Watkins ass, and Hunter slammed down his bottle, stormed across the bar and punched Dominic right on the nose.

CHAPTER 9

Hunter

"What the ever-loving fuck," Carter exclaimed as he pulled me away from Dominic Taylor. "Hunter, calm down man."

"You even look in her direction and I'll punch you again." My face was so close to his we were breathing the same air.

"You damn animal," Dominic spat back. "I didn't do anything."

"You winked at her, you cocky bastard. While you had your hands all over the woman you cheated with."

A small hand wrapped around my bicep and I looked over my shoulder to find Ellie's big brown eyes begging me to pull away.

"Go on, Hunter, boy," a voice I recognized as old man Simpson shouted. "Punch the little ball sack."

"Mr. Simpson," Ellie snapped as she let go of my arm and turned to the old man wearing sweatpants and a hoody. "Keep your nose out of it. You do not need to be getting your blood pressure up again."

Mr. Simpson batted Ellie's pointer finger away and made a punching motion. "Sock him right between his eyes, boy."

"Don't listen to him," Ellie said and pulled me by my arm away from a cowering Dominic. "*He*," she pointed down at Dominic and gave my arm another tug, "is not worth it."

"She's right," Carter added as he placed a hand against my chest and pushed me.

"Don't you listen to them," Mr. Simpson growled as he did a little shadow boxing. "Knock his teeth out."

"Stan, come on, don't encourage them." Mr. Parker patted Mr. Simpson's back, but the old man wasn't having any of it and shrugged him off.

He was evidently desperate to see a fight, despite the fact that no one else in the bar seemed to be. I had to be honest, I had no problem helping Mr. Simpson get his wish, but the way Ellie's eyes burned with anger told me I should probably listen to her rather than the old man throwing pretend punches. I straightened up and took a step back from Dominic. Miss. Watkins had her cell in her hand about to tap out a number.

"Really, Miss. Watkins, you're going to call the cops on me?"

Everyone swiveled to land their gaze on her, and she immediately dropped her hand to her side.

"You don't want to do that," Penny said, her tone hard as she stood with her hands firmly on her hips. "You know that's not how we do things around here, Pamela."

Miss. Watkins' eyes shot to me and then back to Penny. "You are all just going to stand there and let him punch Dominic."

"Yeah," Mr. Simpson shouted. "He's a fucking little dickwad."

I couldn't help the laugh that escaped me. Ellie's shoulders shook too.

"We all know what he did to our beautiful Ellie," Mr. Simpson continued. "And you should know better, Pamela Watkins. You're old enough to be his mother."

I doubted that she was much past thirty-six as she'd been pretty young when she'd started to teach us at high school, but even so, he was right, she should have known better than to mess around with someone already in a relationship.

Miss. Watkins leaned down and pulled at Dominic's hand. "Come on, let's get out of this mad house."

Dominic grunted and groaned as he pushed to his feet. Once he was standing, and Miss. Watkins had an arm around him, he threw me a glare and pointed a shaky finger at me.

"You'll pay for that, Delaney, I promise you."

I threw my hands up in surrender and rolled my eyes. "I'm fucking petrified."

"Dominic, come on," Miss. Watkins said as she pulled him toward the door.

"You're all a bunch of crazy people. I'm glad I got out of here."

"You should never have come back then," Ellie said and took a step forward.

"As for you, you stupid, frigid little bitch," Dominic snarled.

I made a lunge for him, but Ellie pushed in front of me and beat me to it, punching him right on the nose.

"Shit!" She stamped her foot and shook out her fist. "You fucker."

"For God's sake, Ellie," Carter groaned. "You said that you wouldn't fight him."

Ellie's eyes went wide as she cradled her hand. "He called me frigid. I'm the best sex he'll ever have."

Her words and the way she stamped her foot and glared at Dominic was pretty sexy. I couldn't help but notice my dick perked up.

"And you," Carter continued and pointed at me. "What the hell did *you* hit him for?"

I shrugged, but I knew it was the look on Ellie's face when I told her she deserved better than Dominic the Douche. She'd looked so grateful, as if she hadn't believed it up until that point. When he'd taunted her with a wink, well the red mist kinda clouded my judgement.

"Oh, Hunter honey, you're such a hero." I turned to see both my aunts had pushed through the crowd of people gathered around us. I knew they must have missed most of the excitement because like clockwork whenever the final number had been called by Mr. Parker, they both went off to the bathroom. Janice-Ann told me it was because of the anticipation of hope that they could win the big prize that made them want to pee. Like everything they did, they did it with twin synchronization – one needed to pee, they both needed to pee.

"You haven't hurt yourself have you, sweetheart?" Lynn-Ann asked.

"No, Auntie L," I said as I flexed my hand. "But I think Ellie might have."

Ellie still had her punching hand cradled in the other and was arguing in hushed tones with Carter.

"Well, you got the first punch in I heard, so well done you." Lynn-Ann reached up on her tiptoes and kissed my cheek, quickly followed by Janice-Ann. I told you twinchronisity as Pop liked to call it.

"I'm not sure I did the right thing," I said and glanced over to see Dominic being comforted by Miss. Watkins, while he groaned in pain against her chest. "Maybe if I hadn't Ellie wouldn't have either."

"I damn well would," Ellie snapped, pausing her conversation with Carter.

"How the hell do women do that?" I asked. "Have a conversation with one person but listen to another."

Ellie and my aunts all grinned at each other and shrugged.

"Anyway," Janice-Ann said as she linked her arm with mine. "We just wanted to let you know there's no need for you to take us home. We're going back to Brewster's room at Sunny Years to play poker with him and Norm."

I looked over to where Brewster Whittaker and Norm Carmichael were grinning and waving their fingers at my two aunts.

Shit what the hell was in the water that made the older folks in this town act like teenagers at an after-prom party?

"How you going to get home?" I asked, glancing at my cell to see it was almost nine-thirty.

"Norm will bring us back on his scooter," Lynn-Ann replied as she patted the back of her perfectly set silver hair.

It was three miles from Sunny Years to our ranch and Norm's scooter was only big enough for one person to ride. Did he even have headlights on it? I thought about protesting to my aunt, but she already wore a look of grim determination.

"Okay, if you're sure."

She patted my arm and then looked coyly at Norm. "Oh, I'm sure, sweetheart."

I suppressed a shudder and turned back to Ellie and Carter, who were going at it again.

"You should be on my side," Ellie cried. "I'm your sister and he disrespected me."

"I am on your side," Carter replied, glancing over at Dominic who was dabbing a handkerchief to his lip. "But you have a career and punching guys won't look good if the hospital board finds out."

"Hey." I slapped a hand on Carter's back. "No one is going to tell the hospital board."

"Dominic might," he snapped and turned to glare at me.

Ellie suddenly looked scared. It hadn't occurred to me, but Carter was right. Dominic had been punched by a girl who had split his lip, not to mention the nice bruise I'd added to his cheek. Telling Ellie's employers was just the sort of thing someone like Dominic would do. I decided to take control of the situation and moved around Ellie and Carter to Dominic and Miss. Watkins.

"Don't you dare touch me." Dominic took a step back and pulled Miss. Watkins in front of him – damn coward.

"I'm not, I'm here to make sure that this is the end of it all. You know what you did was wrong, cheating on Ellie and then coming back to rub her face in it."

I looked at him and actually wanted to punch him again, but knew that wouldn't help matters, plus he was hiding behind his woman and I couldn't get to him.

"I didn't rub her face in it. I'm entitled to drink in here." Dominic winced as he dabbed at his lip again. "I was trying to be nice."

"Winking at her when you're wrapped up in another woman and then calling her frigid is nice?"

Miss. Watkins winced and took a half step away from Dominic. "*You* didn't need to punch him, Hunter."

"He disrespected my friend," I said, realizing as I said it that it didn't feel as weird as I thought it might by calling Ellie my friend. She'd always been Carter's little sister, but that hadn't been why I'd punched Dominic. "And to be fair, you both have, when you carried on behind her back. Not real good behavior from a teacher now is it?"

Miss. Watkin's face reddened, and she glanced over to where Ellie was with Carter.

"You'll hear no more from us," she replied. "We're only back in town to put my house up for sale. We won't be back."

"Pamela—"

Dominic grabbed her arm, but she pulled away from him and stopped him abruptly. "No, Dominic. I can't afford to have any investigations into our relationship."

A look passed between them and when Dominic nodded my pulse notched up a rate.

"Fuck," I said quietly. "Sex with a pupil, Miss. Watkins, now that is naughty. As for you, Dominic. I had no idea you had it in you all those times at high school when you crashed and burned with the girls. No wonder you didn't put any effort into it if you were already banging one of the teachers."

I braced myself for the punch for disrespecting Miss. Watkins, but the cowardly piece of shit just dropped his head and muttered something about, 'leaving this shithole of a town' and then stormed past me with Miss. Watkins hot on his tail.

"Okay," I said and turned around to face Ellie and Carter, the rest of our audience now gone and tucking into Penny's grilled cheese. "All sorted. We won't be hearing from them again."

"You sure?" Ellie asked hesitantly.

"Yeah, now let's get another beer and talk about the hospital fundraiser."

Ellie's eyes lit up and I couldn't help but smile. She looked like an excited little girl. She knew this was my way of saying I'd help with her damn awful plan to get Carter and Bronte together, and even though I didn't think it was necessary, it might be kinda fun. We never did get around to it though. Penny felt we were a distraction to bingo night, so were asked to leave, which meant one very unhappy Carter.

CHAPTER 10

Ellie

C arter wasn't happy we spoiled his night in Stars & Stripes and was ignoring me. I'd been over to his apartment with a chicken casserole from Mom, but he'd opened up, taken it out of my hands and then slammed the door in my face. Even when I kept banging and ringing his doorbell for a full five minutes, it drew a blank, unless of course you counted his neighbor Valerie. She flung her door open and shouted a string of abusive words at me for a full minute before… slamming the door.

When I got to work and found no one had refilled the coffee jug, it added to my bad mood. I decided to order Carter a dildo online and arranged for it to be delivered to the veterinary clinic where he worked. That would teach him to ignore me just because I'd got us thrown out of the local bar.

Penny hadn't barred us or anything like that, but she had told both Hunter and I to go home and cool off, and as he'd taken me there, Carter had to leave too. I think he'd hoped that Hunter might offer, as he went in the general direction of the street that we lived on, but he was out of there and speeding off in his truck quicker than Mrs. Abbot from the bookstore, on coupon day.

"Why has no one filled up the jug?" I grumbled to my friend and colleague Davis as he walked into the break room.

"It was Joella's turn, but as usual she's been too busy fluttering her eyelashes at Dr. Hotpants."

I laughed and opened up the cabinet where we kept the coffee. "He'll hear you call him that one day."

"No, he won't." Davis sighed. "He doesn't even know I exist. I could faint at his feet and he'd step over me."

"Unlike Joella, who would trample all over you to get to Dr. Andrews."

"Exactly. You totally understand."

Davis had had a huge crush on Dr. Andrews since the doctor had first joined us six months previously, but he was right, he barely glanced Davis's way.

"I think he's scared of me," Davis added. "I mean I'm so openly gay I could hold my own Pride event. I think old Hotpants is worried that I'm going to roofie him or something and take him into the store closet and have my way with him."

At the mention of the store closet, I thought about the last couple I'd found in there – Jefferson and Miss. Watkins. That reminded me not only of Dominic and his smug face, but also that Hunter and I needed to put our plan into action. Which also reminded me of the fact that he'd agreed to take part in the hospital fundraiser.

"I have some news which will cheer you up," I said to Davis who took the coffee from me to get the jug on – he always said I made it too strong.

"What's that?"

"Hunter Delaney is going to take part in the calendar this year."

Davis' hand went to his heart and he took an exaggerated step back. "Tell me you're not joking."

"I'm not joking." I grinned at him and pulled two mugs from the cupboard.

"How the hell did you manage that?" He began to fan himself. "You've asked him for the last two years and he's said no each time. What did you do to persuade him?"

I shrugged. "I kind of tricked him into it. I told Bronte he was going to do it before he'd said yes, and then I guess he didn't feel he could say no"

It wasn't exactly true, but I didn't want to tell Davis about my plan. He had a mouth bigger than that on the Mississippi and would no doubt tell Bronte next time she tinted his eyelashes when he went into the small beauty salon that she owned.

The truth was we'd only been trying to hide our *plan* from Bronte, but it had been the first thing I'd thought of when she'd asked what we were talking about. I'd never once thought Hunter would go along with it, so when he texted me after our night at Stars & Stripes to say he was in on the plan *and* the fundraiser I was more than surprised. I read the text at least five times to be sure I'd read it right.

"I want in on the photoshoot that day," Davis squealed. "I need to see that cowboy's hot bod with those beautiful tattoos."

"How do you know he has a hot bod and that his tattoos are beautiful?"

I turned to get the creamer from the refrigerator, mainly because I didn't want Davis to see my pink cheeks. I'd seen Hunter without a shirt, and he was right, his bod was hot, and his tattoos were beautiful; my favorite being the edgy and cool, zombie cowboy on his left, tight, tanned pectoral.

"Ellie what the hell are you doing?" Davis asked and clicked his fingers in front of my face.

"W-what?" I stammered, pulling my scrubs away from my chest and wafting it to create some breeze around my girls.

Davis let out a roar of laughter. "You were pushing your thighs together girl and circling your damn nipple."

"*I was not!*" I gasped and punched Davis' arm. "You, big fat liar."

He held his hands up, palms forward as if I might be about to shoot him. "Swear on the life of RuPaul, honey. You were having naughty thoughts about Hunter Delaney, weren't you?"

"No." I pushed a mug toward him. "Coffee now. I only have ten minutes of my break left."

"Please would help."

"Please." I gave him a narrow-eyed stare. "Circling my nipple, as if," I muttered.

"Swear to God, and like I said, on the life of Our Lord RuPaul."

I cleared my throat as heat prickled over my chest and back. Okay, Hunter was a good-looking guy, he was sexy if you liked that tattooed cowboy thing that he had going on. If you could even call him a cowboy, he didn't even wear a Stetson, instead favoring a ball cap, often flipped around with the peak at the back and a tuft of his hair poking out the front and a pair of shades hooked in the front of his shirt. And, more often than not he drove a truck, only riding his horse to round up the herd.

"You're doing it again, honey," Davis called as he poured the coffee.

My eyes met his and his eyebrows were high up on his forehead as he pushed a mug to me.

"I'll take this back to the nurse's station," I muttered.

"Okay, honey, you do that."

Davis gave me a look that said he knew my secret, well great for him because I had no damn idea what it was. There was nothing wrong in daydreaming about Hunter, like I said he was handsome and most girls in Dayton Valley had crushed on him at some point – except for me, I'd never seen the attraction. He was just Hunter, my brother's best friend.

"Oh, and Ellie," Davis called as I reached the door. "Maybe wipe that drool from your chin before you do your drugs round."

I chose to ignore him, but still felt my chin, just in case.

CHAPTER 11

Hunter

I looked at Carter and gave him the dead eye, only for him to laugh right in my face.

"A fucking costume party," I moaned. "You know how I hate them."

"And you know that Belinda's birthday party is *always* a costume party. You could have bailed if you really wanted to. I'm guessing the prospect of seeing Belinda Jennings dressed as a sexy schoolgirl *again,* is what had you logging online and buying *that*." He pointed at my outfit and grinned.

"I didn't damn well order this and you know it. How did you manage to change the order without me knowing anyway?'

Carter winked and shrugged his shoulders. "You should know not to leave your account open on your laptop."

"You were supposed to be checking my damn cows, not messing with my fucking costume order. I only slipped out for a few minutes to pee."

I glanced down at myself and groaned. I looked like an idiot.

"Like I said, you could've bailed or not worn it." Carter shifted the box of beers in his arms and pushed through the door into the crowded hallway of the Jennings' house, strutting through in his Top Gun outfit and Aviator shades.

"Carter," Belinda our hostess and birthday girl screeched and ran toward us, her arms waving in the air.

"Belinda, looking lovely as usual." Carter leaned in and kissed her cheek. "Happy birthday."

She was dressed as expected, as a sexy schoolgirl and I was pretty sure that her skirt was a damn sight shorter than the year before.

"You brought beer," she squealed and almost pierced my eardrum as she bounced up and down and clapped her hands.

Belinda could only be described as perky both in personality and tits. Rumor had it that the perky tits had been a twenty-first birthday present from her mom and dad.

"They can go in the kitchen with the keg my daddy organized. Isn't it good of him for doing that? He and Mom have gone away for the night so we can have fun. My brothers are running wagers on beer pong in the dining room if you want to go play."

I was exhausted from just listening to her and when she went quiet, I wondered if she'd actually passed out through lack of oxygen. I looked at Carter who was grinning at her like she was a little kid who was telling some tall tale that barely made sense.

"I need a drink," I muttered. "Great to see you, Belinda, Carter you coming with?"

Carter nodded and gave Belinda another quick kiss and pushed through the crowd of people to the kitchen. With a huff he let the beers drop onto the counter.

"Thanks for your help," he groused, giving me the stink eye.

"I paid for them, seeing how you conveniently forgot your wallet."

Carter laughed. As usual he thought he was damn hilarious when he was actually a pain in my ass. Why Ellie wanted to land poor Bronte with him,

God only knew.

"Hey guys," a deep voice boomed behind us.

We turned to see our old school pal Alaska Michaels dressed as a woman with a blonde wig, chest hair poking out of the top of a pink jacket and a sign around his neck that told us he was supposed to be Hilary Clinton.

"What the hell, Alaska." I looked him up and down feeling a little uneasy at the sight of him.

He shrugged. "Jennifer thought it would be funny. She's dressed as Bill."

"Does she have a sign too?" I asked. "Or is it more obvious."

Alaska grinned. "It's obvious. We rubbed mayonnaise into her crotch."

I bust out laughing at the thought, Carter though looked at me with narrow eyes and a facial expression like he was constipated.

"You don't get it do you?" Alaska said with a roll of his eyes.

Carter shook his head.

"Damn, Carter, for a brainy guy you're totally stupid," I muttered. "Come on let's get a drink and I'll explain it to you later."

Alaska shook his head and slapped my back. "I'll catch you later, I've left Jennifer with Minnesota and he ain't the best company at the moment."

"How come?" Carter asked.

"His girl dumped his ass. He wasn't going to come tonight, but Mom made him. It was a kinda last minute decision, so he's come dressed as a cowboy." He grinned at me. "You should hang out together tonight, you'd be a pretty good pair."

My smile dropped as I was reminded of my costume. I wondered if I could poison Carter in some way and get away with it.

"Pass me a beer would ya?" I held out a hand to Carter and waited for him to pass me one of the bottles. "Is your sister coming tonight?"

"Yeah, her and damn Bronte are coming. One night I hoped I could spend without her giving me shit, but no, she had to agree to come." He popped the caps off two bottles and handed me one. "When was the last time you remember Ellie ever going to a party, especially one Belinda was throwing. They hated each other at school."

"Well Belinda did say Ellie had a fat ass."

I took a sip of my beer and considered whether Ellie had a fat ass or not.

I quickly concluded while it wasn't skinny it wasn't fat, but just the right handful – if I really cared about her ass of course.

"Yeah well, we all know it doesn't take much to get my sister to exact revenge." Carter rolled his eyes at me and I knew he was getting at two nights before when Ellie and I had tag teamed to put Dominic down.

"I was going to call her," I said, a little surprised I'd admitted it to him. It had always been an unsaid rule that you didn't make any moves on a buddy's sister, and I didn't want Carter to think that's what I was doing. "Just to check she was okay, and that nothing had been said about it at the hospital."

I felt the need to clarify my reasoning, but I wasn't sure who I was trying to make a point to; Carter or myself. If I had to be honest, I'd worried about Ellie and whether the whole situation had upset her. She'd been cheated on and then made to look a fool when he'd rubbed her nose in it with Miss. Watkins. I didn't like the idea of that. For all her spit and fire, Ellie Maples could be easily hurt—Belinda's comment about her ass being a case in point. Tonight would be Ellie's first time at any of Belinda's parties for years, she certainly hadn't let it go easily.

"Ellie is always okay," Carter replied. "Don't you worry about her."

"You're not concerned he'll report her?" I asked.

Carter shook his head. "Nope, you saw Miss. Watkins' face when you called them out about being together when we were at school. Dominic knows if he reports Ellie either you or me will tell the school authorities about them."

"Yeah, but we can't prove anything. It was only the fact she went as white as a sheet when I said it. He could still decide to go to the hospital board."

Carter slapped my back. "Hunt, I have no idea why you're worrying about this. Ellie isn't, I'm not, so don't you."

I couldn't believe how damn cool he was being about it. I knew if it was my sister, I'd be doing everything I could to make sure nothing came back to bite her on the ass; but then Ellie wasn't my sister and Carter wasn't exactly the best of big brothers.

I was about to ask him if we should make sure somehow, when I saw his face change. The grin dropped from it and his lips moved into a thin line. I looked over his shoulder to follow his gaze and saw Ellie and Bronte moving through the crowds and greeting people with kisses on cheeks and hugs. I knew he had a thing about his 'little sister' hanging around with him, but Carter's attitude toward Ellie being at the party seemed a little off by the way he was looking at her with narrow eyes and clutching his beer bottle so hard I thought it might break.

Carter shifted a little and I got a better view of Ellie as she started to move towards us.

"*Fuck*," I muttered under my breath as my mouth went dry and I swallowed hard.

She looked as sexy as hell. Every guy in the place had their eyes on her. She was wearing a cheerleader costume covered in fake blood. The tight top, which stopped just below her tits, was slashed and gave glimpses of her tanned skin, while the skirt rested on her hips and just about covered her ass. Even her hair, in two pigtails high on her head, looked sexy as they swung with each step she took.

"What the hell is she wearing?" Carter mumbled and took a step forward.

I stepped in front of him; Ellie'd had enough public humiliation for one week. I glanced over my shoulder at her brother while Ellie turned around and immediately saw me. She stopped dead still, both hands flew to her mouth, and she began to actually shake. Her legs shook uncontrollably, tears sprang to her eyes as her breathing got heavy.

"Ellie?"

I reached out a hand, but she screamed loudly and tried to back away from me, stumbling as she did.

"What the hell?" Carter pushed past me. "*Ellie.*"

I moved with him and as he reached out for his sister, Bronte turned around. "You damn idiot," she spat at him.

As a sexy female version of Freddie Kruger in a real short red and black sweater dress that covered less of her ass than Ellie's outfit, she stormed toward me. I didn't have time to be confused by what was going on. Bronte had a face like thunder and Ellie was shouting at me to keep away.

"What the hell did I do?" I cried. "I only—" Bronte's foot stamped down on mine and then a hand came up and slapped my face.

"Shit, Bronte." Carter reached out a hand to pull her away. "It was just a joke. I didn't think she'd be so upset."

Bronte rounded on Carter as I cupped my stinging face.

"You, absolute dick, Carter Maples. How could you?" Bronte screamed in his face.

"What the hell is going on?" I winced at sharp pain shooting up my foot, pretty sure that Bronte had broken one or more of my toes, never mind left a handprint on my cheek.

"Don't pretend you don't know, you... you... dickwad."

Bronte then turned back to Carter and without any hesitation kneed him in the balls.

"Will someone please tell me what I'm supposed to have done wrong," I begged as Carter collapsed on the ground cupping his junk.

"She's petrified of cows," Bronte roared. "As if you didn't know."

I looked over at Ellie who was being comforted by a couple of girls who she'd been friends with at high school. Her shoulders heaved and she glanced my way, distress still written all over her face.

"I swear, Ellie," I called across to her. "I didn't know."

Bronte stared intently at me and then looked down at Carter who was curled in the fetal position on the floor, his cries of agony far louder than Ellies scream had been.

"He knew," she snapped and kicked at Carter's foot. "He told you to wear it didn't he?"

I thought about the Joker costume that I *thought* I'd bought online.

"I knew it." I'd evidently paused too long as Bronte gave Carter one last kick and then stormed back over to Ellie who seemed to be calming down.

I looked down at Carter writhing around and felt the need to give him another kick to the balls, but Alaska came over and placed a big hand with pearly pink fingernails on my shoulder.

"Wow, you really are a douche sometimes," he said with a grin.

"I didn't know." I held my hands in the air in exasperation. "I swear."

"You idiot," Jennifer, Alaska's girlfriend, growled and poked me in the chest. "How can you not know that the girl you've known since she was a baby is petrified of cows."

Alaska laughed, Carter groaned, and I looked down at the plastic udders that were hanging from my stomach and felt the hood I had on which was shaped like a cow's head.

"Oh fuck," I muttered and scrubbed a hand down my face. Then I tipped my beer over Carter.

CHAPTER 12

Ellie

Watching everyone enjoy themselves, whilst I hung out on the sidelines hugging a bottle of beer, I realized why I never went to parties—I damn well hated them.

At least my pulse had slowed down after a quick shot from the hip flask Alaska had tucked in the leg of the granny pants that he was wearing. Now, I felt stupid. So stupid that I couldn't find it in myself to join in with the fun and had chosen to sit alone, on a wall in the yard, while everyone else stayed inside.

Bronte had gone missing almost a half hour ago. I guessed she was using some poor idiot's tongue and fingers to try and forget her crush on Jefferson. I mentally rolled my eyes and thought about my plan to hook her up with my dick douche of a brother. The wisdom of it was in severe jeopardy. Why on earth would she want to date someone who couldn't father children? When

I got hold of him his nut sack would end up well and truly empty after the stunt he pulled with Hunter's costume. I shuddered at just the thought of it. Shit, my brother really was a Weiner head as well as a dick douche.

"Can I sit?"

I looked up to see Hunter, minus his hideous costume and in ball shorts and a tee, holding two bottles of beer.

"I come in peace, minus cow titties," he said, offering me one of the beers.

I nodded and took the bottle from him, placing it on the wall next to where I was sitting.

"I should also point out, I raided Belinda's folks' medicine cabinet and your brother should be getting the shits in round about…" He looked down at the big sexy watch on his wrist. "Ten minutes.

I grinned but then winced – how the fuck can a watch be sexy?

"Thanks. He deserves it. Where is he anyway."

Hunter shrugged. "No idea, but let's hope it's close to the john. Those laxatives were extra strength and I put two into the hot dog I got him from the grill."

Eyeing him warily, I took a swig of my beer.

"You're forgiven. You don't have to lie about the payback on Carter."

"Oh, I ain't lying." Hunter smiled and tapped his bottle to mine. "It's the least the fucker deserves."

We lapsed into silence, both giving a quiet laugh as Jennifer ran past, chasing a squealing Alaska shouting, "I did not have sexual relations with that woman, Hilary. It's mayo."

"So, how come you never told me you were scared of you know whats?" Hunter asked once they'd disappeared back inside.

"I just figured you knew." I shrugged. "My friends and family know, so…"

Hunter blew out a breath. "Well, I guess that's my bad, for not paying you more attention."

The words made me feel a little strange in my belly, but I decided to ignore it and kept silent. I glanced up at him and couldn't help but think how handsome he looked with his disheveled hair brushing against his eyelashes.

It wasn't that I'd never noticed how hot my brother's best friend was, I'd spotted that at the age of thirteen when he'd given me my first lady boner. The problem was he was fifteen and while he was Zac Efron High School Musical cute, he was a person with a dick, who acted like a dick, talked like a dick and basically was a dick. He hung with my brother, so no mystery why he was so *dickish*. I gave up on liking him after the first time he made me cry, by ignoring me at the town fete and French kissing Bettina Mercer in front of me. It was then that I decided that Hunter Delaney would no longer have an inch of my time or brain space. Him getting hotter as he got older made it a whole lot more difficult, but I'd succeeded – well on the surface, he did have his uses during my self-pleasuring sessions.

"I do feel bad for not knowing," he added. "But I guess that explains why you never came out to the ranch much."

"Nope, not really. That's mainly because I thought you were a dick."

I nudged him with my shoulder and winked. Even so, Hunter snorted a dismissive laugh as if it'd be impossible for anyone to think he was a dick.

"Oh, come on, Hunt, you must know you are." He wasn't entirely, but it didn't hurt to yank his chain a little.

"I am not a dick," he argued, turning to face me. "How can someone who takes their aunts underwear shopping be a dick?"

I turned to face him, a huge grin on my face. "You do not."

"Scouts honor." He gave me the correct salute, but he didn't have me fooled.

"If you were a scout how come I never knew?"

"It never really came up," he replied with a wink. "Just like I didn't know you were scared of cows."

His wink created a little party action in my panties, worryingly.

"So, we both have secrets," I said with a clearing of my throat as I pushed my thighs together. "Who knew?"

Hunter's eyes grazed down my body and then back up again. It wasn't hard to see the want in them. Problem was with Hunter, he might have been hot, and probably packing more than a quarter pound of best beef between his legs, but I wasn't in the market to be the next Hoagie roll of many that he laid it in.

"You look amazing, by the way?" he said, around the neck of his bottle. "Although I was a little surprised to see you here."

"Yeah, well, we're supposed to be getting Bronte and Carter together, so I figured it'd be a good opportunity. And I can't hate Belinda forever. Although there doesn't seem much fun in it now; getting Carter and Bronte together I mean. It's still hilarious hating Belinda."

Hunter grinned and shook his head. "Does that mean you're giving up on the Bronte and Carter project."

I shrugged. "Maybe. Especially as what I really want to do is string him from Archer's tree by a rusty chain from his nut sack."

Hunter visibly winced, making me laugh.

"What was it that mentally hurt, Archer's tree, the rusty chain or the nut sack?" I asked.

"All of the above. The last two would be fucking painful, but if I had to be hung from my nuts with a rusty chain, Archer's tree is not where I'd want to be."

Archer's tree was right on the edge of Archer land and somehow looked like a witch. The branches grew to a point for the hat, there were two gnarly old knots in the trunk that looked like eyes, and a big hole below them for the mouth. Legend also had it that Archer land was haunted by old man Archer. He told his son on his deathbed that if he ever married one of the Perkins girls, the daughters of his old enemy, he'd haunt him and the land forever. As Willie Archer knocked up Dotty Perkins and married her just three months after his dad died, everyone was convinced old man Archer had kept his promise.

"Chicken," I muttered.

"You get yourself hung up from it then. See how you like it."

"Ah and that's where you'd fail," I said, smirking at him. "I don't have balls you can hang me from."

Hunter's eyes immediately went to my girls, earning him a back hander in the stomach.

"Shit, Ellie. You sure you don't have balls? That hurt."

"Good," I replied, shivering as a wind gusted around us, blowing the front of my tiny skirt up.

I quickly smacked it down, but I knew it was too late when Hunter's eyes lit up.

"Never realized that white panties could look so hot."

I lifted my hand to hit him again, but he quickly stood up and moved at least three paces away from me.

"Like I said, chicken."

Hunter laughed and lifted his bottle. "You want another?"

I shook my head. I'd barely drunk any of the one in my hand and still had a full one on the wall next to me. I'd had the one shot of Alaska's bourbon and two mouthfuls of beer and just wasn't feeling it. Maybe it was the cow fright earlier that had put me off.

Hunter disappeared and I wondered whether I should go back inside and join the rest of the party. Looking through the open terrace doors, I could see there was still a game of beer pong going on, and some dancing in the middle of the room. Over in the kitchen area some guy was being held upside down while Belinda's two brothers emptied the keg into his mouth via a funnel – the male of the species never really grew up.

When a roar went up from the beer pong, I lifted slightly to get a better view to what had caused the excitement. To be faced with Mindy Larkins putting her own nipple in her mouth was not what I expected. Don't get me wrong, it's a great skill, but not one I wanted to be a party to. As I sat back down Hunter appeared with a beer and what looked like a cover of some sort.

"Got you this." He put his bottle down and then shook out what I realized was a throw. He reached behind me and draped it around my shoulders. "Better?"

I snuggled into the thick wool and nodded. "Yeah, much."

When he sat down next to me, he was a little closer than before and I could see the goosebumps on his arms. It had gone chilly pretty quick.

"Come on," I said holding out the throw. "I'd be cruel to leave you out there in that wind."

Hunter raised a brow. "You sure?"

"Yeah," I replied with a sigh as if I didn't really want to—total lie.

As fast as a rattlesnake, Hunter was under the throw and squeezing himself close to me.

"Thank fuck for that. My balls were about to freeze off."

"Can't have that," I said, putting my bottle on the floor. "What the hell would I hang you up by?"

Hunter laughed and poked my side. "As if you would, who'd help you with your plan if you did?"

"Yeah, well like I said, I'm not sure it's a good idea now. Why would I push anyone with *him*?"

Hunter inclined his head like he was thinking hard and then shrugged. "You might have a point. But to be fair to him, he'll be better for her than any of those guys on that dating website, or my pop."

"So, you've come around to my way of thinking." I nudged him with my shoulder. "That she's in danger of embarrassing herself and making a real shit storm if she continues with this obsession she's got."

"Yeah, I do. Mainly because I don't want to either hear my pop bringing it home with her or have to start calling her Mom in the future."

I felt the color drain from my face. "He wouldn't get that serious about her, would he?"

Hunter laughed and brushed my bangs from my eyes, his hard, calloused fingertips feeling amazing against my skin.

Shit, I was losing my head over him and alcohol had barely passed my lips. Speaking of which, his were looking pink, pouty and soft.

I closed my eyes to block out how damn inviting they looked, and then without any announcement, they were on mine and Hunter's tongue was pushing for me to open up. I blame it on the shock, because I opened up straight away. Lips, tongues and teeth created a heady and wild kiss, and when his fingers whispered against my neck and jaw, the quiet little party in my panties turned to a full on kegger with fireworks.

"Shit, Ellie." Hunter groaned and wrapped an arm around my waist, pulling me closer to him.

I couldn't speak because the kiss was the kiss of all kisses. It was soft when it needed to be and hard when it needed to be ramped up, it was the absolute bomb. Without considering the consequences of what we were about to do, I pushed myself forward. My legs practically straddled his thighs when something started to vibrate in his pocket.

"Hunter, there's something in your pocket."

He groaned and smiled against my mouth. "I'm just real pleased to see you."

"Hunt, it's vibrating."

"Ah fuck." He pulled away from me and let his fingers linger on my cheek before reaching into his pocket and pulling out his cell. "Shit, it's my pop."

As Hunter talked to Jefferson, I ran a fingertip along my puffy bottom lip, wondering what the hell we'd just done. I couldn't blame alcohol, and really had no excuse. Glancing at Hunter I thought about just getting up and leaving, to go and try to find Bronte, but I might have been a lot of things, but certainly not a coward. So, I patiently waited for him to finish so I could tell him it was great, but it was a once in a lifetime opportunity. I knew that there wasn't any real reason why I shouldn't be with him, if it was what we both wanted – oh except, he was my brother's best friend and a dick by association.

"Sorry about that," he said, and pushed his phone back into his pocket. "We've got a cow struggling to calf and Pop needs my help. I'm going to have to go."

"How will you get home?" I asked standing with him.

"Not sure. I'll try an Uber and hope someone is working tonight."

I looked up at the stars and knew I'd probably regret it, but I couldn't see him struggle to get home when his dad needed him.

"I'll take you. I've barely had anything to drink and I have my car here."

Hunter ruffled his hair. "You sure?"

"Yeah, come on. Let's get you home. We'll just slip out through the side gate, otherwise if we walk through that lot, you'll get sidetracked with Mindy Larkins nipples."

He nodded in agreement, which kind of pissed me off, and then led the way. As I followed him through the yard, I couldn't help but ogle his ass and feel jealous of the horse he rode every damn day.

CHAPTER 13

Hunter

I hadn't expected to be riding in Ellie's car so soon after our last disastrous journey. Being honest, this trip managed to be even more uncomfortable than the last—my fucking dick refused to go down.

Ellie not only looked spectacular, but I could still feel her soft, plump lips on mine. As for her tits, shit they were like two perky, comfy pillows. If my phone hadn't rung out, I wouldn't like to say where we might have ended up. In *my* head it was my bed, shit, any bed, but I was pretty sure Ellie would have put a stop to that. She seemed sober and thinking straight, whereas I had a little buzz and thought, 'I can't wait to be balls deep inside of you.'

Glancing at her as she concentrated on the road, with her glasses on this time. I half expected her to tell me that she fucking hated me, and that the kiss should never have happened. She stayed silent though, except for humming along to *Yellow Hearts* by Ant Saunders, which weirdly reminded me of her.

"No singing tonight?"

She gave a little grunt. "Not after you were so rude about my voice, no."

I grinned but decided to keep it at that. If she flung a hand in my direction, she'd be likely to catch my dick that thankfully had started to stand at ease. That was until she shifted in her seat and gave me a bit more leg to look at.

Fuck, they were tanned, smooth and toned. The thought that they led up to white lace panties just added to my dick's excitement and had him at full attention once again. She sure was beautiful. How could I only now be just noticing? Damn, I must have been walking around with my eyes closed for years. Not only hadn't it registered with me how hot she was, but I hadn't even known about the cow thing, and I'd known her all her life. I really was a self-absorbed dick.

"You can drop me at the top of the track if you like," I offered, pulling at the loose fabric of my shorts as my thoughts helped junior deflate a little. "I can run from here."

Ellie waved me away. "It's fine. Those things will be in their shed thing, won't they?" Her head shot around and she looked at me panic stricken. "They will, won't they?"

"Yeah." I laughed. "They will. So, what made you so scared of them? And why did your brother never tell me?" I asked, determined to pay more attention in the future.

"That'll be because he's a weasel." She shrugged. "I remember being about three or four and Dad brought me with him to see your dad and I ended up screaming the rooks from the trees. Dad couldn't get me to stop and Mom was convinced he'd smacked my butt or something. I couldn't stop crying to tell her he hadn't, but just kept making a mooing noise."

I leaned my head back against the rest. "How come I don't remember that?"

"You'd gone to Dallas with your mom and Carter to see Disney on Ice." She snorted and indicated to turn onto the track that led up to our property.

"I fucking did not," I protested. "You liar."

"I'm not lying," she said, her tone matter of fact. "Carter had a thing for

Aurora, and you were madly in love with Belle. On your eighth birthday you told our moms that you'd marry her one day."

"Fuck off." I snorted out a laugh. "No way I said that when I was eight."

"Oh yes you did. And you must have had it bad, because you'd carried that torch for her for two years."

She had a smirk twitching her lips, which still looked kiss swollen to me. I really wanted to lean over the console and take her mouth again. Unfortunately, we had the argument over a Disney Princess to finish.

"You're such a liar."

"I'm honestly not," she retorted. "I can't believe you've forgotten it."

"I was obviously so traumatized I wiped it clean from my brain. I'm still going to check with Carter though."

Ellie shrugged and giggled. "Whatever, but he'll tell you I'm being honest. He still has the brochure that you both bought. I think he still likes to throw one out over the picture of Aurora doing a spiral."

I eyed her warily, not at all sure whether she was telling the truth or not, but damn sure my best friend would be getting a call in the morning. As we fell into silence, with me contemplating that Ellie looked a little like Belle—something else, like a tool, I'd failed to notice before—we pulled up outside the house. As soon as we had, the door was flung open and my two aunts came rushing out. Auntie J holding a thick checkered shearling jacket and Auntie L a pair of jeans and boots.

"Oh, thank goodness you're back." Auntie L was breathless as she ran down the porch steps. "Your pop is really struggling."

"Has he called Lance?" I asked, toeing off my sneakers and pulling the jeans on.

Lance was Carter's boss at the veterinarian clinic, and as grouchy as a bear with a boil on its ass, but he was a damn good vet. There was no secret he was going to hand everything over to Carter when he finally retired, despite the fact that at twenty-six Carter had only been qualified a couple of years – the clever bastard had fast-tracked his last year at Veterinary School. However, Lance was currently making my best friend wait by still working, even though he was almost seventy.

"Yes, but he's doing an emergency operation on Muriel Steiner's dog,

Booboo because he's swallowed a pair of her pantyhose." Aunt J offered me the jacket as I pushed my feet into the boots. "You might be out there a while," she added when she saw me roll my eyes.

Zipping up the jeans, I looked over to Ellie who'd rolled her car window down.

"Thanks for the lift, Ellie. Appreciate it."

"No problem. Hope you manage to save the…" she shuddered. "The thing and its baby."

God she was cute.

Fuck. What the hell was going on in my head at the minute?

"Oh, Ellie, honey," Auntie J said, walking up to the car and laying a hand on Ellie's arm. "You can't ride back to the party without something warm to drink. Come on in and we'll make you some cocoa."

"Oh, I'm not going back to the party," she replied. "I'm going to get home and have an early night."

I looked at my watch; only just gone nine. It seemed like hours since I'd scared the shit out of her and then kissed the shit out of her.

"Now you know your momma and daddy will be fooling around," Auntie L added, sidling up next to her twin. "You don't want to walk in on that, do you? No, you do as Janice-Ann says, come inside and let us make you some cocoa."

Lynn-Ann peered inside the car and then pulled back out, her eyes blinking rapidly.

"I mean, you're practically naked. You must be perished child."

And at the thought of Ellie naked, my dick jumped again, making me curse under my breath. It had to damn well stop. I'd known her for years, why was I suddenly getting all hot and bothered by her? It had to be the alcohol. Oh, and maybe the way she wore that tiny little cheerleader outfit with sass and style.

"You should stay, El," I said with a deep sigh. "They won't give up until you say yes."

Ellie shot me a glare, but when her lips twitched, I knew she wasn't really mad.

"Okay, a cocoa would be nice, Auntie L."

Janice-Ann clapped her hands like Ellie had just told her George Clooney was coming to stay—yeah, my aunts had a bit of a thing for George—and pulled open the car door while Ellie turned the engine off.

I watched a long, tanned leg appear and held my breath.

"You shoo," Auntie J said, waving her hands at me. "Go and help your pop before he busts a blood vessel."

With one last look at Ellie's ass swinging in her skirt, I rushed off to help Pop, hoping that some physical work might just calm my testosterone down.

***

After three hours and a lot of cussing, pushing and pulling we had a new cow to add to the herd. She was a big girl which was why the mother had struggled, but she battled to the end and finally birthed her calf. Thank God, both were fine, although we had one very tired momma.

When Pop and I rounded the corner back to the house, Ellie's car still sitting outside surprised me.

"Ellie stayed." Pop scrubbed a hand down his stubble, but his voice seemed to lift a little with excitement.

"Please tell me you're not interested in her."

My heart must have been beating fast because I was so tired, and the sickness in my belly was definitely due to the beers I'd had and then all the hard work of delivering the calf. *It had to be, right?*

Pop burst out laughing. "Jeez son, she's young enough to be my daughter."

I let out a long breath and made a mental note to let Ellie know that we probably didn't need to go ahead with 'Operation Bronte', not if that was Pop's view.

"I was thinking of you," he said, nudging me.

"Me?"

When I stopped in my tracks, Pop carried on walking toward the house and chuckled to himself.

"Pop, what did you mean, you were thinking of me?"

"Use your brain, son," he called and without breaking step beckoned me toward the house over his shoulder. "C'mon let's get inside, I need a hot drink and my bed."

Frowning I followed him up the steps and into the house, almost barreling into his back.

"What the he—"

"Shush," he whispered, putting his index finger to his lips and nodding toward the couch.

I looked over his shoulder to see Ellie curled up with one of my hoodies on. It was so big it covered her thighs and almost reached her feet with the short, white socks on. One hand was under her cheek, while the other was clutching the loose fabric of the top.

"She looks like an angel," Pop said quietly. "Kinda reminds me of your mom when she was that age."

When I looked down at Ellie, she stirred and rubbed her nose. Pop was right, she did look like an angel.

"I'm going to get me a glass of milk and then go up to bed. Tell Ellie she can stay in the spare room if she wants."

Pop slapped my back and left me to it. With my hands on my hips, I looked down at her, wondering whether to wake her, or just cover her with the knitted blanket my aunts had made one winter. It lay over the back of Pop's chair and more often than not after a long day, I ended up covering him with it after he fell asleep in front of the TV; or I had until he'd started his lady killing ways.

I was still in two minds what to do when Ellie turned over, and as she did, she showed me a good deal of a white lacy ass. Then the said white lacy ass let out a toot like a quick blast of a trumpet. It was so loud she jostled and sat bolt upright.

"What was that?" she gasped, one eye open and one still closed with sleep.

My laughter busted to burst out, but I reckoned she might be embarrassed. But damn it was funny.

"Oh my God, El," I gasped, grinning. "You just passed enough gas to light your mom's double oven."

She sat up straight, totally affronted. "I did not. I don't do that."

"Sorry to disappoint, cutie pie, but you really did."

My laugh echoed loud until I heard Pop's footsteps on the stairs. I quickly toned it down to a quiet chuckle.

"You're such a liar." Ellie narrowed her eyes at me and dropped her legs to the floor and stood up.

Disappointingly my hoodie dropped right down over the cute short skirt and her thighs, but I was not disappointed to see that even through the thick fabric, her nipples were hard.

"I should go," Ellie said, rubbing sleep from her eyes. "Your aunts must have put something in the cocoa because that's the best sleep I've had in ages."

"Pop said you can stay in the spare room," I replied trying not to ogle her too much as she stretched her arms and pushed her rack out. "It's a forty-minute drive back home and it's gone midnight."

Ellie hesitated for a few seconds, obviously thinking about it, but then shook her head.

"I'd better go. I have an early start in the morning."

"You working?" I asked.

"Nope, but I need to be up early to come up with a plan." She padded toward the door and picked up her sneakers and pushed her feet inside of them.

"Hey about that, I really don't think we have much to worry about. Pop said something that made me think he'd never be interested in Bronte."

"What?" she asked, with a little shrug of her shoulder.

What the fuck did I say? 'I thought he might be interested in you and it made me green with jealousy, so I called him out on it, and he told me you were young enough to be his daughter' – fuck no.

"Just that he'd never be interested in anyone under thirty." A lie, but I didn't plan on telling her the truth.

"Well, that won't stop Bronte. Anyway, that's not what I'm planning." She reached for the door handle and pulled it down. "I'm going to be planning on how I can kill Carter and get off scot free. That douche isn't getting away with his little joke from tonight. In fact, my plan may not include murder, but will definitely include mutilation, his balls and possibly an eggplant."

She gave me an evil grin which made me shudder.

"Okay, I'd better go." She opened the door, allowing the cool breeze inside.

"If you won't stay, at least text me when you get home."

Ellie rolled her eyes. "Hunter, I'll be perfectly safe. Just like I am when I travel home from the hospital after a late shift; I don't text you then."

"I just feel responsible, okay? So, do me a solid and send the damn text, El."

"Okay, okay, but don't blame me if it wakes you from your beauty sleep."

"I might not be asleep." If I carried on thinking about her legs and those panties, I'd likely be whacking one off.

"Hunter, you look like shit. You're dead on your feet. You'll be asleep."

I followed her down the porch steps to her car and when she got inside, I wondered whether we should maybe talk about that kiss. Problem was she was back to being sassy Ellie, soft, kissy Ellie had well and truly up and left the building.

Ah fuck it.

"Hey," I said as she turned the engine over. "About earlier—"

"No need," she said, stopping me with a hand up, palm toward me. "Forget it."

"Forget it?" Shit I felt kind of rejected, if not a little hurt.

"Yeah," she said, pulling slowly away. "Carter is the one to blame and he'll pay don't worry."

With a wave of her hand she was gone, driving off up the track leaving me feeling a little disjointed.

When I got into my bed fifty minutes later, after as expected, whacking off in the shower with images of Ellie in my head, my phone buzzed on the nightstand.

Ellie: I'm home. Don't tell the Sherriff but I broke the speed limit. Now tucked up in bed. See ya soon x p.s. thanks for the hoody. I may just keep it

And that was it, images of her tucked up in bed in a tiny pair of sleep shorts and maybe my hoody, had me hard again.

"What the fuck?" I groaned and rolled over forcing images of Ellie right out of my head, because it was something that could never happen, no matter how hot she was

CHAPTER 14

Ellie

Well, that was weird.

That was my first thought when I woke up. I wasn't sure whether the kiss with Hunter had really happened, or it'd been some sort of psychotic episode I'd had after seeing him dressed as one of those awful things.

Shaking my head and then rubbing my eyes for good measure, I realized it was indeed true. I'd kissed Hunter Delaney and boy had it been good. Okay, so he'd been slightly inebriated, and I hadn't, but this made me even more stupid. Hunter though, well he seemed to kind of like it too, if the hard on in his shorts all the way home was anything to go by.

I'd always thought him hot, always wondered, but now, all of a sudden, thoughts of me underneath Hunter, or even on top of Hunter, were increasing. Not only were they increasing but they were getting hotter too. The lilac colored dildo wrapped up in my duvet was testament to that. Don't judge me, don't all girls enjoy a little me time and then have another forty winks when they have nothing to get out of bed for on a Sunday morning?

Looking at my phone, I saw it was almost ten and I'd slept in a lot longer than I'd planned. I'd been telling the truth when I'd told Hunter I needed to plan Carter's demise; I needed to come up with something good. What though, I had no clue. We were too old to be still playing tricks on one another, so I'd be the better person and chalk it down to his douchery. Anyhow, planning to get him and Bronte together was giving me enough of a headache.

The idea of it had made me feel a little squeamish when I'd woken during the night. Why on earth would I want to land my best friend in the whole world, with my donkey head of a brother? Maybe there was someone else I could fix Bronte up with. The conclusion I'd quickly come to was that there wasn't. Bronte liked a challenge and none of the other men in our town, or the next three towns along would be a challenge – they'd all give their right nut to spend a night with Bronte Jackson, she was that beautiful.

It had struck me that maybe Hunter would be a good option instead, but two things made that a no go. One, if they did get together, she'd see Jefferson all the time and her crush could start up again at any time. Two, the idea of the two of them together made me even more squeamish than her with Carter; so, Carter it was.

I padded into the kitchen, still wearing my pajamas. Mom and Dad were sitting at the island, Mom reading the newspaper while Dad concentrated on his coloring book—yeah, apparently it helped him to relax.

"Morning, baby," Mom said, looking up and giving me a beautiful smile. "How was the party?"

I shrugged and curled my lip as I opened the refrigerator and pulled out a carton of juice. "Okay, except for Carter is the biggest dick head on this earth."

Dad sighed. "What's he done now?" He pushed his coloring book away and swiveled on his stool to face me.

He opened his arms and I gladly walked into them, snuggling into his big chest, while Mom stroked my hair.

"Did he say something to embarrass you?" Mom asked.

"Nope. Worse than that."

"Tell Daddy, honey." Dad kissed the top of my head and then let me go, taking the carton of juice from me and pouring it into a clean glass next to the sink.

Shit, I loved my parents when they went all Mommy and Daddy on me.

"He didn't show his wiener, did he?" Mom asked as Dad passed me my juice.

"Hey," Dad said, wagging a finger at Mom. "That boy has the Maples wiener and that is nothing to be embarrassed about."

I rolled my eyes and poked Dad in his rock-hard stomach. "No, it has nothing to do with his tiny wiener."

Dad growled making Mom and me giggle.

"So, tell us, what did he do." Mom settled her hands in her lap, waiting for my tale of woe.

"He got Hunter to dress up as a… ugh I can't say it." I screwed my eyes up and shuddered.

"What?" Dad asked, placing a comforting hand on my shoulder. "Because if it was Norv Turner, I'll kick his ass real hard."

Mom sighed and rubbed Dad's back. "Sweetheart, you need to let that go. Norv did what he had to do for his career."

"Fucking traitor," Dad muttered. "Y'all do not go from the Cowboys to the Redskins, no matter what. Damn right he got fired in the end."

"Whatever," I said a little impatiently. "But no, he didn't get him to dress up as *Norv Turner*."

"What then?" Dad asked, his breathing calming down.

"A… one of those things that Hunter has on his ranch." I whimpered. "He tricked him into dressing as a ugh… cow. I had a panic attack, almost passed out and made a real show for everyone. I was humiliated, Daddy."

I pouted and fluttered my lashes, knowing my dad would take the bait.

Three, two, one… he pulled his phone from his pocket and stabbed at it. "The little dick. He knows that's unacceptable."

Mom pulled me into a hug and kissed my temple. "He's a horrible brother, and I'm sorry I ever saddled you with him, baby."

I pulled away and looked up at her with a frown.

"But he was born first."

"Semantics baby, semantics."

"Carter," Dad yelled down the phone. "What sort of trick was that to play on your sister, you little douche canoe."

Ah shit, I really did love my parents.

***

Bronte and I were walking around the shopping mall, aimlessly wandering from store to store, neither of us having any idea why we'd even gone there.

I'd called her after my breakfast, half expecting her to ream my ass for leaving her at the party, but she'd been cool about it. Apparently, she'd found 'something to play with'. When I asked who, she gave me a rough description of some guy who had gone to the party with a friend of a friend of Alaska Michaels. She said he was hot and had the most amazing fingers and tongue and that was when I'd groaned and said, 'let's go shopping'.

"Let's go to the cosmetics section. I need concealer," Bronte said around a huge yawn.

"No what you need is an early night and less partying."

"Shit you sound like my mom. Seriously though, I do need some. Apart from the dark circles around my eyes, I'm getting the biggest break out."

I studied her clear skin carefully and knew by the little jut of her chin there was no point in arguing with her.

"Mac has a sale on."

I led the way past through the perfumery section of the store and when we came upon the Dior counter my heart did a little skip. The special offer scent of the day was Miss Dior and I could only think about Hunter's face when he told me about Jefferson buying it to remind him of Sondra.

"Wait up."

Bronte glanced at me over her shoulder. "Catch me up, I'm gonna go pee."

As she wandered away, I moved closer to the counter and picked up the tester bottle, holding it to my nose. It did smell like Hunter's mom, which was weird because I'd never realized before that I knew her smell. But, as I inhaled, memories of her hugging me at get togethers, or her coming over to our house and laughing uproariously with my mom and Darcy, flooded my memory banks. They made me happy and a little bit sad too. No wonder Jefferson and Hunter chased their own memories by spraying her scent.

"Can I help you at all," the overly made-up assistant asked as she approached me with a bottle, pointing at me like it was a gun.

"Just having a little trip down memory lane." I sprayed some onto each of my wrists and smiled at her.

"Would you like to buy some? We have a special today."

I shook my head. That was the last thing I would ever do. This was Jefferson and Hunter's way of remembering the woman they'd lost, and it wasn't something I would ever take away from them.

"I'm good thanks."

With one last smile, I went to find Bronte, feeling a deep ache in my heart for Hunter.

CHAPTER 15

Hunter

"**M**y dad chewed me *two* new ones this morning," Carter complained as he skimmed over the menu in Café Au Lait. "He actually told me I was fucking grounded."

"Is that so," I replied, barely listening to him.

He'd been bitching since I'd picked him up, about his dad calling him about the trick he'd played on Ellie. To be honest, I'd switched off after the tenth time of hearing it.

"If I'd known that she was scared of them, I wouldn't have worn it," I added, sitting back in my chair. "It was a pretty shitty thing to do."

Carter clutched a hand to his chest and stared at me, his mouth wide open.

"What? It was."

"I know, that's why I did it and you're supposed to be on my side. Since when have you ever been on Ellie's side?"

Since I realized she was fucking hot and kissed like a porn star—not that I'd ever kissed a porn star, but I had an imagination.

"Since that was the shittiest thing you've ever done to her. She was real scared and it made me feel bad."

"Hey boys, the usual."

I smiled up at Delphine who ran the café with her husband Garth and earned myself a beautiful one in return. Delphine and Garth were in their late fifties and didn't have any kids, so for the thirty years they'd been running the café, every kid in town had been unofficially adopted by the sweet couple.

"Hello, darlin'," Delphine said, scuffing my already messy, Sunday morning, had a few drinks and delivered a calf the night before, hair. "How's your pop doing? I haven't seen him in here for a few weeks."

"He's good, Delphine. We're busy on the ranch and when he's not busy, he's kinda busy if you know what I mean."

Delphine's cheeks blushed a pretty pink; she was another one who thought the sun shone from my pop's ass and dimples.

"What about you, sweetheart?" She turned to Carter. "Has Lance decided it's time for you to take over yet?"

Carter pouted and shook his head, earning him a hug.

"Oh, my lord. When will that man see sense?" Delphine pulled away from Carter and took a pen from the mess of hair on top of her head. "Usual, boys?"

Carter looked at the menu again and I knew he was contemplating going healthy, as he did every other Sunday when we went in for lunch. But like every other Sunday…

"Yep, all-day breakfast, and some of your amazing coffee please, Delphine," he said, rubbing his stomach.

"Coming right up."

Once she was out of earshot, I nudged Carter with my foot.

"So, tell me, who'd you hook up with last night?"

"Who said I did." He frowned. "Did Ellie tell you, because she's a sneaky little liar if she did."

What the fuck was wrong with him? He normally couldn't wait to tell me every last little detail of who he'd banged or nearly banged at a party.

"Well did you?"

"No. After you bailed on me, I spent the night talking to Minnesota, well listening to him cry into his beer to be more truthful."

"Really?" I asked. "Rather than get your hands into some girl's panties you spent the night talking to Minnesota who'd just been dumped. Jeez man, way to have a good night."

"Tell me about it. He cornered me. You should have asked me to come help with the calf."

"You'd had more beers than me so would have been useless, plus it was your night off. I know you've been busy these last few weeks helping down at the O'Reilly ranch."

The O'Reilly's bred cattle like us, but they bred Longhorn's which were beef stock, whereas our Beefmaster were good for milk and meat. The O'Reilly's also had a much bigger herd than me and Pop. It was probably three times the size, so while they had a few ranch hands they tended to call on Carter and Lance, but specifically Carter, much more than we did. I also had a fancy that Marie O'Reilly, their middle daughter, had taken a liking to Carter which was why he was called so often. Declan O'Reilly was desperate to see all five of his daughters married and Marie and sixteen-year-old Bernadette were the only two left.

"Hey," I said, having a thought. "Marie O'Reilly was there last night, wasn't she?"

As soon as Carter colored up, I knew I was right.

"You didn't. Shit tell me you didn't go there with Marie O'Reilly. If you did you know Declan will have you down that aisle faster than I can say, 'you're a dick'."

"Fuck off," Carter snapped, checking around the café. "No, I didn't, and don't even joke about it. I don't want Declan, Eamon or Pat knocking on my door wanting to know if the rumors about me and their daughter and sister are true. I told you I spent the night talking to Minnesota, so drop it."

I grinned getting the distinct impression my best friend was telling me a great big fat lie. No matter, I'd find out soon enough.

"Fuck's sake," Carter groaned. "Can't I get a break from her."

I looked over my shoulder to see he was talking about Ellie. She was huddled in some sort of girly chat and laughter with Bronte and they were walking into the café.

If I'd thought the kiss and my raging wood the night before had been purely down to the alcohol and a cute cheerleader outfit, I was sadly mistaken.

Fuck she looked amazing.

Her face was bare of makeup, her hair in one long braid over her shoulder and she had on a flannel shirt that I knew she'd had for years. Her jeans were ripped at the knees, and not those trendy ones bought like that, and on her feet were a pair of old scuffed cowboy boots. She looked like she hadn't made any effort, yet still managed to look more beautiful than anyone I'd ever seen.

"Well look who it is," Bronte sighed as they reached our table. "Carter the unstoppable douche machine."

"If you must reference crap British Indie bands then get the name right."

Bronte huffed. "You're hardly an unstoppable sex machine, from what I hear."

"Yeah, and that's your problem, Bronte. You'll only *ever* hear."

Carter leaned back in his chair and smirked. I for one wondered how either of them knew about British Indie bands.

"Thank the lord. You're such a douche even the Douche Club think you're overqualified to join."

"Oh, give it a rest, Bronte," Carter sighed. "The fact that you kicked me in the balls last night should be enough."

"You deserved it. Hi there, Hunter."

Bronte flashed me a quick smile and then turned to Ellie.

"I'll get us a table while your brother apologizes to you."

As Ellie stepped forward smirking at her brother, the smell hit me. It was like I'd been hit by a truck straight in my chest. The pain slashed sharply and took my breath away.

That smell, that scent, it was home, it was fun, it was love, *it was my mom.*

"What the fuck, Ellie," Carter complained. "Isn't it enough that Dad gave me shit on the phone this morning."

I watched Ellie's mouth move but didn't hear a word she said. I was too busy allowing the musky floral scent to invade my senses. I could smell her. I could feel her. And I could hear her. Ellie had done something that the bottle of perfume my pop had hidden away couldn't do; she had brought Mom back to life.

I should have been glad, happy and joyful, but all I wanted to do was tell her to get out and take a shower. It was all too fucking much. I needed her away from me.

"Ellie, he apologized so just leave it," I growled. "Now if you don't mind, we want to eat in peace."

I nodded toward Delphine who was carrying two coffees to our table.

"Hey, Ellie, darlin. You and Bronte staying to eat or just a coffee?"

Ellie didn't take her eyes from me, her mouth dropped open not unlike her brother's had been earlier. I knew I'd been sharp with her, but I couldn't handle all the feelings her smelling like my mom did to me.

"Ellie?"

She shook her head and turned to Delphine. "I think we're having cake… I don't know… erm I'll ask Bronte."

Delphine put the coffee down. "It's okay, darlin' I'll go ask her."

"What the hell, Hunter," Ellie snarled, turning to me. "What woke you up biting your ass this morning? And how come what he did is suddenly okay with you?"

"Duh, because he knows it was a joke," Carter replied, sounding like a dick.

"I didn't ask you," she shot back. "I asked him."

Brown eyes bored into me and I couldn't help but think how hot she looked. Then the smell wafted over to me again and I rolled my eyes.

"Just go eat cake with Bronte, Ellie."

"You're as big a dick as he is," she replied, her eyes full of fire and brimstone. "I have no idea why I even speak to you."

"Suits me fine," I scoffed not able to stop myself from sounding like Regina fucking George.

Okay, so I knew *Mean Girls,* but it wasn't something I spread around.

My mom had made me watch it with Ellie when she was about eleven and I was thirteen. Everyone was over at the ranch and for some reason Ellie didn't want to go outside and sit in the yard. Because I had sunburn, I'd been the one designated to watch the damn movie with her. Ellie had given me a lecture practically the whole way through how mean girls like Regina George didn't deserve to be happy. She went on for so long, the damn name stuck in my head.

Of course, I also now got why she didn't want to go outside, it was the fucking cows. I was still messed in the head though and wasn't in the mood for playing nice with her.

"You finished?" I asked, forcing my eyes wide to make the point I was done.

Ellie's eyes however went narrow as she looked at Carter.

"This is for you," she said as she flipped him the finger. "And this one left over is for you. Oh, and forget about the calendar, I don't need your help." She then turned to me and flipped me again before turning on her scuffed heels and storming over to the other side of the café.

"She's a damn spoiled brat," Carter muttered as he took a sip of his coffee.

As I watched her yank out the chair and start to tell Bronte everything, I kinda wanted to agree with him, but she was a damn sexy one that was for sure.

CHAPTER 16

Ellie

Damn Hunter Jefferson, what a big douche canoe. How dare he speak to me like that, especially considering we'd kissed the night before. Well, he wouldn't be getting any more of my sugar, not unless hell froze over or I needed CPR and he was the only man around to give it.

"What the hell did he say to you?" Bronte asked, halfway out of her chair.

"Leave it, sweetie. He hangs around with a douche, so he's a douche, no mystery there." I glanced over my shoulder to see Hunter looking over at me, so I did what any normal twenty-four-year-old woman would do and stuck out my tongue.

"Oh, it's Hunter you're mad at. Not your brother." Bronte's eyes gleamed with mischief. "That says so much."

"Like what?"

"Like you want in his pants *real* bad."

She elongated the word real and wiggled her perfectly shaped eyebrows.

"I do not." I snatched up the menu. "Are we eating, eating or just having cake?"

"Don't you dare change the subject, Eleanor Mary, but both."

"I'm not," I protested, looking up at her with a frown. "I'm hungry is all."

Bronte leaned across the table and whispered conspiratorially. "He's watching you. Did you know that? In fact, he can't take his eyes off you."

I buried my head further into the menu. "Don't know and don't care. Now, please can we just decide what we're eating."

With a sigh and a smack at my arm, Bronte flopped back into her seat. "You spoil all my fun. First off I'm not allowed to think about Jefferson and now I'm not allowed to talk about how you and Hunter have hot panties for each other."

"Sheesh, will you give it a rest."

I hoped that she couldn't see how pink my cheeks were, because her talking about me and Hunter and Hunter's eyes being on me, *was* getting me hot under the collar. I licked along my lips, remembering where his had been the night before, and cleared my throat.

"Did Carter apologize?" Bronte asked, taking the menu from me and stuffing it back into its little wooden holder.

"No, why would he? When has he ever apologized for anything he's ever done or said to me?"

"Ugh that boy irritates me beyond belief."

Bronte craned her neck to look over my shoulder toward my brother and when I saw her give the universal sign of dick head, I knew he was looking over.

"Stop it." I giggled. "Just let them be a pair of idiots together."

"Ugh boys are so stupid, and you wonder why I want in Jefferson's pants."

My stomach churned as she reminded me that Hunter and I were supposed to be working together on a plan.

"Made your mind up, girls?" Delphine asked as she placed a coke and a glass of milk on the table.

"I'll have a chicken salad sandwich and a piece of Garth's chocolate brownie cake, please Delphine," I replied and smiled up at her.

"Tuna on rye please, Delphine, but same cake." Bronte sighed. "God, I love that cake."

Delphine laughed. "I'm pretty sure that Garth's chocolate brownie cake is the only reason most folks come in here." She turned to walk away and then suddenly turned back. "Oh Ellie, I meant to tell you, my nephew Dylan is coming into town next week. I thought you could use him in the calendar if you're short of men."

I shifted in my seat, remembering the last time I'd seen Dylan about four years previous. He had a bag of donuts in one hand and a single donut in the other which he'd devoured with two bites.

I was short of Mr. March, but without being mean, I wasn't sure Dylan was the kind of guy the ladies of Dayton Valley would want to welcome Spring with.

"I don't know, Delphine, I think I might have the right number."

I didn't need to mention I'd fired Hunter only minutes before.

"Oh no you don't," Bronte butted in. "Cooper Wyatt dropped out, his fiancée told him it was her or the calendar, so the ball-less idiot chose her."

Bronte frowned, crinkling up her tiny button nose. Sometimes she was so damn cute, yet I also wanted to strangle her.

"Oh wow, that's amazing," Delphine gushed as she reached into her apron pocket. "Have I shown you a picture of him lately? He's lost 72 pounds."

My ears pricked up a little, but only because I wanted to fist pump his endeavors for losing weight. I'd been a chubby kid up until I was around twelve and it wasn't nice to be made fun of. That was why I'd gone total freak out on Belinda's car when she'd called me fat ass.

"Here you go," Delphine said, passing her phone to Bronte. "How cute is he?"

Bronte let out a long, low whistle. "Wow, Delphine. He looks fine."

Delphine beamed with pride and taking the phone from Bronte, passed it to me. I expected to give it a cursory glance, but when I looked down at the blond, bronzed god looking up at me, my vajayjay did a little gallop. I didn't usually like longer hair on a man, but jeez Dylan certainly wore his well.

"Woah," I exclaimed. "He's hot, Delphine."

"I know, right." She raised a brow and grinned. "And single."

"Oh my God," Bronte screamed. "Delphine, you have to introduce him to Ellie. You have to."

"We are so in tune," Delphine said and high-fived Bronte. "Which is why I think he'd be perfect for the calendar. You get a cute guy and I get to introduce you both. Win, win, Ellie."

"Oh no," I said with a shake of my head. "I'm not sure I…"

"Come on, Ellie," Bronte replied. "He's hotter than Satan's ball sack."

I rolled my eyes, thinking that description actually applied more to Hunter, and turned to Delphine. "I'd be glad of his help with the calendar, but as for anything else I'm—"

"Who's that?"

Hunter's voice cut into mine as he leaned into Delphine and stared down at the picture.

"My nephew Dylan." She practically preened as Hunter actually took the phone and peered more closely. "He's coming to stay and I'm going to introduce him to Ellie. He's going to take part in the calendar."

Hunter's head shot up and he stared at me, his eyes dark and intense.

"Thought you had enough guys for that?" he asked, holding the phone out to Delphine without taking his eyes from me.

"Cooper Wyatt pulled out," Bronte replied brightly. "He likes his fiancée to hold his balls for him when he's taking a leak."

I straightened and automatically my chest pushed out. I didn't fail to notice Hunter's eyes dropped to it and my damn nipples got a little hard at the thought. *Stupid bitches!*

"I may ask him to do two now, seeing as you're not helping out."

"Why?" Bronte asked at the same time as Hunter shouted, "I damn am."

"No, you're not, Hunter," I replied, giving him a shake of my head. "I don't need you."

"I think you do," Hunter said through gritted teeth.

"You do," Bronte whined.

"No, I don't, not after he spoke to me like I was the dirt under his shoe, I don't."

Bronte slapped him on the arm, while Delphine slipped away mouthing that she'd be back with our food.

"You idiot," Bronte said. "Apologize immediately."

"I don't want him to apologize. I'm not putting him in the calendar."

I knew he'd be a great asset and would probably be the selling point for half the ladies in town, not to mention the other towns the hospital serviced, but he was an idiot, and I was standing my ground. I was determined. I didn't need Hunter Delaney for anything, least of all a titillating calendar shot of him in just his underwear.

As I jutted my chin out with determination, Hunter leaned down, his mouth close to my ear.

"No calendar, no help in getting Carter and Bronte together," he whispered. "In fact, I might just go back over there now and tell him your little plan."

I gasped like I was a shielded Southern Belle and he'd just told me the dirtiest joke ever.

"You wouldn't."

He didn't speak but raised his brows and nodded slowly.

"Okay," I said, the fight going out of me. "You're back in."

Bronte clapped like a sea lion while Hunter grinned and then carried on to the men's room. Me, well I cussed and cursed under my breath and realized that the stupid idiot had me tightly by my lady balls.

CHAPTER 17

Hunter

Not a fucking chance would Ellie be getting introduced to Delphine's damn nephew.

Fucking pretty boy.

Nothing else was going to happen between me and her, that much was pretty evident after I pissed her off in the café the day before, but that didn't mean that I was going to sit back and let some Thor look alike cozy up to her. Stupid prick needed to get a haircut anyway.

"Hey, son you got a minute?"

"Hang on."

I forked the clean hay around the calving pen and then turned to Pop. "What's up?"

He frowned and I knew I wasn't going to like what he had to say. "L and J want to go into town. Was wondering if you could take them."

"Why me?" I asked, rubbing my forehead with my forearm. "Can't you? I was going to ride out to the far pasture and check whether we need to cut down that storm damaged tree."

Pop rubbed the floor with the toe of his boot. "I'm kind of avoiding someone."

"Shit, Pop," I groaned. "You've dumped Jojo."

"Yeah, and she didn't take it too well."

"Why does that stop you going into town? I thought she worked at Tatum's Grocery Store at Jennings Bridge."

"Yeah, she did, but they asked her to cover here for a few weeks. And," he sighed, rubbing a hand down his beard, "because she thought we were seeing each other, she agreed. Thought she'd get to see more of me."

"You don't have to take Auntie L and J into the grocery store."

"That's kinda where they want to go, and you know I can't leave them on their own in there. Remember last time and they came home with twenty cans of Chicken a la King, just because it was on special."

I couldn't help laughing, mainly at the pained look on Pop's face. "Yeah, we have beef on hand, and they bought canned chicken in case we had a winter storm and needed supplies."

Pop shrugged as if to say, *'told you so'*.

"So, will you take them?"

I'd been looking forward to giving Dante, my horse, a blow out, but Pop looked as though the idea of him going into town was about as popular as a fart in a spacesuit.

"I'll let you have the afternoon off tomorrow," he said, almost pleading with me.

Liking the idea of a few hours down time, I nodded. "Okay. As long as you go and check the tree and take Dante instead of Jezebel."

"Fine. No problem." Pop replied. "I'll let him blow off some steam. I know he's been frustrated, stuck in the stables for the last two weeks because of that abscess on his tail."

We had four horses in total, but we rarely used our two older mares Dolly Parton and Tammy Wynette. They'd worked hard over the years and deserved their time in the pasture opposite to the house. To say they'd been mad at having to work had been an understatement. Dolly had even tried to throw me the day before.

I handed Pop the fork and was about to walk out of the barn, when something struck me. *Him and Ellie.* It just blasted from nowhere, right out of left field.

"You're not after someone else, are you?"

"Fuck no. I think I'm going to stay away from the ladies for a little while." He grinned at me and smoothed back his hair. "Well until singles night on Friday at Stars & Stripes."

"Really? Pop, you do know that you've probably had most of the single women in this town."

"Yeah, but according to Mack from the feed store there's a bus coming in from Middleton Ridge."

"Like you've not got enough women to be going at," I muttered and shook my head. "Seriously Pop, I hope you're wrapping up because you're gonna catch something nasty one of these days."

"Of course, I am. What sort of idiot do you think I am?"

"A sex crazed one," I replied with a roll of my eyes. "I'll see you later."

"Later, son, and I really appreciate it."

I waved him away and went to wrangle my aunts into the truck, for what I knew was going to be an afternoon of hell.

***

Leaning onto the handle of the cart, I yawned loudly as we went into minute four of my aunts arguing about which was the best toilet paper.

"We keeping you awake?" Auntie L asked, arching a brow at me.

"Well, does it matter. As long as I can wipe my ass without poking my finger through, I don't care which is softest."

"Of course, it matters," Auntie J exclaimed, hitting me with a pack of two rolls. "When you ride out on your horse every morning, you don't want to have a sore butt before you've even started your day." She turned and put the pack back. "We'll come back to them later."

"What?" I threw my hands in the air. "You're kidding right?"

They both looked at me like I was the most stupid person on earth. Being that I'd agreed to bring them shopping, I think they had a point.

"We need to take our time choosing." Auntie L tutted and then moved past me with her nose in the air.

"Take no notice, sweetheart," Auntie J said. "She's hormonal."

At this point I knew I'd done something bad in a former life.

Shuddering, I followed them with the cart only to find they'd stopped again. This time though they weren't arguing about which was the best of something, they were talking to none other than Ellie. Ellie who was dressed in jean shorts which cupped her ass cheeks to perfection and showed off her slim, tanned legs – images of which in a short cheer skirt were still invading my dreams.

As I reached them, Ellie gave me a cursory glance with, if I wasn't mistaken, a little curl of her top lip.

"Ellie.'

I knew she must still be mad at me for how I'd been in the café, but I didn't expect her to ignore me totally.

"Okay, that's rude," I grumbled.

Ellie's head shot around and she levelled me with a deadpan stare. "Because you'd know."

"Oh my, Hunter, what did you do?" Auntie J asked, clutching her purse close to her chest.

"Nothing," I remonstrated.

I wasn't about to tell her why I'd lost my shit with Ellie in the café. That would open up a whole can of worms that I didn't want to sift through. It was hard enough coming to terms with the fact that I'd suddenly started fantasizing about my best friend's little sister, never mind the fact that her smell reminded me of my dead mom.

What a mind fuck.

"Oh, Hunter," Auntie L sighed. "I thought you were more of a gentleman than that."

I startled, wondering if she could read my dirty thoughts, especially as I was trying to avoid looking at Ellie's tits in the tight white tee she was wearing.

"I'm always a gentleman," I argued.

Ellie crossed her arms over her chest as though she also knew what was going on in my head. She probably did to be fair, the last couple of times we'd met she'd had to tell me to keep my eyes above chin level.

"Not so much in the café," she replied with a smirk.

Auntie J smacked my arm. "I'm so disappointed with you, Hunter Meredith Delaney."

As she full named me, I drew in a breath the same time that Ellie burst out laughing.

"No way," she laughed. "Your middle name is not Meredith. Oh shit, that's hilarious. Does Carter know."

Of course, my best friend knew. On the very day he found out, during a history lesson about family trees when we were thirteen, he caught his dick in a coke bottle. Okay weird I know, but he was keeping watch outside the school sports hall while I got my first sexual experience from Paulette Benedict who was two years older than us. That meant we both had shit on each other.

The fact that Ellie now knew at least meant that all bets were off with Carter. I could hold that juicy little nugget over his head without any fear for ever more.

"Yes, Carter knows," I replied through gritted teeth.

Ellie had tears edging at the corners of her eyes as she continued to laugh and held her stomach. To add insult to injury, both my aunts joined in with her.

"It was Sondra's uncle's name. He left her quite a sum of money, on provision she promised to name her first child after him," Auntie L explained with a giggle.

Auntie J looked at me with a huge grin. "She didn't really want you to have it, but it *had* been his last will and testament, so she had no choice really."

"Yeah, I'm aware," I said, flashing narrow eyes at Ellie who was still braying like a fucking donkey. "Mom told me the story many times." Usually when she was a little tipsy and apologizing profusely for landing me with such a shit name.

"Oh my God, Hunter," Ellie sighed, her laughter finally dying down. "That's the funniest thing I ever did hear."

"Well, never mind that," Auntie J said, laying a hand on Ellie's arm. "Why don't you tell us how he upset you."

Ellie shook her head. "Oh no, it's fine Auntie J. It was nothing and I'm sure he's sorry. Aren't you, Hunter?"

Her words were pointed as she raised both her brows, almost to her hairline.

"I'm sorry," I breathed out. "And I promise to be a gentleman in the future."

I couldn't be bothered with arguing with her about it. Anyway, she was right, I had been a bit of dick.

Auntie J smiled. "That's good, so how about you apologize properly by taking Ellie to the singles night on Friday."

Ellie giggled nervously. "That's okay. It's fine."

"You don't really take someone to a singles night, Auntie J."

"Only if it's a date you don't," she replied, her lips twitching as she tried to hold back a smile. "It's not a date, is it?"

"No, she hasn't even said yes." I pushed the cart away from them. "Anyway, come on, you still have a whole list of stuff you need to get."

"She hasn't said yes, *yet*. Ooh, Janice-Ann, do you think that means they're going to the singles night together."

"Now, Lynn-Ann, don't put the cart before the horse. Hunter hasn't asked Ellie yet."

"I wasn't going to," I declared.

"Why?" Ellie asked. "What's wrong with taking me to singles night? It's not like it'd be a date Hunter... Meredith."

My nostrils flared as I looked at her. She was sucking on her bottom lip and one hip was cocked out. She had the same fire in her eyes as a wild mountain horse and I wondered how the fuck I'd never seen her before. I mean I'd known she was hot, but I'd never really *seen* her. Yet for the past couple of weeks, she'd been *all* I could fucking see, especially when I was jacking off.

"It wouldn't be a date," I stated.

"I wouldn't want a date with you." Ellie screwed up her nose and looked like she could smell shit.

"It'll be great," Auntie J said. "You'll be there, so will we and then there's Bronte."

"Bronte's going?" Ellie exclaimed.

"Yes," Auntie J replied. "I spoke to her this morning. I booked in for us to have our nails done, so they look nice for Friday night."

"Don't forget Jefferson." Auntie L beamed at us. "All there together, just like Janice-Ann said, so much fun."

"*You're going.*" I almost choked on the gasp of air I took in. "You can't. It's singles night."

"Well, we're single," Auntie L said with a defiant tilt of her chin. "So, why shouldn't we?"

I raised my palms to the ceiling. "Because… well because…"

"Your Pop is going?" Ellie muttered, looking like her eyes might burst out of her head. "*And* Bronte."

I ran a hand through my hair. "Yeah, Ellie, I heard."

"*Your Pop.*" She leaned forward and poked me in the chest. "So maybe we should go."

"Fuck, not this again," I muttered under my breath. "Really?"

"Yes, really," she replied with a shake of her head. "Sometimes I wonder about you."

"What does that mean?" It was now my turn to cross my arms over my chest.

Ellie leaned closer to my ear and got on her tippy toes. "We have something we *have* to do, *remember.*"

"How the fuck can I forget," I whispered back.

"What are you two talking about?" Auntie L asked with a starry-eyed smile as she nudged Auntie J. "Is there something you need to tell us."

"No." Ellie and I shouted at the same time.

"Oh, that's a shame, isn't it, Janice-Ann. I was hoping we might have a little love story going on."

Ellie took a step back, clutching her t-shirt like she'd just been shot, and I felt stupid for feeling disappointed, yet again, by her reaction. I had no clue what was going on in my head, or why how Ellie felt about me was important all of a sudden.

"Yeah well, we don't," I snapped back. "Come on let's go."

"But you haven't finalized your arrangements for Friday night yet?" Auntie L complained.

I heaved out a frustrated breath and pushed the cart past Ellie. "I'll pick you up at seven-thirty," I called over my shoulder. "Be ready.'

The last comment wasn't necessary, I knew that, but she'd pissed me off.

"Oh Hunter," Auntie L sighed. "You could have asked her in a more gentlemanly way than that."

Damn women, who the hell needed them?

CHAPTER 18

Ellie

"I thought you said it wasn't a date." Bronte winked just as she ripped the muslin strip from my vagina.

"Shit." I winced and blew out a shuddering exhale. "I never get used to that."

"Maybe if you got your hoo-hah waxed a little more often than twice a year, you wouldn't feel such pain." She tsked and shook her head. "Honestly Ellie, I'm ashamed to call you my friend. It's bad for business when people see my best friend walking around town with pubic hairs showing at the bottom of her shorts.

I rolled my eyes and braced myself as Bronte flattened the strip against the warm wax again.

"Stop exaggerating," I replied with only the tiniest of gasps. "I'm really neat down there, I just need a tidy up."

"Yes, because I'm damn good at my job. When I get rid of those hairy little critters, I get rid of them good." She did one more rip and I swear she pulled harder that time. "Okay you can put your grey granny panties back on now."

"They're not granny panties," I objected as I swung my legs off the bed and onto the floor.

Bronte snorted a laugh, evidently disagreeing. "They're granny panties, darlin' believe me."

As I slipped back into my roomy and comfortable panties, Bronte set to cleaning up her station and threw out all the rubbish, including the pink, latex gloves she'd been wearing. She worked quietly and I felt pretty unnerved. There wasn't a minute go by where Bronte didn't have something to say.

"Which cat got your tongue?" I asked. "You're awful quiet for someone who is desperate to know all the gossip."

She swung around to face me. "I'm a conscientious worker. I like to be sure everything is clean and tidy."

I started laughing. "Okay, tell me what's wrong."

"Nothing." She frowned and went back to her cleaning.

"Bullshit. I know you too well, now spill it."

Bronte blew out making her bangs blow in the breeze as she flopped down onto her stool.

"It's just if I go to singles night and Jefferson is there, and he leaves with someone, I know it's gonna hurt real bad."

My head dropped back onto my neck and I gave a silent prayer, coupled with a few chosen curse words.

"What?" Bronte asked.

I levelled my gaze with hers. "Enough of the crap about you and Jefferson. It can't happen."

While I zipped up my jeans, Bronte stared at me wide-eyed like I'd just taken a crap on her beauty couch.

"I don't get why you think it would be shit for me and Jefferson to be together," she said with a shrug of her shoulders.

"Our parents. *Your* parents," I declared. "They've all been friends for years. Can you imagine the size of the turd that would hit the fan? It would be epic, Bronte. Shit would be splattered to all four corners of Dayton Valley and maybe even as far as Middleton Ridge."

A thudding started in my temple as I looked at Bronte, despair in my tone and pleading in my voice, only to see a huge damn grin on her face.

"Bronte, this isn't funny."

"Oh, but imagine Thanksgiving and Christmas, when its mine and Jefferson's turn to host the party." Her eyes twinkled as she hugged a towel to her chest. "Do you think Jefferson would call my mom and dad, Mom and Dad, or would I call them Darcy and Jim?"

"Neither," I replied. "Because you are not getting together with Jefferson."

"Well, I kinda need to point out, you can't actually stop me." Bronte gave me her most sugary smile and gently pulled at a strand of my hair. "Don't be such a spoilsport anyway."

"I thought you just wanted a quick roll in the hay with him – literally," I said, trying a different tact. Hoping if she was only interested in a quick round of sex, I'd be able to dissuade her. "Not a full-on relationship."

"Yes, but I kinda like the idea of being the second Mrs. Delaney. I mean, I know Hunter would spit feathers about it, but that boy needs a momma."

My mouth dropped open, disbelieving what I was hearing. There could not be one brain cell in her head that thought the words it had just formed were sensible, valid or obtainable. Surely? Any minute now, my best friend would slap her thigh and shout, 'just kidding'.

Taking a minute to gather myself, I smoothed down my shirt and popped my feet back into my flip flops. When I finally had my purse on my shoulder, I cleared my throat and looked up at Bronte.

"Okay," I sighed. "I know you have to be joking about the being Hunter's mom thing, so I'll ignore it for now."

"But I—"

I showed Bronte my palm, silencing her.

"No," I replied evenly and with a smile. "I know you're joking, so I'll take the joke in the good faith it was offered. Please, don't let me ever have to hear you say those words ever again. The thought is just—" I stopped, thinking I might gag at the thought of Bronte being Hunter's step-mom.

Imagine it, him having to kiss her goodnight, or hug her and thank her for dinner or for the Christmas gifts that she and his dad bought him. What if spending more time with Bronte, gave Hunter time to see how adorable she was. Then he'd make a move and knowing Bronte, she'd be bored of Jefferson by then... shit, Jefferson would be heart broken and he and Hunter would never talk again.

"Crap," I muttered and gave myself a little shake at my ridiculous mind ramblings. Mostly though I needed to whup my own ass for even caring. "Okay, I'm going home to get ready for tonight."

"For your *date*."

"I told you, it's not a date."

"What is it then?" Bronte asked not looking at me but messing with her phone instead.

"We're just going to singles night together, company for each other. Plus, it's Hunter's apology for being a dick in the café on Sunday."

"Who the hell goes to a singles night on a date?" Bronte asked, turning back to me. "That boy needs his pop to show him a thing or two when it comes to women."

I really didn't want to say it again, so I pulled her into a hug and turned for the door, pausing as I reached it.

"If you do go tonight, please don't make a play for Jefferson."

Bronte opened her mouth to say something, but before she spoke, I jumped right on in there.

"It won't be pretty if Hunter sees you." I gave her my puppy dog eyes, laying on every bit of cuteness I had. "Show him a little respect."

Bronte thought for a couple of seconds and then nodded.

"Okay, if I go, I'll stay away from Jefferson."

With a sigh of relief, I left, pulling the treatment room door closed behind me. As soon as I reached the parking lot, I pulled out my phone and dialed Hunter's number.

"Hey," he greeted me. "What's up? You changed your mind about tonight?"

"No," I replied, glancing towards Bronte's salon. "We need to step things up, so as well as getting Carter and Bronte together I have another idea for the plan."

I heard Hunter groan quietly and wished he'd been in front of me so I could stamp on his foot.

"Go on," he sighed before I had a chance to lose my shit with him. "What's this new piece of the plan."

I grinned, pretty pleased with myself.

"Tonight, at singles night, we make sure your dad gets fixed up with someone."

Hunter laughed on the other end of the line, almost deafening me.

"Hunter," I snapped. "What's so funny?"

"We don't need to make sure Pop gets fixed up, Ellie."

"Yes, we do." I pulled to a stop and slammed a hand against my hip. "Bronte is…" Damn. How did I tell him she was fixin' to be his new mom without him either laughing until he peed his pants, or losing his shit?

"Bronte is what?" he asked.

"She's definitely going tonight." I improvised, not wanting to give the whole of Bronte's sordid plan to make him her stepson. "So, we need to make sure she's not even on Jefferson's radar.

Hunter replied with a frustrated "I know, I was there when the twins told us, remember."

"Oh, and by the way, Carter is going too," I offered.

"Yeah, I know. He said."

"And he was okay about us going together?" I asked, wondering what Carter would be like about his friend hitting on his sister. Okay, it was immaterial; Hunter wouldn't be hitting on me and Carter barely tolerated me himself, so probably wouldn't care.

"Yes," Hunter replied sharply. "Because it's *not* a date. Now can I go? I need to help round up the herd and bring them in before I shower."

Pressing my key to open my car, I once again glanced over at the salon wondering if I could actually lock Bronte inside until Monday morning.

"Fine," I replied. "And don't be late picking me up."

Before he ended the call, I was pretty sure I heard Hunter say something about me being a dictator, but wasn't sure, so let it go.

It was only once I was in my car that I let myself relax and realize that it wasn't hunger swilling around in my belly. I was excited and it was actually a hundred, thousand butterflies doing a synchronized dance.

CHAPTER 19

Hunter

When I pulled up outside the Maples house, I didn't expect Ellie to be running down their driveway, coatless, in a tiny dress with her shoes in her hand. I especially didn't expect her to be closely followed by her dad.

"What the fuck, El?" I asked as she yanked the door open and hauled herself up into the truck.

"Drive!"

"What's going on?" I peered out at Henry who was laughing and waving his arms around.

"Just go, Hunter. Go."

I turned the key in the ignition, but before I managed to put the truck into drive, a six-feet-two, ex cornerback plastered himself to the hood.

"Hang on a damn minute," Henry called with a shit eating grin. "I need to talk to you."

Ellie shrank down into the seat, burying her face in her hands. "Just drive over him. I won't hold it against you, I swear. We can tell the Sheriff it was an accident."

I glanced at her and couldn't help but smile. The dress she was wearing was not only short but tight and gave me a great view of her legs. Her hair was up with wispy bits hanging down and on her knee was a pair of hot pink pumps, with the thinnest and highest heels I'd ever seen. I was about to adjust myself, when a banging in my left ear stopped me from putting a hand to my dick.

I buzzed the window down and turned to Henry. "Hey, Henry. What's up?"

"Dad, no," Ellie yelled, loud enough to bust my eardrum. "Don't you dare."

Henry held up a pacifying hand. "Come on now, Ellie Belly, I wouldn't be fulfilling my duty as your daddy if I didn't do this."

My stomach flipped as I looked at Henry's face. He wore a frown and had me pinned with a stare that would have made a marine shit his combats.

"What's going on?" I asked, trying to hide the nervous quake in my voice.

"Dad if you do this, I will hate you forever. I will never cut your toenails for you ever again. Never give you a foot rub and most definitely never, ever get rid of those knots in your back after a long day in the office."

My head whipped back to Ellie who had her chin tilted in defiance.

"Sheesh," Henry replied, getting my attention again. "That's harsh, Ellie, but I'm sorry, honey I have to."

"Will someone please tell me what's going on."

I looked between them both. Ellie was all sulky and pouty, while Henry was still grinning at me.

"I want to know what your intentions are toward my daughter," Henry replied. "I need to know whether they're honorable or if you're going to try and get into her panties."

"*Oh my God, Dad*," Ellie cried, loud and painfully. "I hate you. In fact,

I'm divorcing you as my dad."

A deep chuckle was followed by a huge hand landing on my shoulder.

"So, Hunter, what is it? Are you a good virginal boy, who doesn't believe in sex before marriage? Or do I have to come at your nuts with a pair of pliers?"

My fucking balls actually shrank as I inhaled sharply.

"It's not a date, Dad. I told you this."

"You say that," Henry sighed. "But I know what these young bucks are like. I was one. Shit, me and your mom were always—"

"No, Sir." I butted in to avoid having to hear something that may have scarred me for life. "I'm not going to try and get into Ellie's…" I glanced at Ellie's legs and then I just couldn't help it—come on, her tits were heaving, and her dress was tight.

"Hunter." She snapped her fingers and nodded toward her dad.

My head turned back to Henry whose face quickly morphed into one of all seriousness.

"My intentions are strictly honorable."

I felt a sharp elbow in my side. "You don't need to tell him, he knows," she replied, with an exasperated huff of breath. "He's just being an idiot because him and Mom popped the wine at dinner."

When she leaned across me, I sank back into my seat as far as I could. Her tits looked totally on point as the rounded swell of them pushed against the low neckline of her dress. I knew if they touched me, Henry would most definitely be pulling me out of the truck and beating my ass. I knew this for fact because my dick would be a pretty good indicator that there was not one inch of honor in what I intended to do to his daughter, if I ever got the chance.

"Can you please go back inside now," Ellie said to him through gritted teeth. "You've had your fun."

I inhaled her perfume, which was rich and sexy, and I was glad she didn't smell of my mom again. All I wanted to do was drag her across the console into my lap and kiss the fuck out of her.

Making a little growling sound, she lifted a hand to pry his fingers from the window, but as she did, she lost balance and her face landed right next to my damn dick. My dick that thought it was a good idea, at that very moment, to drain all the blood from the rest of my body and keep if for himself.

"Fuck, Ellie," I groaned, as I scrambled to lift her under her arms.

"Oh my God, Hunter," came her muffled response.

"Get up, get up now."

As she wriggled, she created friction between my pants and dick, and the fact that her lips were dangerously close to the goods, just made things worse.

Frantic and desperate, I managed to pull her up and find myself face to face with her. I figured we were both the same crimson color. Although, when Ellie put her hand down to steady herself and brushed my hard on, she may have gone a shade darker.

While we scrambled to get ourselves sorted, Henry's deep rumbling laughter echoed around the cab of my truck.

"Well, glad that's all sorted," he said as he banged twice on the roof. "You kids go have fun, but remember I have pliers, Hunter."

He then strode off, back up the driveway, his shoulders shaking with laughter.

"You okay?" I asked as Ellie straightened her dress and pushed her tits back into place.

She didn't look at me but gave a tight nod. "Yep. Now drive."

As we pulled away, I gave her a quick look and I knew that if I didn't do something about this newfound crush soon Henry wouldn't need pliers for my balls—they'd fucking explode of their own accord.

Maybe banging someone else would help?

Yeah, that'd be the answer and singles night might just be the perfect place to find someone to fuck Ellie Maples right out of my head. That's what I'll do, I thought, find someone tonight and then Ellie and I could get back to being just friends.

Perfect plan.

CHAPTER 20

Ellie

How the hell was I supposed to concentrate on the plan when Hunter looked so damn delectable. If the grey dress pants and black dress shirt weren't enough, the fact that he had his sleeves rolled back to show off his tanned forearms and chunky watch almost finished me off.

Ovaries – Boom – Exploded.

"You okay?" he asked, tilting his head to one side and frowning.

"Yup." I nodded and clenched my thighs together.

"You sure, because you look kinda strange?"

"Strange in what way?" I thrust one hand to my hip. while the other smacked at him with my clutch.

"What the actual fuck, Ellie," Hunter complained and took a step back. "I need danger money when I'm with you."

"If you didn't insult me all the time, I wouldn't feel the need to slap you." I narrowed my eyes at him and then pushed to the bar. "What do you want to drink?"

A big, rough hand landed on my upper arm and pulled me back.

"Nope. No way you are buying me a drink, or any drinks for that matter."

Hunter pushed past me, his arm brushing the side of my boob and my belly swooped down close to my toes. In fact, I was so caught up in the smell of his cologne and the fact that I could see the outline of strong back muscles under his shirt, I forgot to complain about him being a chauvinistic pig.

"Beer or vodka?" Hunter asked over his shoulder.

I considered it for a few seconds. I was rostered onto a late shift the next day so…

"Vodka please."

How the hell did he know I drank vodka occasionally, anyway?

Contemplating it momentarily, Jefferson soon pulled my attention by strolling into Stars & Stripes. Looking good in a white dress shirt and pants, he, like Hunter, had his sleeves rolled up, showing off his tattoos that far outnumbered Hunter's which were only on his biceps and chest.

His chest!

Shaking my head to get Hunter's chest out of it, my attention went back to Jefferson. He was talking to a tall guy with a shock of black hair; a guy whose name I didn't know, but knew he worked at the seed store – a while back Bronte'd had a thing for one of the guys who worked there. They were both laughing, but I could see that most of the ladies' attention in the bar was drawn to Jefferson.

He was tall and broad, his grey hair and beard were stylish and even from where I was standing, I could see the twinkle in his eye. Yep, he was striking alright, and it was clear what Hunter would look like when he got older.

"Oh my," I whispered to myself, exhaling deeply.

Licking my lips, I glanced over at Hunter, who was laughing with Penny as she handed him his card back. When he reached around to slip his wallet into his back pocket my eyes were drawn to his ass. It was not so high it looked like a girl's, but high and firm enough that I thought about bouncing a nickel off it just for fun. I was pretty sure it was the nicest, firmest male ass I'd ever seen.

My nipples began to ache as they rubbed braless against the fabric of my dress, and there was a distinct throb between my legs. While it all felt pretty nice, it felt weird too. This was Hunter Delaney, my brother's best friend. The guy I loved giving shit to on a regular basis. The guy I'd known all my life. Why the hell was I suddenly having dirty thoughts about him?

I couldn't give it any more consideration because Hunter was walking toward me with a large glass of alcohol.

"Vodka and diet," he said, passing it to me.

Our fingers brushed and I couldn't help my sharp intake of breath.

"Okay?" he asked, a smug smirk on his lips.

I rolled my eyes. He damn well knew what he was doing to me. If that stupid gasp hadn't given it away, I was pretty sure my nipples almost poking him in the eyes had.

***

Hunter and I were pretty tight and well on our way to being drunk. In fact, drinking, laughing and talking were the only thing we'd done in the hour and a half we'd been in the bar. We'd done nothing to put our plan to get Jefferson hooked up into action. Reason being, we didn't need to. He'd managed that all by himself, just like Hunter said he would.

"Oh my God," I snorted leaning into Hunter. "He's got his hand on her ass."

Hunter lifted his bottle to his lips and grinned around it.

"Hunter, he's squeezing it."

I started laughing. Jefferson had been talking to this particular lady, a tall, curvy redhead for around twenty minutes, and was already putting the moves on her. She didn't seem to mind though, because as we watched, her hand snaked up his chest and rubbed seductively against it.

"My Pop is the shit," Hunter groaned. "He only has to look in a woman's direction and she's melting at his feet."

"Pity he didn't pass on his expertise to you."

Biting my lip, I tried not to smile, but when Hunter's mouth dropped open, I couldn't help it.

"You little shit," he said, pulling me closer and poking a finger into my side. "You know how fucking good I am with women."

He added a couple more fingers and started to tickle me, making me giggle and squirm.

"Say you're sorry," he demanded.

"Nope."

I could barely breathe for laughing, but I didn't care. It felt good to be actually enjoying spending time together. While we stood at the high table, we watched everyone around us, neither of us even considering finding someone we might like to hook up with. I hadn't gone there for that anyway, but that didn't mean Hunter wasn't interested. Yet he'd only strayed to the bar and back, never any further, and I didn't think his eyes had either.

That thought gave me a little warm feeling inside my chest and a few more butterflies in my belly.

"Want me to prove it?" Hunter asked.

"W-what do you mean?"

My heart went boom-dah-dah-dah-boom as I waited for him to put the moves on me. Then he looked around the room, looking discerningly at all the women.

The boom-dah-dah-dah-boom was replaced with a pathetic bump and I moved away from him. It wasn't me he was going to put the moves on. Every single one of those beautiful butterflies I had flying around my stomach, just went and dropped to the pit of my stomach and died.

"I can prove it to you that I have my Pop's skills with the ladies."

Swallowing down the bitter taste of disappointment, I pushed my shoulders back and nodded. I'd been stupid to even start to feel an attraction to him, never mind consider what a few drinks and giggles together might mean.

"Okay," I said, feeling a new determination to get him out of my head. "Let's have a wager."

My eyes skimmed the room until they landed on a tall blonde woman wearing a gorgeous red dress that fitted her like a wetsuit. She was talking to a preppy guy who although good looking was a little too smooth for me. His golden blond hair looked like it may actually have been sculpted, it was so neat and tidy.

"See that couple over there."

Hunter followed my gaze. "Yep."

"Let's see who gets asked to go somewhere quieter first. Winner has to clean the other one's car. Inside and out."

Hunter snorted and carefully placed his bottle of beer down onto the table.

"It's a deal," he said, holding out his hand for me to shake. "Easy."

I placed my glass next to his bottle and then shook. I was determined I'd win. For one, I didn't want Hunter to beat me, I really didn't want to have to clean that monster of a truck of his. For two though, maybe chatting to preppy guy would help me to forget that I wanted inside Hunter's boxer briefs.

Oh God, was it possible that Hunter went commando? No, he was definitely a boxer brief kind of guy. The chafing while riding Dante every day would be awful.

"Quick," Hunter said as he started to move away from me. "The guy has gone to the bar. Now's our chance."

***

"Oh, my goodness," I sighed, with what I hoped was a seductive lick of my lips. "That's amazing. Wait until I tell my Dad."

It turned out that preppy guy, Conrad, had been to the same college as my dad and had also played on the football team as cornerback. That's what he'd said, but he hadn't heard of my dad and as he was in their college hall of fame, I wasn't quite sure Conrad was telling the whole truth. He was cute though and as I wasn't interested in anything after tonight, I'd forget his white lie.

"So, how come you're here tonight? I mean I would have thought a good-looking guy like you would have lots of girls falling over themselves to date you."

I'd glanced over at Hunter a few minutes earlier and he seemed to be doing better than I was. The blonde was pushing her girls up against him and had flicked her hair enough times to create a tornado.

"I do okay."

Conrad raised a brow and winked with the opposite eye. He looked like he was trying to pass wind, but hey if he thought it looked sexy and I might be interested then so be it.

We continued to talk, well Conrad did, and for another ten minutes I listened. It was totally boring. I couldn't give up though because every time I looked over at Hunter, Miss Red Dress had pushed even closer to him. She was so close I was holding my breath and waiting for her to mount him like a spider monkey.

"So," Conrad said, taking one of my wisps of hair and running it through his fingers. "Tell me about yourself."

Finally.

"Well, I'm a pediatric nurse and… sorry, I…" I trailed off as I noticed Miss Red Dress' hand that had been on Hunter's chest had moved around to his ass and given it a squeeze, just like Jefferson's had done to the redhead earlier.

"Go on," Conrad urged, chucking his glass of wine with my vodka.

I tried to move my attention back to him, but I couldn't take my eyes from Hunter. I was waiting to see how he reacted. Would he see her hand on his backside as his sign to make a move?

I didn't get a chance to find out, because the bar doors flew open and Lynn-Ann and Janice-Ann strolled in waving at everyone, like they were the Queen of England only in duplicate.

"What the hell," Conrad said around a laugh. "What have they come as?"

My gaze spun to his and he was literally looking down his nose at the two old ladies dressed in coordinating pant suits. Janice-Ann was in baby pink, while Lynn-Ann was in sunshine yellow. They both had on white pumps and carried purses the color of their outfit. They looked like walking candy bars, but not one of the few locals in the bar batted an eyelash. The only people really staring were those who'd come in from out of town.

"They're my friend's aunts," I replied with a hint of snark to my tone. "They're extremely lovely ladies."

Conrad laughed and took a delicate sip of his wine and watched as the twins parted the small crowd on the way to the bar.

"Do they think they're actually going to pick someone up here tonight?" he asked.

"There is some older gentleman in." I nodded to a small round table where three older guys I didn't recognize sat.

"Forget them," he said as he trailed a finger down my arm. "How about we get out of here? I have my Porsche out front; I can take us wherever you want to go."

I shook my head and glanced over at Hunter, sensing his eyes were on me. I was right. Miss Red Dress was on her tippy toes and bending her body around Hunter so that she was able to put her face into his. Hunter though had his gaze firmly on me.

"Thanks, Conrad, but I think I'm going to stick around."

"Oh, come on," he urged as he edged closer, his nose skimming down my cheek. "You know you want to."

I gave him a tight smile, pushed my glass between us and tipped it to my lips, giving him time to move away from me. Unfortunately, he didn't take the hint.

"We could have a great time."

His soft hand – ugh yep, soft – took my arm and gave it a gentle tug.

"Conrad," I bit out, teeth gritted. "You want to get your hand off me?"

The fuckhole grinned and kissed my cheek.

"Hey," I said, taking a step back. "When I said get your hand off me, that didn't mean put your lips on me instead."

"Ah c'mon, Elsie. You know you want me to."

He did not just wrong name me!

First, he put his putty soft hands, and slimy lips on me, and then he *damn well wrong named me.*

"I'm sure you've never had anyone with a Porsche show you any interest before. Just think of how you could boast to your friends."

"I'm sorry?" I took a step back and stared at the stupid douche with my mouth wide open.

He winked and pulled me to him, slapping a hand onto my ass. "You know you want it. I bet a girl like you has never been with a guy like me before."

Okay, so wrong naming me was one thing, acting like a dick about having a Porsche was another, but touching my ass and intimating I was a sure thing because he had money... well.

"You really are a dick," I said, resigned to the fact I was going to have to hurt him.

Still not getting my drift, Conrad smiled as I put my drink down and took a step back, clenching my hand into a tight fist.

"I certainly haven't met anyone like you. You're quite right."

"Count yourself lucky then." He veered toward me, his lips already wet and pursed.

Before he was able to do anything else smarmy, I landed a punch right on his nose.

"You fucking little..." He clutched his face and stamped his foot cursing as he did. "I'll fucking kill you."

With one hand still holding his nose, he advanced toward me, his eyes burning with anger as he cursed and reached out a hand to grab me. I stepped back, but he caught hold of my arm and roughly dragged me toward him.

"You want to fight me, do you?" I asked, pulling my arm back ready to strike again.

"Try it, you little bitch."

His hand shot out like he was going to slap me, but before it reached my face he was pulled back, and Hunter crowded into his space.

"Please tell me you weren't going to hit a woman," Hunter growled, his nose almost touching Conrad's. "Because if you were then you're a bigger piece of shit than those tight pants and ridiculous hair make you look."

"Get off me," Conrad hissed and tried to pull away from Hunter.

"Let me at him," I screeched as I tried to push into the space between the two men. "I'll show him what a girl like me can really do."

"He hurt you?" Hunter asked without looking at me.

"Hurt *her*, she fucking broke *my* nose."

Hunter peered at him. "Your nose ain't broken, but if she punched you, she had a reason. And, if Ellie had a reason, then I think maybe I should finish the job."

Hunter curled his hand into a fist, and I saw red. It was my nose to break not his.

"No," I cried and pulled down on his arm. "I want to do it."

Hunter turned to me, there was fire in his eyes and his nostrils were flared as he spoke. "I'm finishing this piece of shit. He was going to hurt you. That's not right."

"But I-"

If I'd thought that Conrad would stick up for himself, I was wrong. The yellow, pansy-ass, dickweed took advantage of Hunter's attention being on me, pulled away from him and ran. Literally ran. He shoved past Miss Red Dress, almost pushing her over and like a pinball flying between flipper bats, he bounced through everyone in the bar to get to the door.

"*Fucker!*" Hunter yelled. He turned to me, looked me up and down and raised a cupped hand to my cheek. "*Did* he hurt you?"

"No, he did not," I replied indignantly. "And even if he had, I could have handled him. You didn't need to rescue me like I'm some pathetic little woman who can't look after herself."

Raising his brows, he slammed his hands to his hips. "Say that again."

"You heard," I snapped. "I had it under control."

"You had it under fucking control. Well, it sure didn't look like it to me. He was about to slap you."

"And if he had I'd have hit him back." I copied his stance and leaned into his space. "You did that so that you'd win the wager, didn't you?"

The words sounded stupid as soon as they left my mouth. When they registered in my brain, I realized how ridiculous they really were. It also crossed my mind that maybe I was being a little hasty. *However.*

"You know I could have taken him. I could easily have punched him." I shook my head and added flared nostrils for good measure.

"You are one ungrateful little turd; you know that, right?"

Hunter ran a hand through his hair, and I couldn't help but watch the way his biceps flexed against the cotton of his shirt. Then, when he chewed his lip, something went pop inside of me and my sensibility up and left.

My libido had rubbed the bottle and let the sex Genie out. Just like that, I wanted his lips on mine. I wanted his hands in my hair and I was pretty certain I needed his dick inside my vajayjay. It was most probably the alcohol, but I didn't care. There was a beat throbbing between my legs that could easily challenge Taylor Hawkins' expertise.

Without thinking any more about it, I grabbed a hold of Hunter's shirt and dragged him to me. By the time his mouth hit mine, I was already breathing heavily with my nipples screaming to get in on the action. Instantly, Hunter's hands went around my neck, his thumbs cradling my jaw, and his tongue insisting that I open up for him.

My hands went to his slim hips and pulled him closer, and when I felt how hard he was through his pants, I let out a low moan. Without saying anything, or taking his mouth from mine, Hunter started to walk me backwards. Where we were going, I had no idea, but I just about had the wherewithal to snatch my clutch up and let myself be led. When my back hit a door, Hunter reached around me, pulled down the handle and maneuvered us inside another room.

I was slammed against a wall causing something to fall and my tongue paused in its exploration of his mouth.

"Forget it," Hunter growled. "It was just a yard brush."

I opened one eye and saw we were in the bar's storeroom; a faint smell of antiseptic invaded my nostrils. Did I give a shit that I was about to have sex with Hunter Delaney in a cleaning cupboard?

Like hell I did. I threw my clutch to one side and went straight back in.

CHAPTER 21

Hunter

As a yard brush fell to the floor, I almost had second thoughts about what Ellie and I were doing, but she tasted too good to stop. She was into it as much as I was, at least I thought she was. Ignoring any doubts, I walked us backward toward a high bench that had packs of paper towels stacked on top and swept my arm across it, pushing everything onto the floor. I then lifted Ellie and deposited her on the bench with a little gasp of surprise.

With my concentration back on her, my lips brushed up and down the smooth, sweet skin of her neck and with each nip or kiss, her fingertips dug harder into my back.

"You feel so damn good," I groaned. "Your dad could walk in here now and I don't think I could stop."

"Oh my God, do not... oh that's amazing... talk... oh, shit Hunter...

t-talk about my dad."

I grinned against her skin and let my hand move up her thigh toward the hemline of her short dress. Her thighs were as silky as her neck, and my dick was harder than it had ever been during a make-out session. It must have known what was to come, because this was not going to end in us leaving the storeroom without me being inside of her. Unless she said no of course, but the way Ellie was pulling my shirt out of my pants with one hand, I doubted she wouldn't be willing.

Then she spoke and I knew I was right.

"Hunter, please tell me you have a condom," Ellie gasped as her other hand went to the button on my pants.

I paused wondering whether I did. When was the last time I'd hooked up with someone unexpectedly?

"Fuck, I don't know."

"What? You idiot," Ellie huffed pulling away from me. "Do you not know the diseases you can catch? Diseases which can make you infertile and worse, you doofus."

She smacked at my chest, staring at me while her fucking perfect tits rose and fell in a beautiful rhythm of heat and lust.

"I didn't say I never use them, did I?" I reached into my back pocket for my wallet. "Just that I wasn't sure I had one. Contrary to what you probably think, not all my sexual experiences are casual hook-ups."

"Just most," Ellie said with a wry smile.

I chose to ignore her comment. "I'm normally prepared with a *box* of condoms, some nice wine and maybe Sam Outlaw's '*Tenderheart*' on Spotify."

Ellie laughed loudly and went back to unbuttoning my pants. "Whatever, now do you have a condom, or do I need to get on my knees?"

Woah.

Thank you, Jesus.

While the thought of Ellie's pretty pink lips around my dick was a fucking hell of an idea, me being inside her topped it. I flipped open my wallet and searched through it.

"*Yes!*"

"Thank God," Ellie sighed. "Much as I would have, that floor looks nasty. And for the record, I don't believe a word about your bedroom technique."

Feeling a wave of need sweep through me as Ellie pulled my zipper down, I groaned.

"I swear to God," I replied on a moan. "I know how to treat a lady."

"Yet you bring me into a cupboard," she sighed.

Her eyes were smiling, so I knew she was joking, but even so, she was right. I pulled back a little and cupped her face in my hands, bringing her eyes to mine.

"You want a bedroom with wine, and Sam Outlaw, I'll give you that."

Ellie rolled her eyes and pushed down my pants. "Nope. I want you to fuck me, Hunter. Albeit with the smell of floor cleaner in my nostrils."

Her hand went behind my head and pulled me to her into an amazing kiss, full of lips, tongue, teeth and the promise of mind-blowing sex.

I slipped the strap of her dress off her shoulder and pulled it down to reveal the perkiest, roundest and most beautifully golden tanned tit I had ever seen. Hungry for her, my mouth latched onto her nipple and sucked hard.

"Oh shit, that's good."

Ellie's back arched, like she wanted to give me more, so like the gentleman I was, I obliged. I pulled down the other strap and gave that nipple the exact same attention.

Fingernails scraped across my scalp as she whimpered quiet little mewling noises. When I nipped with my teeth the noises grew louder. She definitely liked what I was doing, and it made me even needier for her. My balls were aching as my hard on pushed against my boxer briefs and for a moment I worried they might fucking burst if I didn't give my dick some action soon.

I reached up under her dress and hooked my fingers in the sides of her panties.

"Lift your ass," I demanded.

"Such finesse," she batted back, yet lifting up. "Thought you knew how to treat a lady?"

"I do," I breathed out as I dragged her underwear down. "But maybe you ain't a lady."

"We'll see," she replied and sucked on my neck.

"Oh, my fucking God." The feel of Ellie's lips on my skin made my dick even more excited. So much so that I knew if I didn't get inside of her pretty quickly, I'd blow my load. Leaving the cleaning cupboard with a wet patch on my pants was not on my agenda for the night.

Sensing my need, Ellie pushed her delicate hand inside my briefs and grabbed hold of me, then she gasped and pulled her lips away from mine.

"Woah." She looked down between us and let out a whistle. "How the hell did I not know you were like…" She looked up at me with wide astonished eyes. "Like fucking huge."

I grinned and shrugged. "Not something I brag about."

And I didn't. Yeah, I was bigger than average. In fact, I was a triple threat. I was long, had good girth and I fucking knew what to do with it. Even in my head though, that sounded shit, so had chosen to never ever repeat it – to anyone.

"I sure hope it's not like red apples," Ellie replied, her eyes back on my dick, but her fingers of one hand working the buttons on my shirt.

"Red apples?"

"Yeah," she said, slicing her gaze back to mine. "Look *real* tasty, but when you bite into them they're all mushy and tasteless."

I didn't reply but swallowed hard at the thought of her taking a bite out of my dick and handed her the condom instead. Ellie grinned and wiggled her eyebrows.

"Tonight has been so much more fun than I expected."

"Yeah," I groaned out as she ripped the foil between her teeth. "And it's gonna get so much better."

I pulled her panties, which were a sexy red lace, from the end of her legs and threw them behind me.

"I need to fucking taste you first."

When I pushed her legs apart, Ellie fell backwards, stopping her fall with her hands and then leaning up on her elbows. With my eyes on her, I pushed her dress up to her waist and then pulled her legs apart.

"Shit," I groaned, feeling the pull of my balls again. "That's got to be the prettiest pussy I've ever seen."

She was bare apart from one thin strip of hair and I could see a faint outline of tan. Then I got images in my head of her in a skimpy bikini in my head and my need for her quadrupled.

I stooped down and parted her lips and with one long stroke of my tongue licked from back to front. She was so damn wet I wondered if I might drown in her.

"Oh. My. God."

Ellie's breathing and chest shuddered as her fingertips dragged along the wood of the bench, clawing at it as I gave her another lick.

She tasted sweet and I knew that even if that was all I got from her I'd be able to use the memory to jerk off to for years. Fortunately, though, me licking her pussy was not enough for Ellie.

"Hunter." She breathed out a shuddering breath. "Get this damn condom on now."

She thrust out a shaky hand, presenting me with the torn foil packet. I snatched it from her, just as desperate as she was, and rolled it onto my dick in record time.

"You ready for me?" I asked as I pulled her to the edge of the bench.

"So ready." She brushed her hands up my bare chest and pushed my shirt off my shoulders. "Fuck me now."

As Ellie's teeth sank into the corded muscle between my shoulder and neck, I pushed inside of her and every fucking planet, star, moon and sun collided with the pleasure I felt.

"Oh my God," Ellie gasped. "That's—"

She didn't say any more but wrapped her legs tight around my waist and took every hard, and fast thrust I gave to her. Fingertips clawed at my muscles and teeth and tongue explored my skin. My head dropped to take her nipple and with my hands at the small of Ellie's back, I pulled her closer each time I drilled into her.

"*Fuck.*" I groaned, never having felt anything like it in my life.

The tightness of her, the way her hips kept rhythm with mine and how she took each and every thrust, heightened every sense and nerve ending in my body. Her moans and cries were muffled as she sucked and kissed my skin and I knew if I ever got her in a bedroom sex with Ellie would be wild and earth shattering.

There wasn't much of her, but she was more than a match for me. She was perfect. She was everything a man would want in a partner. The pull in the pit of my stomach was a steady drum, building and building to the inevitable crescendo and I felt more alive than I'd ever done before. My skin was on fire from her touch and I was sure if I'd jumped off a high building in that moment, I'd be able to fly.

Knowing she could take it and needing to give it, I thrust harder as Ellie's hand reached for my ass and squeezed it hard.

"I knew it," she hissed and dropped her head back, giving me better access to her tits.

"Knew what?" I asked around a mouthful of nipple.

"Your ass." She didn't say anything more but let out a long moan and reached between us for her clit. "So good."

Looking down to see Ellie's fingers scissoring her bud and rubbing sent me onto a higher plain. I didn't think it possible, but it made my hips go faster. It made me harder and it made me even more desperate.

"Ellie, fuck, you're so damn good. Best fucking lay ever."

She lifted her head and gave me a lazy but self-assured grin and when she trapped her bottom lip in her teeth, I knew I was going to blow like a volcano.

I kissed her and my tongue fucked her mouth to the same tempo as my hips until I felt her body hitch and her legs tighten around me.

"Hunter," she gasped. "I'm gonna come."

"Come," I demanded, never once lessening what I was giving to her.

Her hands came to my hair and with a keening cry she tugged hard and shuddered beneath me.

"Oh my God."

Fuck, she was loud and at that moment I made myself a promise to get her to come louder one day.

Shaking and shuddering, Ellie's hips bucked wildly, and it was enough to send me over the edge and I came too, roaring just as loudly. My hips thrusting until there was nothing left, until she'd milked me of every drop of cum in my body and we were left staring at each other breathlessly.

"Well," Ellie finally said. "That was kind of unexpected."

"I guess so," I replied, not really sure what it all meant.

I'd loved every damn single second of it, but she was right, despite how I'd been feeling about her recently, mind blowing sex in a storeroom hadn't been on my list of things to do for the week.

She was also Carter's sister and I had no idea what that in itself meant. He was my best friend, how the hell would he feel about me fucking her into oblivion?

"Anyway," Ellie said as she slapped my ass. "As great as that was, I think we both know it was the alcohol that got us here."

Woah. Weren't girls supposed to get all clingy and talk about feelings after sex?

Okay then.

"Alcohol does seem to play a part in us getting hot and heavy with each other," I replied giving her a wink.

Ellie shook her head and curled her lip. "Exactly. Which means of course it won't happen again. I think we've explored every avenue now, don't you?"

"Not necessarily," I said as I tucked a piece of stray hair behind her ear. "I mean first time we kissed, tonight obviously we had sex, so does that mean next time we get drunk together we get ass play?"

I grinned but despite being cocky and flippant, I wasn't quite feeling it. I kinda liked the idea that she might want to feel clingy enough to ask what amazing sex might mean for us.

Ellie pushed at my chest and huffed out a breath.

"We need to clean up. Pass me some of those towels please." She pointed to the paper towels I'd pushed to the floor.

"Brace yourself, honey," I said and laughed as I pulled out of her.

"Oh my God, you are such a jerk."

Yeah, I probably was, but it was better to be a jerk than a clinger who wanted to know if she'd just had the best sex of her life, like I had.

I reached for a pack of the towels and ripped them open, passing a handful to Ellie, before taking one and wrapping the condom in it.

"Where the hell are my panties?" Ellie asked as I tucked myself back in and began to straighten myself up. I looked over my shoulder and then smiled at her.

"Over there on the floor. Hang on I'll get them for you."

I fastened the last button on my shirt, dropped the condom into the trash and then picked up Ellie's panties. As I held the red lace, I almost wished I'd pushed them into my pocket and kept them, but that was the sort of perverted thing Carter would do.

Shit, and there was that thought again—*Carter*. Oh well, it was too late now.

I threw the panties at Ellie, who now had her tits back in her dress and watched as she wiggled into the tiny piece of underwear. She looked thoroughly fucked and not just because her hair was coming a little loose, but the heavy lids and twinkle in her eye gave it away.

"Let's hope no one saw us come in here," I said as she finally smoothed down her dress.

"I think they were all too interested in hooking up." Her voice was quiet and if I didn't know better, I'd have wondered if I'd hurt her in some way. "Okay I'll go first."

She snatched up her purse and without looking at me she flung open the door and strutted out into the hallway, as if the last twenty minutes had never happened. Sure no one had seen us, I didn't bother hanging around, but followed her out.

When Ellie reached the main bar though, she stopped, and I almost barreled into the back of her.

"What's…"

I didn't say anything else because the whole bar erupted into cheers as everyone began to clap and holler. Even my aunts were waving their arms around.

"Have a good time?" some guy I didn't know shouted.

Without missing a beat Ellie waved a hand at them all and stepped forward.

"It's really not what you think," she offered, opening up her purse. "I'm a nurse and Hunter needed a hemorrhoid as big as a grape pushing back up his ass. It was not pretty, so if you don't mind, I need a drink."

With that she sashayed toward the bar and my dick got hard all over again.

CHAPTER 22

Ellie

Shit, shit, shit.

What the hell had I done? Obviously, I knew what I'd done, I'd had sex with Hunter in the storeroom of the Stars & Stripes – on singles night. It had been loud sex too, if the cheering crowd had been anything to go by. Although, I was pretty sure we'd managed to persuade them otherwise with the story of Hunter's hemorrhoid, at least I hoped so.

Luckily most of the locals had already disappeared and only the bus load of people from Middleton Ridge were still hanging around, waiting for their ride home – oh and Hunter's aunts. It seemed however, they had no idea what they were cheering for and were only following everyone else's lead. Jefferson was also missing, thank goodness. According to Penny who had taken the bartender's vow of silence, so we didn't need to worry about her,

Jefferson left with the redhead about the same time Hunter and I had started kissing.

Therefore, I figured we were clear to keep our little assignation secret. It wasn't that I hadn't enjoyed it or wished it hadn't happened – well I kinda did. In any other circumstances however, I'd have called Bronte and spilled all the gory, delectable detail, particularly the part about that huge amazing penis of his. However, this wasn't normal circumstances. This was Hunter Delaney, my brother's best friend and serial one night only banger of women. At least I'd always thought he was, but Sam Outlaw. Who knew?

"Hey good looking." Stopping me from my brooding, Davis dropped a chart in front of me, on the desk and yawned. "That's the latest spirometry result for little Millie in bed four."

I picked up the chart and gave it the once over and then smiled. "An improvement, that's good."

The poor little thing was only seven but suffered badly with asthma. She was in with us after having a real bad attack while playing in her grandparent's yard.

"Yeah, I think Dr. Andrews will let her go home tomorrow." Davis' eyes lit up at the mention of his crush. "I'm still hopeful of storeroom sex with him you know."

I almost choked and felt my face heat up at his words. I hadn't told Davis about the night before and had no intention of doing so. I hadn't even told Bronte. She was my best friend, no doubt, but had a mouth bigger than Davis', which was saying a lot. But shit, I really wanted to tell her how big Hunter's dick was. A girl shouldn't have to keep those kinds of secrets, but I guessed needs must.

"You okay?" Davis asked. "You've gone a little red there. Is there something you're not telling me?"

Shit, he was too sharp for his own good, even after a twelve-hour shift.

"Nope. Why would there be?"

I busied myself with putting Millie's chart away but could feel his eyes on me.

"What?" I asked when I looked up to see he was indeed staring at me.

"Please don't tell me you've had sex with him. I'm not sure I could forgive you if you had."

His lips were pulled into a sulky pout and he had a hand clutched against his chest.

"Don't be so ridiculous," I replied with an over emphasized eye roll. "He's not my type and I'm pretty sure that while you may scare the pants off him, he'd more likely go for you than me."

Davis gasped. "Oh my God, you really think he's gay?"

I'd had my suspicions over the last couple of shifts I'd worked with him, but I hadn't mentioned it before because I knew how fixated Davis could get. If he thought our new doctor might be gay there was a huge chance my favorite colleague would step up his flirt and even buy the good doctor a subscription to Gay Man magazine. Subtlety was not Davis' forte, but I wasn't averse to throwing Dr. Andrews under the bus, if it meant Davis didn't guess my secret.

"I think he may be," I replied and wagged a finger at him. "But you need to be restrained. Not everyone is like you; out and proud. Let him have his privacy if that's what he wants."

Davis rolled his eyes. "I know, I hear you, Momma."

"I'm serious."

He nodded and actually looked genuine. "I know. I'll dial it down, I swear." He yawned again.

"Now, go home and get some sleep." I looked up at the big red and yellow clock on the wall. "It's thirty minutes after your shift ended."

"I know and I'm going. Joella is sitting with Bobby by the way. He had a bad dream."

My heart hurt as I thought about the four kids we currently had on our ward. The youngest was only three and the eldest was Millie at seven. Their parents were allowed to stay with them, but Bobby's mom was a single mom. She had temporarily swapped to a night shift at the canning factory in Jenningstown so that she could be with Bobby in the day while he got over his appendectomy.

"He goes home the day after tomorrow, doesn't he?"

Davis nodded and smiled. "Yeah, but I'll miss the little guy. That smile of his is beautiful. He's such a happy little thing."

I agreed. It was real hard to see the kids in the hospital, but it was also difficult to say goodbye to a lot of them too.

"Right, go." I pointed to the door.

Davis saluted me and turned on his heel. He was about to disappear into the locker room when the buzzer went on the ward door.

"I'll go," he sighed. "The intercom is faulty."

"Really? Do Maintenance know?" I looked down at the intercom console on the desk to see he was right, there was no light of any color shining from it.

"Yeah," Davis called over his shoulder. "They're coming tomorrow."

While he moved out of sight, around the corner, I busied myself with reading the medication list for the night-time meds round. I was beginning to think Davis had got rid of whoever it was and then gone off home, when a large hand smacked down on the desk. My eyes shot up from the sheet I was reading to be met with gorgeous pools of chocolate brown.

"What are you doing here?" I hissed, as I craned to look behind Hunter.

"Came to see you." He crossed his arms over his chest, and I could see he was full of determination. "We have things to discuss."

What he was determined about, I had no idea, but the narrow eyes, straight back and slight tilt to the head told me that he was.

"W-what about?" I whispered hoping just a little bit that he wanted to discuss his penis.

He bent over at the waist and put his mouth close to my ear.

"Davis is in the locker room, so you don't have to whisper."

"He has the hearing of a bat. I think I do. Now what do you want?"

I could feel his breath on my cheek, and I could smell his soap and cologne and damn it, I wished I could turn the clock back twenty-four hours. I wouldn't change a damn thing, except maybe savor the hot sex a little bit more. Oh, and maybe take a photograph of his huge wang.

"Like I said, we need to talk."

Hunter straightened up again and shoved his hands into his jeans' pockets. He still had a steely look in his eyes, but he didn't have the Hunter Delaney confidence I'd grown used too.

"Nothing to talk about." I wheeled my chair away from the desk and put the meds list into the top tier of a yellow tray and then wheeled further back to flick the switch to dim the ward lights.

"Ellie, stop messing around back there and get back here now."

He pointed a finger down at the desk and let out a long, slow exhale.

"Messing around?" I asked, trying hard to regulate my breathing. "I happen to be working, not *messing around*."

Hunter let his head drop back onto his shoulders for a moment and let out a groan.

"You know what I fucking meant," he replied, shifting his gaze back to me. "Now move that cute little ass of yours back here so I can talk to you."

I opened my mouth to protest, but the locker room door burst open and Davis swanned out ready to go home.

"Okay, I'm off home to dream about a certain someone." He wiggled his eyebrows and leaned in closer to Hunter. "Please don't tell her you've changed your mind about the calendar shoot. She's in a strange mood already tonight, so poor Joella doesn't need you spreading bad vibes around."

"I'm not," Hunter retorted with his eyes on me. "Quite the opposite."

I frowned, but Hunter carried on talking and saved me the trouble of working out what he meant.

"I'm offering to do two pictures, three if necessary. That way you won't have to ask Delphine's nephew. Him not being a local and all."

"Delphine has a nephew?" Davis asked, eyes wide. "Is he cute? We need to get her fixed up with someone cute." He pointed at me.

"Oh yeah," I replied enthusiastically. "He's real cute."

"Why do we need to fix her up with someone? And did you not hear me say, he's not local." Hunter practically added 'duh' to the end of the sentence, he was so agitated.

Davis didn't bite but grinned at me. "He kinda has a point. Would Mrs. Callahan be happy with looking at someone she doesn't know throughout the month of May? I think not. You know how she likes to perv on all the local boys."

Hunter shuddered. "She's eighty."

"Seventy-six," Davis corrected. "But the point is, she's excited to see the flesh of the locals, so that she doesn't have to imagine it when they visit her gas station. Some non-local won't give her that joy, Ellie."

"Yeah, what Davis said," Hunter agreed with a grin.

"I promised Delphine and I don't go back on my promises. Now," I said turning to Hunter. "If there's nothing else I have work to do. Davis can walk you out."

Hunter glanced at Davis and then shook his head. "Nope. I have other stuff we need to discuss. Night, Davis."

Hunter's eyes were firmly back on me, so my colleague took the hint and flicked his scarf over his shoulder.

"See you tomorrow then," he said to me with a look that said: 'what the hell is going on and I will interrogate you when we meet again'.

I didn't have a chance to argue because he was gone.

"Right," Hunter growled. "Let's get to it."

I had no idea why suddenly I'd caught a load of weird feelings about Hunter, but I was pretty sure his ability to make me wet just by the sound of his voice meant I was in real trouble. That and his… *okay, so I was obsessed*!

"To what?" I asked, just so he'd speak or growl again.

"Talking about me and you and the sex we had last night."

I clenched my thighs and wondered whether it was medically possible to orgasm by speech alone. Maybe I'd Google it later, along with 'which is the biggest penis in the USA?', but in the meantime, I had one moody cowboy to listen to.

CHAPTER 23

Hunter

"I'm working, Hunter. I don't have time to talk." Ellie waved a hand over her shoulder without even turning around. "Sorry."

There was not one ounce of her that was damn sorry. Still, her walking away at least gave me a great view of her ass in her scrubs.

"Fucking pain in my—"

I didn't say anything else because her colleague, who I think was called Joella came from the direction Ellie had gone. She smiled at me and it was one of those 'hey handsome, want some company?' smiles, so I left, determined to get fucking Nurse Maples to talk to me at some point.

No sooner was I back in my truck than my phone buzzed. When I fished it out of my pocket, I was surprised to see it was a text from Ellie.

"What the actual…"

She couldn't discuss the sex we'd had but she could text me damn *instructions* on 'our plan' the minute I left the hospital building.

Ellie: Call Carter and get him to meet you at Stars & Stripes tomorrow night. I have a plan

Hunter: Bossy much!

Ellie: Someone has to be if this plan is going to work. Will you do it?

I had to be some sort of sap, because after a couple of minutes of sulking and pretending to myself that I wouldn't, I texted her back a simple **OK**.

Now we were in the bar and I handed my card to Penny while she gave me a knowing smile.

"What's got into her?" Carter asked as he took one of the bottles that Penny had placed on the bar. "She looks like she's got trapped gas."

I cleared my throat and hoped to hell Penny stuck to her word regarding keeping mine and Ellie's storeroom 'meeting' to herself. All I wanted was a drink with my buddy, not to end the night in a punch up with him.

"There you go, honey," Penny said, giving me back my card. She then turned to Carter. "How's your sister doing?"

I cleared my throat as Carter frowned, his beer paused halfway to his mouth. "Err, okay."

"That's good." Penny winked at me and then walked away to another customer, chuckling to herself.

"I thought you and Ellie were in here the other night, when you were apologizing for being a dick to her – not that I thought you were of course." Carter grinned and took a long swig.

"Yeah, we were. Just having a friendly drink, me apologizing like you said."

"So, why's Penny asking after her?"

I shrugged and started to walk toward the tables at the back of the bar. When I reached an empty one, I dragged out a chair for Carter and then one for myself.

"Pretty busy in here tonight," I said to change the subject.

"Yeah," Carter replied. "I guess everyone is building up for Thanksgiving. Getting in the mood, you know."

"It's two weeks off yet and what the hell is there to build up to?"

"You have to prepare for Thanksgiving," Carter replied, frowning at me. "Get in some training for all the alcohol you'll be drinking."

I shook my head in disbelief. "So, your sole purpose for Thanksgiving is to get wasted?"

"Well, yeah. I'll stay over at Mom and Dad's as per, get up around ten for Dad's pancakes, eggs and bacon and then I'll sit and watch TV with Dad, drinking beer, while Mom and Ellie make dinner."

I slowly blinked, twice. "Carter, you did that when we were teenagers. You don't still do that do you?"

He didn't answer but shrugged again.

"How the fuck did you even graduate Kindergarten, never mind High School or Veterinary School?"

He grinned at me and winked. "That my friend is a total fucking mystery."

I couldn't help but laugh at him, feeling myself relax a little. That was until my phone buzzed and I saw it was Ellie with instructions for her diabolical plan.

She was like a damn chicken pecking at my head.

Ellie: Okay, I'm with Bronte. Send a text from Carter's phone saying something nice to her so I can gauge how she reacts. He has her number under Annoying Blonde

I sighed and was just about to put my phone back in my pocket when another text came in.

Ellie: And make it snappy

Why the hell I had thought for one second that I *wanted* to talk to her and suggest we could date, I had no damn idea. Maybe I'd wanted to talk to her about it at the hospital, but that idea was now something I'd filed under *'Bad move, don't fucking think about it'*, in my head. She was bossy enough without me being romantically involved with her. I imagined if we did date, she'd be ten times worse. Shit, I'd be visiting garden centers and shopping malls every weekend without any choice in the matter.

I looked up at Carter, who funnily enough was scrolling through his own phone. I guessed it was as good a time as any.

"Hey, can I check your phone out? I want to see if I should get one."

He frowned, pressed at his screen, and passed it to me. "You do know that Cell Center at the mall lets you try them out? And they have experts who know abso-fucking-lutely everything there is to know about phones."

"Yeah, but I can get it online if I know what I want. You want to get another beer by the way?" I showed him my half empty bottle.

"Okay, Mr. Impatient."

Once he'd left the table I clicked on the screen, only to find he'd locked it. I thought about what he might have as his passcode and typed it in.

Blake Lively's birthday. It had to be. He'd told me often enough what it was and that they were compatible star signs. He was obsessed with her and even had a framed picture of her next to his bed. At times I wondered why I was actually friends with the damn weirdo.

I typed in 08-25-87. Bingo!

I didn't have much time, so typed out the text message to Bronte, the first thing that came into my head.

Carter: Bronte, I really liked the shoes you were wearing last time we spoke

Quickly, I put the phone back onto the table and then realized I'd better delete the message, so snatched it back up again.

"For fuck's sake," I muttered to myself, not for the first time wondering how I'd let Ellie get me involved in her crap.

Anxious at being caught, I looked up, but Carter was still at the bar. He'd been stopped by Jim Wickerson, a local pig farmer. He was no doubt discussing his veterinary bills and trying to get Carter to give him a discount.

The mean old coot did it every time we saw him. Grateful for once that Jim was as tight as a newborn's exit path, I put Carter's phone down, determined not to touch it again.

I wasn't so damn lucky. *My* phone buzzed.

Ellie: Shoes! Shoes! Frickin' Shoes. You dick!

"I'm a dick?" I muttered as I stared down at my phone.

"Kinda," Carter said, surprising me. "Not all the time, but why'd you ask?"

My gaze shot up to him and I ground out a smile. "Oh nothing, just thinking about something I said to my pop."

Carter frowned, like he really didn't believe me, but like the self-centered prick he could be, he didn't question me any further and started going on about how busy his day had been. His commentary of his last twelve hours had reached between the hours of ten a.m. and eleven when both of our phones buzzed at the same time. Instantly I knew it had to be Ellie. Eyeing Carter warily, I picked up my phone and read the text.

Ellie: Look and learn mother fucker, look and learn

I looked over to Carter who was reading his text and grinning before he let out a huge belly laugh. After a few seconds of looking down at his text, he locked the screen and dropped it into the pocket of his jacket, which was hanging off the back of his chair.

Hunter: What did you send him? He's laughing

Ten seconds later.

Ellie: Your hair looked real sexy today

Really?

Hunter: Hair! Hair! Frickin' hair! You dick!

Ellie: Abort mission. You obviously have no idea how to sext and are just embarrassing yourself

Was she for fucking real? I had no idea how to sext. Did she not remember I was famous in high school for bringing Rhian Cade to orgasm during French class in our sophomore year? Admittedly it wasn't by sexting, and it involved her pink pen with a feather on the end, but if I had those skills then I could damn well sext. I was determined I'd show her so tapped out a message back to Ellie.

Hunter: You know I'd like to lick your pussy and then kiss you so you can taste yourself before I push inside you

I threw my phone down and sat back in my chair, feeling pretty proud of myself. No way would she be able to resist that. I was almost sure at that moment she was pushing her thighs together to ease the ache I caused her. She didn't think I knew, but I'd seen her do it before—many times.

"How come you're looking like you've just grown another dick?" Carter asked as he looked over at the door where two girls who I didn't know had walked in.

"Nothing, just thinking about the calf we had born yesterday."

Carter gave me a funny look and then shook his head. "You're fucking weird tonight. And who the hell keeps texting you?" he asked as my phone buzzed again.

I shifted, feeling a little uncomfortable, but just smiled. "My pop. Think there's another calf on the way."

"We need to go and help?" he asked, half out of his seat.

"Nah, he's got it."

Carter nodded and sat back down, glancing over at the two girls while I checked my phone.

Ellie: You dick!

I couldn't help but laugh. She was such a little turd at times, yet her breaking apart and screaming through her orgasm, was pretty much the only thought I'd had for the last forty-eight hours.

Hunter: You have the most amazing tits and perfect nipples. In fact, your whole body is out of this fucking world

When a girl sends you a smiley face and a kiss in response to a text about her tits and nipples, you know you're a damn God in the sexting stakes.

CHAPTER 24

Ellie

"What do you think?" Jacob Crowne from the print shop asked as he pinned up the final backdrop for the calendar.

"Oh my God, they're amazing," I replied as my eyes scanned over the beautiful scene of snow-covered hills and pine trees. "You really didn't have to."

Jacob shook his head. "My pleasure, Ellie. The proceeds from the sale all go to a good cause. I'm glad to help."

When I'd taken over the 'Hunks of Dayton Valley' calendar shoot the year before, I'd been real disappointed with the state of the backdrops we had to use. They were old and faded and had more holes in them than a piece of Swiss cheese. I'd mentioned them to Jacob when he'd brought his little boy in to get a cast on his broken arm changed and he'd told me that he'd sort it.

"I never thought for one minute that you'd get me anything this good." I sighed as I pulled Jacob into a hug. "Thank you."

"Like I said, no problem. Now I'd best go before I get dragged into the damn photoshoot."

I wiggled my eyebrows and gave him a big grin. He was at least seven years older than me, but I'd heard he'd been a bit of a heartthrob at high school. He'd have been a good addition, but before I could even try and twist his arm, he was gone.

"You seen these?" I asked Bronte as she moved up beside me.

"Wow, that looks so real," she exclaimed pointing at the beach scene. "I can just see Jefferson in his board shorts in front of that blue sea."

I groaned. "What are you doing here anyway? I thought you were sleeping all day seeing as it's Sunday." As if I'd really needed to ask why my best friend had decided to help.

Her eyes twinkled and she clapped her hands together. "Jefferson of course. Have you decided what month he's going to be? Please say a summer month."

I looked down at the sheet of paper in my hand. "May. He's going in front of that." I pointed to the Spring backdrop with its carpet of Bluebonnets and green hills in the background.

"May? Shit Ellie, give him July so I can see him with no shirt on."

"Sorry but that's…" I feigned looking down my list, knowing full well who it was. "Hunter." I kept my eyes down so she didn't see the excitement in them. I'd given Hunter March and July, that way I'd get to see him topless *and* maybe a nice sweater and jeans that cupped that huge dick of his. Shit, why the hell did that *thing* keep popping into my head?

Bronte snatched the list from me and studied it. "Well swap Bobby Jenkins out from August."

"No, I'm not. They've all been given instruction on what clothes or props to bring with them, so it's not happening. Bobby isn't being swapped to spring when he'll no doubt bring his surfboard with him."

Bronte huffed and shoved the paper against my chest. "Like he knows how to surf. Like anyone in this county, this damn state, knows how to surf."

"He goes out to Hawaii every year, you know that. Now, stop sulking and go home if you're not here to help. If you are, sort those out into seasons for me."

With a roll of her eyes, she picked up the box of props that I'd brought along and moved over to a long table on the far side of the community hall. Hopefully it would keep her occupied for a little while until all the guys arrived, because I was sure once they did her attention would be fully on them.

***

The shoot had been going well, everyone had turned up, except for Billy Daniels QB1 at the high school. He'd caught the stomach flu so was confined to bed. Proving once again that December was a damn curse. Billy was my stand in for Cooper with the tiny balls that were well and truly owned by his fiancée. That was also why Hunter and Dylan, Delphine's nephew, were fighting over it.

"Honestly, I don't mind," Dylan said and flashed a perfect smile. "It'd be my pleasure to help out."

I felt Bronte nudge me in the back, urging me to say yes. I was surprised because her focus had been on Jefferson the whole time since he'd arrived, but then Delphine's picture of Dylan hadn't really done him justice. Bright blue eyes the color of cornflowers shone from underneath golden blond hair that flopped sexily across his lashes and skimmed his shoulders.

"I think the locals would maybe like someone, well local, for the holidays," Hunter cut in. "It's a special time of the year. I think I should do it."

"Honestly, it would be my pleasure." Dylan flung an arm around Hunter's shoulder and I saw him stiffen immediately. Since Dylan had walked through the door, Hunter had made beady eyes at him and pretty much shadowed his every move.

"That's real good of you, *buddy*," he ground out, ducking away from Dylan. "But we got this."

I sighed and sagged a little. "I don't care who does it, as long as someone does. Now if you don't mind, I need to get Jefferson set up."

Bronte giggled as I turned on my heels and strode away.

"They should both just get their dicks out and piss on your leg," she said as she caught up to me. "And I just want to say if you do not go on a date with that hot piece of ass, you'll regret it."

"Who, Dylan?" I asked, sounding snappier than I'd intended.

Her eyebrows arched. "Who else would I mean? Unless of course you think Hunter is a hot piece of ass?"

"God no," I squawked and then looked around the room, realizing I'd gone a little high pitched.

Bronte didn't say anything, but grinned and walked off to greet Carter who'd just arrived.

"Please don't upset him," I called out to her. "It was hard enough getting him to agree to this."

She didn't answer but waved me away. Within seconds I heard my brother shout, 'You're so fucking annoying'.

"Okay, Jefferson," I said as I reached him. "You're up."

"Whatcha got for me, sweetheart?" he asked with a huge smile and a glint in his eye.

"The ladies are going to die for this one," I replied. Turning, I whistled for my brother.

Carter looked up from whatever argument he was having with Bronte and gave me a chin lift. Holding up a finger he mouthed he'd be one second.

"Are they arguing again?" Jefferson asked with a laugh.

"Yeah, as always."

I watched as Bronte wagged a finger at my brother and wondered why I even thought it was a good idea to get them together. Then, when Bronte spotted Jefferson unbuttoning his bright blue, short-sleeve shirt to reveal a definite four-pack and toned pecs, I knew why. She actually feigned a swoon and fanned herself *with Carter's hand*. Giving her a look that would wither most people, except Bronte, to dust, Carter snatched his hand away and came over to me with a grey pet carrier.

"Hey, Jefferson."

"Carter, how you doing, son?"

Jefferson fist-bumped my brother and I couldn't help but laugh. If Dad had done that to him, Carter would have gone crazy and told him to act his age. Jefferson was evidently far cooler than our dad.

"Here's what you asked for." Carter put the carrier on the floor and opened it up, pulling out a cute grey rabbit with white ears. "Be careful with him, little Amy Thornton has no idea we have him. As far as she knows, he's relaxing in the surgery before having his balls chopped off in the morning."

Jefferson winced. "Shit." He reached for the rabbit. "What's his name?"

Carter colored up. "Carter," he murmured as he passed the rabbit to Jefferson.

We both burst out laughing but Bronte, who had now joined us clucked her tongue in disgust.

"Because you fuck like a rabbit I'm guessing," she muttered.

Carter's nostrils flared. "No because she likes me. She has a crush on me. Okay?"

Now it was Bronte's turn to laugh. "Little six-year-old Amy Thornton? Well, I guess that's about your level."

By the way my brother looked at my best friend, I figured it would probably be better to try and part them, but then that wouldn't get them together.

"Bronte, can you take Carter to where his stuff is laid out for him, while I set Jefferson up?"

She opened her mouth to protest, but then grinned and nodded. "Sure can. Come on dickweed, follow me."

"Jeez," Jefferson said as his big hand slowly stroked down Carter the rabbit. "I hate to say this but those two just hate each other don't they. In fact, I can't remember a time when they didn't. Even when you were all little kids, they wound each other up. The times your dad and Jim had to separate them." He shook his head and looked over to where Bronte was thrusting a bag of stuff at Carter. "Great times."

As his eyes glassed over and his thoughts evidently went to his late wife, I felt a huge lump form in my throat. I couldn't imagine what he had gone through, was still going through, at having lost Sondra.

"You okay?" he asked me and rubbed a hand down my back.

"Yeah, sure. You ready?"

He nodded and holding bunny Carter tenderly in his arms, he took his place and let Annie the photographer snap away while Whitney Houston's *'How will I know'* played through her Bluetooth speaker.

"Wow," Bronte sighed beside me. "He looks so sexy holding little Carter."

We looked at each other and burst out laughing.

"You show *big* Carter what he's wearing?" I asked, unable to keep the smirk from my face.

"I gave him the bag. And three... two... one."

"Ellie!" my brother shouted from across the room. "Just because I'm October, if you think I'm fucking dressing up like a Halloween Pumpkin you're damn well mistaken."

Bronte and I silently high-fived each other. My good mood was quickly broken though when I heard a ruckus behind me and turned to see Dylan and Hunter playing tug-o-war with the damn Santa suit.

"You see," Bronte said as she pointed at Jefferson posing like a professional. 'That is why I want him. He actually acts like an adult."

And at that moment I kinda had to agree with her.

CHAPTER 25

Hunter

I f you asked anyone to describe me, I'm pretty sure they'd say easy going. I rarely lost my cool, okay so Dominic Taylor was an exception, but he'd hurt Ellie. Dylan 'Fucking Thor' Whatever his name was, was quite possibly another exception. If he didn't give up the damn Santa suit soon, I'd have to punch him.

"Seriously man," I huffed. "I think it's best for me to do it."

"But you're already doing two, I'm only doing November so I can easily slip this on with the same backdrop."

My nostrils flared as I gripped the suit a little tighter. I wanted December, because I had brought something a little special with me. There was no way he was benefiting from it.

"I offered to do two because Ellie was a guy short. She's now another one short since Billy can't make it, so it's only right I help out again." I gave him a smile that could probably be called a snarl and tried to pull the Santa suit toward me.

"It's fine," Dylan replied through gritted teeth, holding the red jacket and trousers tight. "Like I said, I'm November so will be one of the last to go. It stands to reason I should do it."

"Ellie," I shouted over my shoulder without taking my eyes from Thor. "You wanna swap me and Dylan over? I'll do November and he can do July."

I heard her sigh heavily and then the clicking of her heels on the wooden floor.

"I don't care who does which month, just decide because March is coming up and I need you for that."

Distracted by watching Ellie's tits heave up and down, Dylan managed to wrangle the suit from my hands. Not only the suit but the bag I was holding.

"Is this the rest of it?" he asked, opening it up and looking inside. "Ooh what's this?"

"*No!*" I made a grab for the bag, but it was too late.

"Woah, cute little Mrs. Claus outfit. Is this for you, Ellie?"

Ellie's eyes went wide as she took a step back. "I don't know where that came from."

"Well, it would be a shame to waste it," the smug little bastard said. "Why don't you do December with me?"

"Oh, I don't know about that," Ellie replied a little blush coming to her cheeks.

"I don't think that's El's sort of thing," I offered, desperate for Dylan to drop the subject.

Ellie's head almost swiveled off her neck as she flashed narrow eyes in my direction.

"It's not?" she asked, as she tapped her foot. "What makes you think that?"

I wanted to smash myself in the balls. Ellie Maples was never told what to do. If you wanted her to do something you told her not to. Carter and I had learned that a long time ago when we were about thirteen. We didn't want her hanging around with us when we went swimming at the creek, seeing as we were meeting Tiffany Anders and Louisa Carmichael and Carter had a plan to get them to go skinny dipping. I can't remember what the plan was, but it'd have been a shit one if Carter had been behind it. We'd told Ellie she couldn't come but of course she turned up anyway. So, the next time we were meeting girls, I chanced it by begging her to come with and guess who told me she'd rather suck a coyote's hairy ball sack – yeah, she'd always been a delicate little thing.

So, with my head back in the game, I gave her one of my sweetest smiles. "No, it probably would be good if you did it. Would add something different."

Ellie studied me with her head cocked to one side. "You think do you?"

"Oh, yeah." I nodded my head enthusiastically. "I really do."

Her eyebrows arched real high and I was pretty sure she was going to ream me out and then storm off. I gave myself a mental pat on the back; I'd averted having to watch her cozy up to Dylan while she wore a short little red dress.

"That's good then." She turned to Dylan and smiled sweetly at him. "Let me have the dress, Dylan and I'll be ready when it's your turn. Hunter hurry up and change, we're ready for you."

With that she snatched the bag, turned around and walked away from us, adding a little more swing to her hips and ass if I wasn't mistaken.

"Wow," Dylan said behind me. "That's one sexy woman."

I turned to finally plant a punch on him but when I did, he was walking away too, and I was pretty sure he was laughing.

***

March's picture was going to be pretty tame. At least it was meant to be. Ellie had suggested that I wore a flannel and jeans and maybe a cowboy hat – which I didn't even own, but as soon as I'd realized I wasn't getting my way with Santa, I pulled out my other outfit. The outfit I'd taken along just in case. Just in case of what I had no idea, but I was glad I had, because when I appeared from the men's room in it, Ellie's eyes nearly popped out of her head.

"Really?' she said with an eye roll. "You had to wear your '*I'm easy, come get me*' outfit?"

As Kid Rock's *Cowboy* began to play, I shrugged and walked over to my spot in front of the backdrop that had a roaring log fire on it. My grey sweats were low on my hips, my white, sleeveless tee stretched tight against my muscles, I'd pulled my ball cap down low. I knew I looked hot and I also knew Ellie's eyes were firmly on my dick which was swinging free and easy after removing my boxer briefs.

"How do you want me, Annie?" I asked the photographer.

"I think some skin would be nice," she replied from behind her camera. "Just lift your shirt a little and show me your stomach."

With one hand I lifted my tee and with the other touched the peak of my cap, giving what I hoped was a sultry look with hooded eyes and my bottom lip between my teeth. When I heard Ellie let out a long exhale and mutter, 'Fuck,' I knew I'd succeeded.

"Okay," Annie said, still snapping away. "Let's get rid of the shirt."

That was more than fine by me, particularly as Ellie hadn't moved an inch since I'd stepped in front of the camera.

I pulled off my cap and grabbed a hold of the hem of my shirt and slowly lifted it. With the words 'I wanna be a cowboy baby' booming out, I dragged the white cotton up my skin.

"Hold it there," Annie said as I heard her shutter going. "Okay carry on."

When I finally had the shirt off and hanging from my fingertips, I gave the camera a sideways glance with my head tilted downward.

"You… erm… you got enough?" Ellie asked a little breathily.

"A couple more. Hunter, put the ball cap back on."

Doing as Annie asked, I did, but with the peak at the back, like I usually wore it on the ranch. I then looked over at Ellie and noticed her fingers twitching at her sides. She was breathing heavy and her legs were most definitely squeezing together. Shit she looked beautiful and I felt a bit of a twinge in my chest.

"Okay," Annie said as Kid Rock sang his last note. "That's great, Hunter, thanks."

Snagging up my tee, I gave Annie a nod and walked over in the direction of Ellie.

"That okay for you?"

She was staring at me wide-eyed, her mouth gaping, a little like a fish, but with lips I'd love around my dick.

"Ellie, did you hear me? Was that okay?"

"W-wha… yep, yep all good. All good."

Yep, all fucking good alright. Let's see what you've got Dylan, you cheap Thor look alike.

CHAPTER 26

Ellie

"**G**reat job, honey," Jefferson said as he passed me a bottle of beer. "I think this year's calendar is going to be the best ever."

"Aww thanks." I grinned at him and tapped my beer against his. "Thanks for doing it."

"Not sure why you asked me, but I enjoyed it." He pulled me in for a hug and kissed the top of my head. "Did me good."

Watching Jefferson as he took a swig of his beer, I noticed how sad his eyes looked. For all the women he had, it was obvious he was still absolutely crazy about Sondra. Just thinking about how lonely and grief stricken he must have been when she died, gave me little painful flutters in my chest.

"Where'd my boy get to anyway?" he asked, looking around Stars & Stripes at all the people who'd helped with the photo shoot.

I shrugged and turned to look over to the door. "No idea. I saw him just before Dylan and I did the December shoot, then he disappeared."

My eyes focused back on Jefferson while my heart remained focused on the door, hoping that Hunter would wander through it. Self-hatred was pretty high on my feelings at that moment. I'd vowed after Dominic I'd never feel like that again. I'd sworn to myself I wouldn't feel like my day was less than stellar if I didn't see the guy. I'd told myself I'd never, ever feel like a kid at Christmas while I waited to see them. I even vowed I'd die a spinster and spend my life just having sex for fun, but like an idiot I'd started to renege on all those promises I'd made myself.

It must have been the size of his penis. It had to have hypnotized me. Maybe it was some sort of magic wand and when he'd got it out of his pants, Hunter had waved it around and whispered a spell. It had to be that because I'd known him for twenty-four years and apart from realizing he was hot – because I wasn't blind – I'd never once thought about him as anything other than Carter's best friend. It was only when Bronte accused me of ogling him at my parents' summer cookout that I'd considered I might have a mild interest in him. The last few weeks though things had ramped up considerably. Mainly my sex hormones.

"I don't think he liked seeing Delphine's nephew's hands on you." Jefferson chuckled.

Startled, I looked up at him. "W-what?"

"Hunter. He didn't like it when Dylan grabbed you in that clinch."

I thought back to when Dylan had bent me backwards and leaned in as though he was going to kiss me. Not at all fitting behavior for Santa and Mrs. Claus, but Annie had said it was a great shot for December.

"I think that was when he kinda stormed out," Jefferson added. "Boy must have it bad."

I almost choked on fresh air at his words and began a coughing fit. Jefferson slapped between my shoulders, grinning at me the whole time.

"Don't tell me you didn't know?" he asked.

"No," I croaked out.

He shrugged. "Well, it ain't like Hunter knows either, so how are you supposed to."

My stomach rolled and a wave of nausea passed over me. Just as I was about to throw up my beer, the door to Stars & Stripes burst open, and in walked the man himself.

"What's wrong?" Hunter asked. "You look kinda green."

"I think she's had a shock." Jefferson turned toward the bar. "You want a beer, son?"

"Yeah please," Hunter answered, but his eyes were on me. "What's happened? What's shocked you?"

My eyes flicked toward Jefferson. "He knows," I hissed.

"Knows what?"

"About me and you."

Hunter's head swiveled to look at his dad and then straight back to me. "How? Penny?"

"I don't know, he didn't say. All I know is he knows. Could be because you stormed out of the photoshoot, or so I heard."

Hunter's lip curled. "Yeah well, fucking Thor had his hands all over you. I didn't like it."

"Evidently. Not that it's up to you who puts their hands on me."

He took a step back and thrust his hands to his hips. "You do remember what happened in this very bar a few nights ago?"

My skin got heated as I did indeed recall what had happened to me and with what.

"So, I kinda think I do have a say in who puts their hands on you."

I slapped a hand against his chest. "Who says? Putting that inside me once." I pointed in the general direction of his dick. "Does not make me yours."

Hunter caught hold of my hand and pulled me closer to him. He smelled delicious and his hair was damp at the ends.

"Did you go all the way home and shower?" I asked, a little mesmerized by him.

"No, I went to Carter's place. Do you know he has throw pillows on his bed?"

"You're kidding right?"

"No and they match his blinds."

"Oh my God," I gasped. "What is wrong with him."

"His towels smelled clean too." Hunter's brows furrowed. "You think he's got a girl?"

I thought about it for a second and then remembered we were arguing. "I don't know, but you ignored what I said. Stabbing me with that huge appendage of yours doesn't make me yours."

Hunter's eyes went dark and predatory and I couldn't help but feel excited and lustful. Thankfully, Jefferson returned with a bottle of beer and handed it to Hunter.

"Here you go. I'm just gonna have a quick chat with Dusty about my truck."

He nodded over to my Mr. September, Dusty Chalmers, and walked away, leaving Hunter and I alone.

After a few seconds of staring at each other, I began to feel a throb in my panties and decided it was best if I left.

"Where are you going?" Hunter asked.

"Going to rescue Carter before Bronte smashes that bottle of wine over his head."

We both looked over to where Bronte was in a heated conversation with Carter and his and Hunter's old school friend Timothy Reagan, my Mr. February.

"Carter can handle himself," Hunter said softly as he caught hold of my hand. "We need to talk."

He let out a breath and rubbed two fingers against his temple, causing his bottle of beer to rest against his cheek. His eyes looked cautious and gone was the cocky cowboy who'd given me one hell of a show earlier.

I knew I could so easily get lost in the chocolate pools of his eyes. I could allow myself to believe any words he'd whisper to me, but I knew if I was smart I wouldn't.

"Nothing to talk about, Hunter," I replied, pulling my hand from his. "What happened was great, but it won't happen again."

"Why the fuck not? It was amazing, you know it was."

"Yeah, it was but look at them Hunter." I turned and pointed to Carter and Bronte arguing as Jefferson talked to Dusty but had half an eye on them.

"What about them?" Hunter asked, taking a step closer to me.

"They're our family, they're our friends. We're one big group of people who are interlinked in each other's lives. Carter and Bronte hate each other, but it's kind of funny because we know that they don't mean it. That's just the way they are."

"And yet you want to get them together?"

"Like I said," I replied with a shrug. "They're different."

"I'm really not with you, Ellie." He sighed.

"If we got together, when it ended, I would hate you, and that's not fair on our family and friends. If they split it would just go back to normal. It would be so much harder if it was us. Me hating you would be awful for everyone."

He leaned back; surprise written all over his face.

"How do you know you'd hate me? What if you were the one that ended it?"

I let out an empty laugh and scratched my forehead. "Because I know you, Hunter. You don't do relationships. You do one night, or maybe a whole week, but not a proper relationship and I've realized, that's what I want. I want to be loved and cherished and you couldn't do that."

I paused hoping against hope that he might challenge me, but he didn't. It hit me hard, just like the realization that Hunter was *the* person I wanted to be loved and cherished by; nothing less would do.

"Nope, I didn't think so." I smiled and looked over my shoulder at Jefferson. "He's so sad, Hunter, so very sad and if he lost his friends, he'd be even sadder."

"Why? What the fuck—"

"You'd break my heart and then my dad would kill you and Carter would hate you and that would hurt Jefferson so much. That's why we won't ever be anything except for one amazing fifteen minutes."

Swallowing hard, I turned and walked away unable to stop wondering if I'd just done the most stupid thing ever.

CHAPTER 27

Hunter

I t had been two weeks and I'd seen neither hide nor hair of Ellie. In those fourteen days I'd whacked off more than I'd ever done before, *and* I'd acted like a sulky, hormonal teen the whole time. To top my perfect three hundred and thirty-six hours, we were all spending Thanksgiving at her house.

In their wisdom Melinda and Henry had thought it would be a great idea for everyone to go to them for the holiday. We hadn't all got together for Thanksgiving since before Mom died, so I wasn't sure what had prompted them to suggest it. What I did know was that I was a mixture of pissed and excited at the prospect.

"Why now after all these years?" I asked Pop as he pulled up on the Maples' driveway.

"I don't know." He shrugged. "Melinda just said something about it being time."

"Got to say, I for one am excited," Auntie L piped up from the back seat. "It'll be lovely spending it with a lot of people."

"You bored with our company?" I asked, looking over my shoulder at her with a grin.

"No sweetheart," she replied, ruffling my hair. "But I think you and Jefferson need some more laughter in your lives."

"You give us plenty of laughs," Pop said. "And we love you both for it."

"We love you too, honey," Auntie J added. "Now let me at that peach wine I know Henry makes."

Before I had a chance to get out and help them both down from the truck, both my aunts were at the door and banging on it.

"Someone is excited."

"Yeah," Pop replied, sounding a little reflective. "You don't think we neglect them, do you?"

He watched his sisters as they were greeted by Melinda on the front stoop and let out a sigh.

"I'd hate to think we were no fun for them to live with."

"Pop, they fucking love living with us. You really think Uncle Miller would let them knit him a damn awful sweater every Christmas, or that Aunt Debra would let them use her kitchen to concoct soup that tastes like horse shit, and then eat it with a smile on her face."

Pop grinned. "No, I guess not."

"So, stop worrying about it. They're happy."

He nodded and gave my shoulder a squeeze, then we followed my aunts into the house.

Once inside, I had to be honest, it felt pretty good to be there; it was warm, happy and homely. The house was already decked with Christmas decorations, although no tree as I knew the Maples all went together on the twenty-third to buy it and then decorate it as a family – even Carter got involved. A gorgeous smell of turkey cooking permeated into the hallway and all I could hear was laughter and chit-chat. It felt exactly how Thanksgiving should be.

"Hey, Hunter," Melinda said as she came over to me with arms open wide. "I'm glad you came honey. Ellie said you might have to stay on the ranch with the herd."

Oh, she did, did she? Wished more like.

"No, we got the Williams brothers to come in. We usually do when we want some time off. Their fruit farm being seasonal and all, it gives them some extra cash."

"Yeah," Pop added, landing a huge hand on my shoulder. "They're struggling to compete with that huge big farm that's started over in Middleton Ridge. I'm even thinking of employing them full time in the new year."

"You are?" Melinda asked, genuinely interested.

"Yeah, well I ain't getting any younger, and we think we might increase the herd come January."

"That's a great idea, honey," Melinda said softly and pulled Pop in for a hug. "I'm so glad you came."

When she pulled away, there were tears in her eyes and her visible emotion hit me in the gut. This sudden invite and Melinda getting tearful had me worried.

"You okay?" I asked.

Melinda gave me a tight smile and nodded. "Yeah, sure. Just… I don't know, this year I'm kinda missing your mom a little more than usual, you know?"

She looked up at Pop, whose Adam's apple bobbed as he ran a hand over his hair.

"I'm just gonna catch up with the guys," Pop said, clearing his throat.

Melinda watched him go and then turned back to me.

"Is he okay, honey? Only Ellie said she thought he seemed sad, more so than usual."

Ellie. My heart thudded in my chest as I realized why the sudden big get together. She was worried about my pop. Evidently making sure he was happy was more important than keeping Bronte away from him. The idea that she'd got her mom to do this for us made me feel as though my lungs were about to give out and that maybe my heart was too big.

"I think he is," I replied honestly as I took a breath. "But he never really talks about stuff much. He talks about Mom a lot, and how much he misses her, but that's about it as far as emotions go."

Melinda's eyes twinkled with unshed tears and I felt a lump rise in my throat, as it always did when I spoke about my mom.

"I hear him crying sometimes." I sighed and looked over to Pop who was shooting shit with Jim, Henry and Carter. "Not for a little while though."

Melinda dragged me into a hug. "We're always here for you, honey. I know I'm not family, but I loved her like a sister."

"Yeah, I know." I squeezed her back and as I did saw Ellie standing in the doorway, watching us. "I think I'll go get myself a drink now."

"You do that." She patted my back and let me go. "Right, I need to check the potatoes."

I watched her go and was just about to join the guys, when I felt a hand on my arm. Turning around I was a little surprised to see Ellie, particularly as I'd ghosted her for the last two weeks. Yeah, I'd been the bitchy little princess who'd ignored her text messages and sent her calls to voicemail, not that she ever left one.

"Ellie."

"Hey, Hunter. I'm glad you came. I thought you might stay home." She looked down at her feet which were covered in fluffy red socks.

"Why because you were a little bitchy last time we spoke," I replied in a low voice, even though deep down I knew she wasn't.

Her eyes went wide, and her sweet pink lips parted. Images of them parting as she orgasmed around my dick hit me between the eyes; that didn't help with my promise to stay mad at her.

"I was not. I was only being honest," she hissed, giving a cautionary glance over to where her Mom was talking to Darcy just a few paces away.

"Yeah, well there's being honest and there's being a bitch, and I think you were the latter."

And yep, snarky Ellie was back in the room. Hands went to her hips and nostrils flared as she leaned into my space.

"You tell me that isn't what would happen," she snapped. "That you wouldn't hurt me."

"Well, I guess we'll never know now, will we?" Like a dick, I patted her on the head and walked away and I could practically hear the steam coming from her ears with each step I took.

***

To play Cards Against Humanity was not what I considered the best activity. Not in my opinion, as someone who was fucking mad with the sassy little miss who was sitting next to me. At least it gave me an opportunity to be a dick to her; and I had, whenever possible.

"During sex," Ellie read from the card. "I like to think of blank."

I had the perfect fucking card for her, and I was so damn glad I'd held onto it for most of the game. I'd been waiting for the ideal moment and this was it.

Ellie read out the first card. "A bag of magic beans."

No one really reacted, except for Austen, Bronte's youngest brother who sighed and looked at Ellie like magic beans were the worst kind of thing he could have put in front of her.

She then picked up another card. "Dory, the lesbian fish."

Everyone laughed and Bronte bounced up and down in her chair giving it away that it was her card.

"Good one, sis," Shaw, the eldest of Bronte's brothers said before he took a long swig of his beer.

Ellie picked up the next card and rolled her eyes. "My future husband."

"Sorry lame I know," Shaw replied with a grimace.

"Okay, next one." Ellie grinned and picked up the next card. "Oh nice."

Her eyes immediately went to me and then back to the card.

"Hurry the fuck up and tell us," Carter said irritably. "The game starts in an hour."

"Alright, impatient some." She cleared her throat. "A big sloppy blow job from a mean and tired cowboy."

Everyone laughed, well everyone except Austen who at fourteen probably shouldn't have been playing, but all the fucking 'grown-ups' were out on the patio getting drunk on pear wine and JD, so what did they expect but for us to lead the kid astray.

"Oh my God," Bronte said around a laugh. "That's hilarious."

"It's not that funny," Ellie replied, glancing at me as she picked up the final card. "Okay, so during sex I like to think of a *web of lies*."

"What the hell is that?" I said, totally bemused. "It's supposed to be funny."

"It is," Carter replied a little sulkily. "Anyway, it's all I had left."

"I don't understand the question." Austen sighed and scratched his head.

"You're not supposed to squirt." Shaw rubbed his head. "And don't tell Mom and Dad I let you play. I vote that Bronte's lesbian fish wins that one."

"Yeah, me too." Ellie gave me a sarcastic smile, like I gave a shit I hadn't won the round.

"Okay," Carter said as he dragged all the cards toward him. "What shall we do now? I vote, drink beer and have some guy talk about the game."

He stared at Bronte who flipped him off.

"No. It's Thanksgiving, we should stay together," Austen said giving moon eyes at Ellie. "Hunter, Ellie, think of something to do."

Ellie and I shrugged, but a wicked gleam came over Bronte's face.

"Let's get the folks back in and play Sardines."

Ellie's mouth dropped open. She knew and so did I why Bronte wanted to play Sardines, and with all the parents.

"I don't think so," Ellie said as she pushed up from the table. "We have American Trivia, let's play that."

"No," Austen replied, his eyes shining excitedly. "I think Sardines is better. Shaw, you prefer Sardines, don't you?"

Shaw smiled at his brother and shook his head. "I've got a call to make, squirt. I'm gonna do that before the game."

Austen groaned. "He has a girl."

"Yeah?" I slapped Shaw's back. "Something serious, buddy?"

Shaw shrugged. "I don't know, man. She's hot and real smart, but... I'm twenty."

"Look at Mom and Dad," Bronte said as she helped pack up the cards. "I know they didn't start dating seriously until after college, but Mom said Dad took her on a couple of dates in high school. Melinda and Henry actually met *at* college."

"And my mom and pop were real young too," I added.

Shaw gave Austen a sideways look and then patted him on the back. "Hey, Aust', why don't you go ask Dad if you can have one beer?"

Austen's face lit up. "You think he'll let me?"

Shaw shrugged. "You never know."

Austen raced off and Bronte rounded on her brother. "He's only just let you start drinking at home, there's no way he's going to let Austen."

"I know, but I needed to get rid of him."

"Why? You need some advice on the fairer sex?" Carter asked with a grin.

Bronte rolled her eyes and turned to her brother. "If you do, don't ask him."

"No," Shaw replied. "It's about something else."

"What is it?" What's wrong?" Carter frowned and placed a hand on Shaw's shoulder.

"You not noticed how Mom and Dad barely speak to each other?" he asked, turning to his sister.

Bronte shook her head slowly, but when she flopped back down onto her seat with the color draining from her face, it was obvious that it wasn't news to her.

"I got up to get a drink real late last night and Dad was sleeping on the sofa."

Ellie immediately rounded the table and nudged Carter out of the way so she could take his place behind Bronte and wrap her arms around her friend.

"It doesn't mean anything," Bronte said, looking up at Ellie. "Right? They probably just had an argument. Or maybe Mom had enough of him snoring. Don't tell me you haven't heard him."

Shaw looked like he was about to say something but then gave Bronte a huge smile instead. "Yeah, that's probably it."

I grabbed my beer and took a long drink. Shit, it didn't bear thinking about Jim and Darcy not being happy. Both sets of parents had been a constant my whole life along with my own and being without Mom had changed the dynamic. Losing Jim or Darcy as well was a hard thought to get my head around.

"Hey, guess what?" Austen came barreling in from outside, breaking the tense atmosphere. "Dad said yes to me having a beer, and they all want to play Sardines."

Carter scrubbed a hand down his face and groaned. "Fuck my life." He bent to speak to Shaw. "You sure you're okay?"

Shaw nodded. "Bronte's probably right."

"Hey guys," Melinda's slightly drunk voice sounded out as she entered the den where we were, stopping any further discussion about the Jackson's marriage. "I vote Ellie is the sardine."

"Yeah, Ellie Belly you go first," Henry replied coming up behind Melinda.

I figured it was my queue to duck out and pretend I needed to make a call to Tom or Sam Williams to check on the ranch. When I looked over at Pop though, his eyes were shining with a laughter and a joy I hadn't seen from him in a while. He had an arm around each of my aunts and he looked happy. Not the 'I just got laid' happy that I'd been used to seeing from him recently, but instead a real unadulterated contentment beamed out.

"Okay," Ellie said reluctantly. "I'll go hide. No cheating, Dad, I know what you're like. *And* I can hide outside or inside, no boundaries."

As Henry argued his innocence, Ellie sashayed out of the room and when she paused at the door to scratch the left cheek of her butt, my phone call was forgotten. I was searching first, and I was going to find her and hope to God no one else guessed where we were.

CHAPTER 28

Ellie

Waiting to be found was boring. I knew what they were all like, they'd be distracted with wine, Jack D and gossip. That was why I'd taken my Kindle with me and was reading the book I'd been losing myself in. The sex in it was pretty hot, well at least I'd thought it had been until I'd had sex with Hunter – now that was totally what I'd call boiling point.

I let out a sigh thinking about it and how since that night I'd been desperate for more. Not even my vibrator, under the covers to muffle the noise, had been enough. It appeared that only Hunter Meredith – that still cracked me up – Delaney's dick would ever be big or good enough for me ever again. The size still astounded me, that and the fact that it actually fit. Sheesh, the phrase baby's arm had never been truer.

The thought of Hunter sticking his penis that was way mightier than the sword inside of me, had me feeling all hot and bothered. The pear wine had me relaxed enough to consider slipping my hand inside my jeans and panties, but the sound of footsteps soon put a stop to that idea. I closed my Kindle and held my breath while they moved around and opened up the cupboard opposite my hiding place. A few seconds later everything went quiet and I was convinced I'd got away with it. Just as I let out my breath, the lid lifted from the wicker basket I was hiding in and I was blinded by Hunter's smile.

"I knew this was where you'd be." He grinned at me and lifted a leg up.

"What are you doing?"

"Getting in. I found you, so I have to hide with you, or have you forgotten the rules?"

"N-No." My heart began to hammer at the thought of being alone with him, in the summerhouse, in the old wicker basket that my mom kept all our old dress up clothes in. "You won't fit."

"Well, you chose it, Ellie, so you'll have to suffer the consequences."

"How *did* you know I'd be here?" I asked.

He shrugged and then lowered himself down. "It's where you always hid when we were kids." His hand reached for the lid. "Comfy. Okay, let's wait."

He wriggled around beside me, groaning a little as he did, and I didn't want to consider the reason why. His body was pretty much plastered to mine, his long leg between mine and one arm over my stomach.

"Lift your head," he said as he wriggled his butt.

Thinking it was easier than arguing, I craned my neck and then dropped my head onto his chest as soon as he let out a sigh.

"Well, ain't this cozy."

Hunter's face was so close to mine that his breath, which smelled of beer and mint, ghosted over my skin and sent ripples of excitement through my body.

"So, tell me, how do you propose we get anyone else in here?"

Hunter edged closer and it didn't escape my notice that you'd barely have been able to slide a slip of paper between our mouths. I swallowed hard and thanked God I hadn't had any of Dad's god-awful onion sauce with my turkey.

"Didn't think that far ahead," I whispered. "I was pretty sure no one would find me. I'm surprised you remembered to be truthful."

I couldn't see his face properly, but I just knew Hunter was staring at me, trying to make out my expression in the darkness.

"Funny," he replied, and I heard him swallow. "I didn't realize how much I do remember about you."

We were so quiet he must have heard my heart banging against my chest bone, begging to come out.

"Nothing to say?"

"Nope," I breathed out.

"Wow, that's different." Hunter chuckled low and pushed closer to me.

I gasped quietly feeling that damn big schlong of his pressing against my leg. Even through his denims I was pretty sure I could feel every inch and every ridge of it against my leg.

"Well, that was rude," I hissed hoping that some sass would break the tension inside the basket.

The thought caused me to giggle.

"What?" Hunter asked as he ran his hand down my arm. "What's so funny?"

"Us. Being in a basket. It's just funny is all."

"I guess we do hang out in some strange places." His fingertips trailed up toward my shoulder and drew small circles causing my stomach to flip. "Storerooms, dress up baskets, wherever next?"

My nipples sprang to life and I knew that Hunter could feel them when his breath hitched.

"I thought we agreed that this wasn't going to happen again," I mumbled into the darkness, not sure whether I was talking to Hunter, myself or my nipples.

"You said that, not me," Hunter replied and shifted even closer, snaking his arm around my back and pushing his hand up my shirt. "And nothing is happening… yet."

Rough fingertips trailed the goosebumps which broke out across my sensitive skin and I started to breath heavily as he reached the fastener on my bra. With a deft flick of the wrist, he unclipped it giving my girls the freedom they were craving – well they were craving his touch, but you can't be too greedy.

"Hunter," I protested a little lamely.

"Ellie."

He mocked my tone and even though our mouths weren't touching, I could feel him smile.

"What are you doing?'

"Well, Ellie, there's this thing called sex and—"

"Don't be such a dick," I replied, but moved my crotch closer to his hard on.

It was like he had a magnet in his dick, and I had a metal plate in my pussy – the damn hussy wouldn't stop moving toward him.

"Do I need to continue with the sex-ed theory, or shall we move straight to the practical part of the lesson?"

As much as I wanted to tell him to go fuck himself, my traitorous vagina sent a message to my brain, which then zapped it to my mouth.

"Just get on with getting me off, Hunter, because you're actually getting on my last nerve."

Hunter laughed low and moved his hand to the button of my jeans.

"Last chance to say no to me making you come all over your Cinderella and Princess Jasmine costumes."

"*Really.* God, Hunter, I was going to donate them to the elementary school. How can I do that with sex juice on them."

"You have heard of dry cleaning, right?" Hunter's mouth found mine and his tongue licked slowly across the seam of my lips. "They've been in this basket for years. They probably smell real bad anyway."

I thought about it for a second. "Yeah, true." I grabbed the back of his head and pulled him to me.

We kissed like we were a couple of teenagers. All teeth, tongues and grabby hands. In seconds my jeans were undone, and Hunter's hand was inside my panties. My hand was around his beautiful appendage and we began to pump and finger in unison until we were both gasping.

"What if someone comes?" I gasped as Hunter pushed another finger inside of me.

"Someone aside from you?"

I didn't want to laugh but couldn't help my breathy giggle.

"Oh fuck," Hunter groaned. "That laugh is just so damn sexy."

Spurred on by his words, I nipped at his bottom lip and began to pump harder. I felt his butt tense under my hand, and I couldn't help but give it a squeeze.

"Love your damn ass," I breathed out.

"Good... damn... to know. Keep going, I'm gonna——"

"Shush." I stilled my hand and listened. "Did you hear that?"

I held my breath, but Hunter grabbed my hand with his that wasn't in my panties—there was no way I'd have let him remove it anyway—and forced me to keep pumping. When he gave a quiet moan, I fused my mouth to his and listened but there was nothing.

"No one there. Sorry."

"Don't give a fuck if the whole town are waiting outside this basket, just keep going."

He moaned against my mouth and increased the speed of his fingers while his free hand moved up my shirt and palmed my boob. A thumb softly rubbed against my nipple and my skin set on fire as I began to come undone.

"Oh my God," I gasped momentarily forgetting I was supposed to be pumping his dick.

Hunter thrust upward, urging me to continue and when my body tensed with my own orgasm, he groaned with his lips against my neck.

"Ah, *fuck.*"

"Hunter."

Breathlessly we both rode out the pleasure, leaving gasps of breathlessness in the air. Our chests were heaving heavily and the atmosphere inside the basket felt electric.

"Shit, I've got jizz all over my sweater."

"Spoil a moment why don't you." I started to giggle. "I think there's a Captain Hook outfit in here. Complete with hook for your hand."

"It'll disguise the smell of my fingers, I guess."

I slapped at his chest but couldn't help but smile. "Sometimes you're too disgusting for words."

He pulled his hand from my panties and sniffed loudly. "Yep, I'll be needing that hook."

We both laughed and then fell into silence, as Hunter gently stroked my cheek.

"We should get back," I said wishing away the euphoria rising inside me. "I don't think anyone is going to find us."

"No, I don't think so," he replied but didn't move.

I wasn't sure how to deal. Did I make the first move to leave, or should I wait for Hunter? Did I tell him it was great—again—and that I was starting to want more for us, or did I act cool? I had no damn clue. The only thing I did know was that the stolen moments were starting to feel not enough. Having sex with a guy and getting off from his fingers were not the sort of thing I did. I'd always been a relationship kind of girl. Yes, Dominic had ruined that. Even though the sex and playing around with Hunter was amazing, I didn't want to be his regular fuck buddy until he got bored and went back to his one-night stands.

"You think maybe this might be a good time to talk?" he asked as he pulled up my zipper. "Like I wanted to after we had sex."

"We did talk."

If we talked now, I knew I'd ask him for things he wasn't ready for, and then I'd be the fool, once again. No, it'd be much better for my heart and self-respect if we didn't talk.

"No, Ellie, we didn't. You told me we weren't happening and then closed me down. You didn't even give me a chance to tell you what I want."

My laugh sounded a little sarcastic. "Oh, I can imagine what you want," I huffed out, unable to hide the hurt that I pre-empted from me wanting him so damn much.

"Really? So, you're a mind reader now?" Hunter sighed heavily and shifted his body to reach for his own zipper.

"No, never said I was, but you're so predictable. I'd be shocked if you wanted anything else other than to have me as a fuck buddy."

I could just about make out his face. He didn't look thrilled at my theory.

"Your opinion of me is so fucking stellar, isn't it?" he said as he shoved up the lid of the basket.

He pushed himself up and maneuvered out. Pausing to fasten the button of his jeans he then pulled a handkerchief from his pocket and rubbed at the white stain on his sweater.

"Has it come off?" I asked, trying to alleviate the awkwardness I felt at lying back in the basket as he stood over me.

Hunter glanced down at me with hooded eyes and sighed. "I'm going back," he replied, not answering my question. "You coming or not?"

I nodded and held up my hand. Hunter tugged on it, pulling me to my feet. I then stepped out and brushed myself down, chancing a look at him as he continued rubbing at his sweater.

"I'm sorry, okay."

"Just forget about," he replied, glancing up at me. "I was stupid to even think you'd talk about what's happening."

"Which is having fun, just like you said. So why do we need to talk about it?" I argued as Hunter pinched the bridge of his nose.

"No, you're right, we don't." He gave me a thin-lipped smile. "It's just fun, nothing at all to discuss."

Before I could respond, he stormed off back toward the house. Feeling a lot of annoyance and frustration of my own, I ran after him. I called his name, but his pace never let up. He flung open the door into the kitchen and then let it slam closed behind him.

When I spun into the den, Hunter was standing in the doorway, with his hands on his hips. Even from behind I could see his anger; his butt was tensed so it wasn't difficult.

"What's going on?" I asked, standing alongside him.

He let out a long exhale and pointed into the room. Everyone was in there, well into a game of Monopoly.

"They look like they've been playing that for an age," I whispered.

"Yeah." He didn't say anything else to me but stepped into the room. "Did any of you actually come and look for us?"

Jefferson looked up from taking a wad of notes from Austen and smiled.

"Oh, sorry, son, we totally forgot. We kinda got engrossed in this game of Monopoly. Your Aunt L is raking the money in."

I looked over at Lynn-Ann who was sitting proudly on one of the love seats with Shaw and counting the huge pile of money she had.

"Yeah, sorry, honey," Mom called without even looking away from the board. "We forgot. There's pumpkin pie just out of the oven if you and Hunter want some."

I growled and Hunter looked at me. His eyes were still full of indignation, but I wasn't sure if it was just down to me or our families as well.

"You want some pie?" I asked, trying to clear the air.

His eyes raked up and down my body and then stopped right at my crotch. He shook his head and then looked back at my face, a wicked grin on his own.

"No thanks just had some."

Chuckling to himself, he turned on his heels and went off toward the kitchen where all the beer was, leaving me with the distinct feeling that I might regret not hearing him out.

I looked back into the den deciding whether to join them or get pie first, when I noticed Bronte staring up at Jefferson, all starry-eyed. Every time he spoke, she giggled and flipped her hair and a feeling of foreboding passed over me. She was down and out flirting and in front of everyone. It was not good.

"Excuse me," Hunter said, coming back from getting his beer, and laying a hand on my waist. "Just need to squeeze past you here."

"Have you seen Bronte?" I asked, barring his way into the den. "She's outwardly flirting with your dad."

Hunter looked over my shoulder and shrugged. "And?"

"*And* we need to step up our plan."

He took a long swig from his bottle of beer and then sighed as he leaned in, so his lips were at my ear.

"I think it's about time I got some recompense for helping with this plan of yours."

Side-eyeing him I snorted my derision. "Recompense for what? I've done everything."

"Well for listening to you in the first place, for doing the calendar."

"Oh, which I've seen the proofs of by the way," I replied excitedly. "And I have to be honest, you look pretty good."

Hunter preened, pulling to his full height. "You doubted me?"

I shrugged but smirked and earned myself a beautiful smile.

"Wish I'd done December though, don't cha?" He nudged me with his shoulder and winked.

"As much as I hate to admit it, you are a teeny bit more photogenic than Dylan." I held my finger and thumb apart to show him how small the gap was. It was a lie of course; his pictures were phenomenal. I had no idea how, but he knew how to work the camera. His eyes looked down the lens as though they were looking right at me and only me.

Phew, just thinking about them made me hot.

"That mean you're going to be buying more than one calendar for yourself?"

"Well, it is for a good cause," I replied with a shrug.

"Sure is." He grinned and took a drink of his beer. "So, I look forward to hearing from you when you've decided what I deserve for helping you."

He moved to go and join the Monopoly game, but I caught hold of his sweater.

"What are you thinking?" I asked. "A few beers, a dinner. What?"

Hunter's eyes crinkled with amusement and he put his mouth close to my ear and whispered.

"I'm sure you'll think of something, but until you do, you're on your own baby."

CHAPTER 29

Hunter

"**W**hat the hell is wrong with you today?"

Pop jumped out of the way as I threw the broken fence post to one side.

"Nothing. I'm fine."

The post slammer went down on the new post with a thud and reverberated around us.

"That post has done something wrong then." Pop shook his head and with a swing of his axe split the broken one in half. "Something happen yesterday at Henry and Melinda's?"

I breathed out deep, through my nose. "Pop, I said I don't want to talk about it."

"Fine but stop acting like a teenage girl who lost her ticket to a Bieber concert."

"Bieber isn't relevant any longer," I replied, lifting the slammer again.

"Whatever, you know what I mean."

We continued to work in silence, but everything that had gone on with Ellie the day before had turned me into a brooding dark cloud. I didn't want to talk about it, but it was also *all* I wanted to talk about. She was driving me fucking crazy with her hot and cold attitude. We'd been intimate twice and both times she'd passed it off like it was nothing. Wasn't that what *I* was supposed to do? I'd tried to laugh it off, make her think I was okay with the fun of it all, but once I got home and thought about things, I was pretty pissed.

"It's Ellie," I blurted out and threw the slammer to the ground. "She's driving me crazy."

The grin on Pop's face said it all. Ellie had been right; he did already know about us.

"You knew?"

He shrugged. "Not the full story but then you've had a thing for that girl most of your damn life. She's grown into a beautiful woman, so why would you have different feelings now."

"What? What the hell are you talking about? I haven't had a thing for her all my life."

"Most of it you have, son. I'd say since you were about ten or eleven and you realized she looked like Belle from Beauty and the Beast." Pop threw his head back and laughed. "I remember you almost walked into the side of that big old tree in their back yard because you couldn't take your eyes off her. She came outside in a cute little yellow sundress and a pair of flower shaped shades, with a book under her arm. Then she plonked her sassy little ass on a sun lounger, pushed her shades up her nose, crossed her legs and started to read. You watched her from the minute she set foot outside, to the moment she picked up that book and you've been watching her ever since."

"Huh," I scoffed. "As if."

Pop smiled and nodded. "Truth. Your mom noticed too."

"She did?"

"Yep," he sighed at the memory. "She grabbed my hand and said, 'he's found his one, baby'."

I started to laugh. "My one. I don't think so, Pop. I mean I like her and all, but my one? Nope we're nothing like that."

"So, tell me, son," he said as he took his work gloves off and shoved them into the back pocket of his jeans. "What are you like?"

Pinching the bridge of my nose I thought about his question. "We just had sex and… well other stuff."

"Don't let Henry hear you say that you've *just* had sex with his girl, but she ain't your one."

"Why not? You have a sex with lots of women and none of them are *your* one."

"I had my one," he replied, a shadow passing over his face. "And I treated her like a queen from the moment I knew she was it for me."

"It's kind of difficult to treat someone like a queen when they act like a bitchy princess most of the time." I kicked at some stones on the floor and sighed before looking up at him. "Truth be told, Pop I have no idea how I feel about her."

He leaned back against the truck and folded his arms over his chest. The tattoos on his arms peeked out from under the cuffs of his rolled back shirt sleeves, both our jackets were thrown to one side when the work got sweaty.

"So, what's got you so hot headed. If you don't know how you feel, how come you're in such a shitty mood?"

"She just shut me down afterward; both times."

"And that's hurt your sweet little heart, right?" He quirked a brow and crossed his feet at the ankle, looking every inch the damn man who knew exactly what he was doing with his life; no regrets.

"No… yes… fuck, Pop I don't know. I just know I'm pissed about it."

"Well, seems to me if you can figure out why you're pissed about it, you're well on your way to figuring out how you feel about her."

I moved over to join him leaning against the truck and looked out over the land. Some of the herd were grazing, in front of us and to the right in a smaller paddock was the bull we were hoping to introduce to them in the next few days.

"I kinda wish I was like that bull," I said, nodding in his direction. "Get introduced to a whole load of females and then just jump whichever ones smell right and take my fancy."

"You can, Hunt," Pop replied. "But something is stopping you and my guess it could be those damn elusive feelings that you have for Ellie."

Watching his profile, I saw his jaw tense and tick as he looked dead ahead. That usually meant he was trying not to get emotional in some way or other. I figured it wasn't anger he was holding back, but maybe sadness seeing as we were talking about feelings and falling for someone.

"How long after you met Mom did you know?" My eyes stayed on him and the tension increased as the tick sped up. "Don't think you've ever told me."

Finally, Pop looked at me and gave me a sad smile. "Your mom would have told you it was the minute she fell off the fence she was sitting on and flashed her panties at me; four weeks after I'd been working on her Uncle's ranch in Connecticut."

"Her Uncle Drake, right?"

Pop nodded. "Yeah. Your Grandpa wanted me and Miller to learn the business from other people, not just him, so he got me a job on Drake's ranch, while your uncle went to Kentucky. Dad knew Drake from way back, from when they went to the same auctions. I was supposed to stay there for eight months in total, but," he sighed and lowered his gaze to the floor, "after five, your Grandpa was killed by a bull that got spooked, so me and Miller had to come back."

"Grandma was already dead wasn't she."

Pop nodded. "Yeah, she died of cancer when I was seventeen." He looked at me and squeezed my shoulder. "Funny how life repeats itself."

"Yeah, I guess so." I hadn't realized Pop had been a similar age as I'd been when I'd lost Mom. It did all seem a little weird. "If it wasn't when Mom said it was, when was it then? When you knew Mom was the one."

Pop's eyes lightened and a huge smile that was brighter than the sun lit up his face. "It was a week after I'd been there. I'd gone into town with one of the other ranch hands. We'd gone to get some supplies for Drake. The guy I was with was in the barber shop getting his hair cut and I was waiting outside because it was real hot and humid and the barber shop had no AC. Well, your mom was walking along carrying some bags and one of them busted open. Everything in it rolled across the floor so I rushed over to help her, but she brushed me away and said she could manage. Said she didn't need my help. I watched her put what she could in the other bags and then stuff the rest down the front of her shirt and in the pockets of her shorts. Once she did, she strutted past me like she had no damn clue who I was or that anything had happened."

"That made you fall in love with her?" I asked, a little surprised. "Sounds like she was too stubborn for her own good."

He grinned at me. "Exactly. So, it was then, but I knew for definite two weeks later when she accidently flashed me her panties."

We both laughed and it felt good to talk about her and not get emotional or feel the need to scream my anger at her leaving us.

"I think what I'm trying to say, son," Pop said eventually. "Is that sometimes it's not the beauty of someone that is the best part of them. Sometimes it's the things that piss you off like their stubbornness. Your mom was one of the most tenacious people I ever knew and thank God she was. If she hadn't been, she would never have stuck up for herself with her folks and come here to marry me. That cost her a relationship with them, but she was steadfast in what she wanted, and praise everything under the goddamn sun, that was me. That damn stubbornness also gave me you because you know she was told not to have kids, but she was adamant. And, without you I don't think I'd have survived losing her, son, I really don't."

I turned away, not wanting him to see the tears glossing my eyes.

"You're right, once she made her mind up," I sighed.

"Yep. So, for all she was the most beautiful woman in the world, it was her stubborn streak that made me realize she was the woman I wanted by my side for the rest of my life. Which means that you may need to look past your anger where Ellie is concerned. Consider why she's being stubborn and pushing you away. And if that all comes from a good place, well maybe you need to give her time and be more understanding."

I let my head drop back and puffed out my cheeks.

"I'm so mad at her though, Pop. She just shut me down and won't even consider what we could be."

"Don't forget the number that ass clown Dominic did on her."

"She didn't care about him," I scoffed.

"She knows that now, and maybe even then, but he still hurt and humiliated her. Plus, you don't have the best track record for long and meaningful relationships, Hunt."

I stared at him wide-eyed.

"Hey, I had the best woman in the world as long as God allowed me to have her. I'm not looking for anything else."

Shaking my head, I slapped Pop's back. "I'll think about it. It's just she's so crazy."

"And the crazy is the best part about women, you should know that."

We moved to gather the tools and throw them in the back of the truck and as I stalked to the driver's side, my phone buzzed in my pocket. Pausing, I pulled it out to see another message from Ellie – number seventeen in the last twenty-four hours.

Ellie: Hunter, if I show you my boobs are you back on the team? Whaddaya say Cowboy?

Yep, fucking crazy.

CHAPTER 30

Ellie

Hunter Delaney no longer existed to me. He was an idiot and a douche, and he'd abandoned me in my hour of need.

Well, it wasn't quite that bad, but he had dropped all my calls and ignored my text messages since Thanksgiving. Admittedly, they were all about our… okay *my*, 'Get Bronte with Carter' plan and his silence had made it quite clear that I was now on my own—unless of course I could think of a suitable recompense for his involvement. Obviously, I knew what he was getting at—more sex and or including the possibility of ass play.

Whatever, he could have at least answered one text message. I didn't even get a response from my offer to show him my boobs if he was still willing to help; things were definitely bad between us.

The plan had evidently become my sole responsibility. That was fine, everything we'd done so far, which hadn't been much if I thought about, had been instigated by me anyway. It was now solely on me to get Bronte's mind off Jefferson and onto Carter. Which was why I was knocking on the door of her house with a devious, some might even say downright evil, plan.

"Hey, Ellie," Darcy greeted me with a small smile.

"Hi, Darcy. Is Bronte home?" I thought she was because her bright pink Chevrolet Spark was sitting on the drive, but she was going through a jogging phase so may have been out.

"She's in her room. Go on through."

Darcy stood to one side and let me in, but I didn't get the usual hug and squeeze from her. In fact, she looked sad and was gray beneath her eyes. Maybe what Shaw had said at Thanksgiving about his parents was more serious than we all thought.

"Hey."

Bronte looked up from the magazine that she was reading and sighed. "Oh hi."

"Hey, what's wrong?" I asked, joining her on the bed. "You look as sad as your mom."

"She and Dad have been arguing again, and last night he actually stayed out all night."

"So, what Shaw said was true?"

Bronte nodded. "Yeah. I think they're going to split up. I wasn't supposed to hear, but I heard Mom say if he didn't want to be here then he should leave."

My heart hurt for her. I couldn't imagine what it would be like to have your parents separate. I couldn't imagine what it would be like to lose a parent.

And Hunter invaded my head space, yet again.

"What did your dad say?" I asked trying to get my mind back on track.

"He said if that's how she felt then he would. He didn't, he stayed home, but last night he didn't come back after he stormed out over another argument. I have no idea where he went, but he came back while I was out getting some supplies for the salon and they haven't spoken to each other since."

I let out a deep sigh, second guessing whether I should put my plan into action. It was kind of mean, and Bronte seemed to be suffering enough.

"One positive," she said, giving me a beaming smile. "I saw Jefferson when I was in Jennings Bridge getting supplies."

My shoulders sagged. "You did?"

"Yeah, we had coffee together." Bronte grabbed my hand and gave it an excited shake. "And he looked super-hot. He was wearing a flannel and jeans and his top two buttons were open and I got a sneaky little glimpse of his tattoos."

She bounced on the bed all worries about her folks evidently gone.

"Bronte," I snapped. "You're supposed to be worried about your mom and dad."

"I am," she replied. "Seeing Jefferson just cheered me up is all."

She pouted but I saw a hint of smile and I knew she was trying to play me which made me even more determined to go ahead with my dastardly plot.

"Shall I get us a coke or something?" I asked, giving her what I hoped was a sympathetic smile.

"I can go." She made to get up off the bed, but I put a hand on her shoulder.

"Let me, you're obviously upset."

She looked deeply sad once more, and I fleetingly second guessed my plan *again* before remembering how she'd had coffee with Jefferson.

"Yeah, leave it to me."

I left her room and furtively checked my pocket with a little pat.

***

"He's going to be okay, right?" Bronte asked Carter.

My brother placed a hand on her shoulder and gave it a squeeze. "Of course, he will. I just want to keep him under observation."

"And you'll call me if he takes a turn for the worse?"

"Honestly." Carter's voice was soft and gentle. He surprised me with just how sensitive he could sound. Probably because it involved animals—

Bronte's cat, Rodrick, being the animal in question. Her shitting cat, Rodrick.

"Why don't you two go over to Stars & Stripes," he said as he looked over his shoulder toward his consultancy room. "I'll come over in a little while when I've kept an eye on him for a bit longer."

"You'll come over?" I asked, thinking my plan was going well. I could bail and get him to give Bronte a lift home.

"I'm supposed to be meeting Hunter, he'll already be there. Tell him I'll get over asap."

Bronte nodded. "Thanks, Carter, I really appreciate it." She stood up on her tiptoes and leaned in to kiss his cheek.

This was getting better and better.

"Let's go, Bronte." I grabbed her hand and pulled her gently toward the exit door.

She gave Carter one last smile and followed me out.

***

"You do think he'll be okay, don't you?"

"Yes, of course he will. With Carter taking care of him he's bound to be. He's a great vet," I stressed. "The best. So good with all animals and such a sweetie when he needs to be."

"Hmm." Bronte pulled a face that asked me if I was talking about the same Carter. "If you say so. Come on let's sit down."

We turned from the bar with our drinks and looked around for somewhere to sit.

"Oh look," Bronte said, instantly moving away from me. "There's Hunter."

Before I even had time to say anything, she'd gone and positioned herself at Hunter's table. He had his head in his hands, a bottle of beer almost empty in front of him.

"Hey, Hunter," Bronte said brightly. "Can we sit with you?"

He looked up at me and then Bronte. "I'm waiting for Carter."

I frowned at the sound of his voice. He sounded sad, and most definitely didn't look like he wanted the two of us for company.

Bronte, however, had other ideas.

"We know," she replied as she pulled out a stool. "He told us to tell you he'll be here as soon as he can."

"Why, where is he?"

Hunter's eyes hit mine and there was questioning behind them. Shit he knew me too well. I immediately felt myself color up.

"He's checking out Rodrick, my cat." Bronte leaned in close to him. "He's shitting for America. I'm pretty sure he could get it through the eye of a needle in one."

Hunter grimaced and took a drink from his bottle, his gaze still on me. "Nice image."

"Yeah. I've no idea what his problem is. He was fine one minute, eating some food Ellie put out for him, then the next, there's shit everywhere." Bronte spread her hands out to indicate how far the shit had spread from one little cat's ass. "And the smell. Damn it was awful."

"Ellie fed him eh?" Hunter's eyes narrowed. "And he got the shits right after?"

"Yeah." Bronte scrunched up her perfect little nose. "About fifteen minutes later. His food must have been an old can, but I didn't think pet food could go off. Carter's taking care of him now though."

Hunter pushed up from his stool, rounded the table and grabbed me by the elbow.

"We'll be one minute, there's something I need Ellie's advice on."

Not even questioning him, Bronte nodded. "Take your time, I got my wine, so I'll be good."

I trailed after Hunter as he strode across the bar, only stopping when we got to a door at the back wall; a door which led to the storeroom.

"Oh no," I said with a shake of my head. "That's not a good idea. Carter could be here at any minute."

Hunter looked at the door as realization sparked in his eyes. "Well unless you've finally decided on my incentive, I'm withholding all favors for a while. Hot sex in the storeroom included. Oh, and for the record, showing me your tits is not recompense for all my efforts. I've already seen them, remember."

I nodded, the memories pretty clear in my mind, which was why Hunter being adamant nothing further would happen flooded me with disappointment. Despite his protestations, I could see the lust and want in his eyes, and I was pretty sure if I pushed it, I could persuade him otherwise. The problem with Hunter though, specifically sexual shenanigans with Hunter, was that it was addictive and I had to cut myself off if I was to survive without extraordinarily expensive rehab. All told, him withholding wasn't a bad thing – not really; okay it damn well sucked.

"What the fuck did you do, Ellie?" he ground out, stooping to look me in the eye.

"Nothing."

"Liar. Now tell me what the hell did you do to Bronte's cat? Because I know you did something."

"What do you care? It's just a cat. Anyway, you gave me the idea when you said you'd dropped Carter some laxative at Belinda Jennings's party."

"I was joking, and Carter is dislikeable most of the time, so would deserve it. This is Bronte's damn pet which she actually loves." His nostrils flared.

"Oh, don't be so judgy."

"If you've harmed it just for this stupid plan of yours, I'll…" He trailed off and rose to his full height, running a hand through his hair. "Shit, Ellie, you're insane."

He turned away from me and cursed some more.

"He's fine," I protested. "Carter is an incredible vet. I mean I know he's only a couple of years out of veterinary school, but he was fast tracked his last year so he's—"

"Enough," he snapped as he turned back to face me. "You are certifiable, you know that? What the hell did you do to the damn cat?"

I shrank back and sucked my lips between my teeth.

"Ellie?" he growled.

"You're pretty scary when you're angry."

Hunter let out a long sigh of frustration and I knew he'd reached the end of his last nerve.

"I gave it a laxative," I replied with a wince. "I mean now I think of it, it does seem pretty bad."

"You think so." Hunter shook his head and stepped closer to me, lowering his mouth to my ear. "You poisoned her fucking cat just to get her in the same room as Carter. Does that not seem ridiculous to you?"

"No," I affirmed as I took a quick glance around the bar to check we weren't being listened to. "She had coffee with your dad in Jennings Bridge."

"So what?" he questioned. "She's known him since she was a baby. He's a family friend, why wouldn't she. I took out a book from the Library and your mom stamped it, that doesn't mean I want to have sex with her."

I grimaced and shook my hands in front of me. "Ugh, nasty visual, Hunt. And how long have you been a member of the library? I didn't know that about you."

He sighed heavily and closed his eyes for a few seconds. "Stop changing the subject, and I can damn read you know."

"I know, I just never imagined you in the library searching through all those books is all. What was it a murder mystery, or some sort of science fiction?"

"It was Jim Warvell's autobiography."

I shrugged, having no clue.

"The Texas Cowboy Hall of Fame inductee?"

"Nope, sorry."

"He and his—fuck will you stop distracting me," he cried. "Just admit what you did was crazy and give my pop some damn credit. He's not interested in Bronte, and if truth be told, you know that deep down."

"I know no such thing," I replied haughtily. "She's pretty, she's twenty-four, why wouldn't he be interested?"

"Because he's forty-eight, and still grieving my mom. He just wants some damn fun, Ellie. He's not going to risk his life-long friendships for a quick fuck-fest with Bronte." He moved closer to me, his breath ghosting over my skin and setting me on high alert. "Now, you're going to go over there and tell Bronte you're stepping out for a few and then you are going over to see Carter."

His words forced me onto the back foot. I put a hand against the wall to steady myself as my heart thudded wildly in my chest.

"I can't," I whispered. "He can't know I poisoned a cat. He'll want to know why and then I'll have to reveal the plan and he'll go batshit crazy on my ass, then he'll tell Bronte and she'll be mad and then I'll—"

"Okay, okay," Hunter ground out. "But you should take responsibility for your actions."

Lots of hot and sexy ways that Hunter could make me pay whizzed around in my brain. I gave myself a little fan with my hand.

"Sorry, baby," he whispered, getting closer to me. "Not those sorts of things. I told you I'm withholding until you realize what I want in return."

"I-I-I have no idea what you mean."

Hunter smirked. "I think your thighs pushed together and those pretty little nipples of yours poking in my direction tell a whole other story."

I looked down and my nipples were indeed sticking out far enough for Reverend Booth to hang his cassock on.

"How do I pay then?" I asked, coughing to disguise the want in my voice.

Hunter wiped a hand backward and forward over his mouth, his gaze bore into me. "I think it only fair you offer to help Carter out."

"Help him? How?"

Grinning Hunter took his phone out of his pocket and punched his long finger at the screen before holding it to his ear.

"Hey, Carter. Just thought I'd let you know that Ellie is on her way over… yeah," his eyes held mine, "she felt bad that she's here and you're having to take care of Bronte's cat when she was the one who fed it." He laughed and then stared at me with a glint in his beautiful brown eyes. "Yeah, that's what she said…he is, woah sounds bad…well Ellie can do that she's used to it… he will, that's great man. So, if she comes over to watch the cat, you want to take her place and drink some beers… excellent. See you in a few."

He pushed his phone back in his pocket and looked at me. His face full of amusement and victory.

"What?" I asked, crossing my arms over my chest.

"Carter says Rodrick's just had another round of the shits, but it was a big one, so he reckons that's the last one."

"That's good." I actually breathed a sigh of relief. Who knew two little laxatives could cause one pussy to splash so much turd around? "So, I don't need to go over?"

Hunter shook his head and smiled, giving me a wink. "Oh no, you need to go. Carter said there's shit everywhere, he didn't get to the kitty litter in time."

I held my hands palms up in question.

"It's pretty rank over there, so I offered your services to go clean it up."

I shook my head and laughed hollowly. "No, no. Not happening. I won't be allowed in anyway. It's strictly qualified people in there, surely."

"You take care of sick kids. How can it be so different? It's after hours so there's no one else around, and like I said to Carter, it's something you're used to."

I started to protest, but Hunter turned me around by my shoulders and pointed me toward the exit.

"Off you go," he said, his lips whispering against the shell of my ear. "Go and clean up Rodrick and his shit. I believe he may need some clingers removing from his ass fur too."

"Hunter, no," I complained trying to turn back to him, but he was too strong.

"Ellie, yes," he replied, and I knew he was smiling. "Because if you don't, I might just have to tell your brother and your best friend about that damn crazy plan of yours and as you said, they won't take it lightly."

The bastard knew he had me. He knew I wouldn't risk having a row with my best friend – Carter I couldn't give two shits about, but Bronte was another matter.

"I hate you, you know that, right?" I jibed.

"Hmm, you may hate me, but you love my dick, so it's a pay-off I'll take."

He then tapped my ass and gently pushed me toward cat shit hell.

CHAPTER 31

Hunter

With my hand firmly around my dick, I pumped it harder. My eyes were closed, yet the images of Ellie were sharp and bright in my head.

I damn well ached for her, but she was clearly going to take some persuading to even talk about what was happening between us. Honestly, her sass made my piss sour at times, yet I damned well loved it too. No wonder I went to sleep hard and thinking about her and then woke up just as hard and still thinking about her.

As I pulled at my hard-on, I imagined her licking along the V of my abdomen, right next to, but not quite on my dick; it made me pant with anticipation. The idea of slamming into her and roaring her name as I came, made my balls tighten. One more pull alongside a memory of Ellie's tits and I came, hard and long all over my stomach.

"Shit," I ground out breathlessly. "Fucking shit."

She wasn't even in my bed, yet she still gave me amazing orgasms.

Reaching for a discarded tee-shirt, I wiped the jizz from my belly and flopped back against the pillow and stared up at the ceiling. The thought running around in my head was how the hell I'd got so caught up on Ellie after years of knowing her. The physical aspect was most definitely a factor in my huge turnaround. I guess you didn't have sex with a girl in a storeroom and then finger fuck her in a wicker basket without catching *some* feelings.

Then again, I'd gotten Rayna Demata off with my fingers once and fucked her twice in the woods at Summer camp in eleventh grade, but *she* didn't take over my every thought. I vaguely recalled having told her I loved her at the time, but I was sixteen. Sixteen-year-old boys lie, especially when they want to have sex with a girl who has big tits.

"Hunter, son."

Pop's voice startled me, and I pulled the sheets up over my dick, just in case he came in.

"Yeah?"

"Breakfast is almost ready."

I picked up my phone and noticed it was almost five-thirty. "Yeah, I'll be down in five."

He didn't say anything else, but I heard his feet padding along the landing toward the stairs. Doing an ab pull I sat up and dropped my legs to the floor and set about getting dressed. Maybe a hard day's work would banish Ellie from my head.

As soon as I walked through to the kitchen, I realized what day it was. The fact that I'd forgotten was also a sharp reminder that Ellie had started taking up too much space in my brain.

It was my mom's birthday and the single, long-stemmed, red rose in the vase on the table was what reminded me. Pop did it every year on her birthday and their anniversary. It was his way of honoring both, rather than go over to the cemetery and put anything on her grave. He kept it clean and tidy, but rarely put flowers there. According to him that piece of ground wasn't where she was, this house, our home was where her soul lived, so that was where he wanted the memorials of her to be.

"Hey, Pop."

I walked up to him and pulled him into a hug, holding on for a few extra seconds. He'd been getting better slowly, but that didn't mean today wasn't going to hurt him.

"I'm good, son. I'm good."

He cleared his throat and pulled away to look me directly in the eye and I could see he was. Yes, there was sadness there, but not the bone deep grief I'd seen for years since Mom had passed.

"Where're the twins?" I asked looking down at the eggs and bacon. The bacon was a little overdone and the eggs were the wrong side of runny. Signs that Pop had cooked.

He rolled his eyes and flung a towel over his shoulder as he turned to pick up the plates.

"Hungover would you believe."

"What?" I asked, picking up my fork and knife as Pop put the plates down. "How come?"

"Damn Henry gave them a bottle of that peach wine he makes. They drank it last night and now can't get their heads off their pillows this morning." His face broke into a grin and he joined me at the table. "Can't say as I mind though. They're too old to be getting up before dawn every day just to make us breakfast."

I bit into a piece of bacon and the snap resounded around the room. "Not sure I agree, Pop," I replied. "Because got to say, your bacon is way below their standard."

***

Still early but having already done three hours work, it was time for coffee. So, when I walked into the house to get the jug on and found my aunts on the sofa watching a film I was a little surprised.

"You're up," I said laughing at their pale faces.

"Barely honey," Auntie L replied. "I know I'm never drinking again."

"Henry's never made it that strong before." Auntie J rubbed at her temples and groaned. "Is it coffee time already?

"Yep, sure is," I replied. "Pop's just penning a cow who's almost ready to give birth."

"You want me to make it honey?" Auntie L moved to get up from the sofa, but I laid a hand on her shoulder.

"No, you stay and watch your film. What you watching anyway?" I asked as I pulled my jacket off, having already left my boots on the porch.

Auntie J looked up and shrugged. "I have no idea, honey. My painkillers kicked in after twenty minutes and I fell asleep."

"I think it's called the Christmas Elf or something like that," Auntie L offered.

"Oh, you mean, Elf." I grinned. "Great movie. I remember going to the movies with Carter to see it. If I recall Ellie screamed blue murder because we wouldn't take her with us."

"But you did, didn't you?" Auntie L said softly, a small smile wrinkling up her pale blue eyes.

"You remember that?" I asked.

She shook her head. "No, honey, but I know you, and I know you would have taken her."

"You're a good boy, Hunter," Auntie J added. "Especially where Ellie is concerned."

I frowned. "You think?"

"Of course," she replied. "You've always looked out for her."

"It'll be that sweet spot she holds in his heart," Auntie L said. "Although from what we heard in the Stars & Stripes that night, the sweet spot she's got might just be somewhere else."

"What?" I swung around to see a huge grin on her face. "You said... that wasn't... what?"

"You heard me, just like we heard you that night. Sounds like you inherited your daddy's ability with the ladies, Hunter."

"Auntie L! You... you can't say stuff like that."

She smiled and shrugged her shoulders before turning back to the TV and Buddy the Elf.

"Oh sweetheart," Auntie J sighed, moving her attention to me. "When will you realize you and that girl are destined for each other. You've been sweet on her for years, even if you didn't know it until now."

I scrubbed a hand over my face. "I never said I was sweet on her *now*."

"Didn't have to," my aunt said, looking up at me and grabbing my hand. "It's in your eyes. Well, that and the fact you did unspeakable things to her on singles night."

"I did not… they were not."

"Oh, hush yourself." Auntie J slapped my hand. "Just make sure you tell her how you feel before it's too late. Your pop will tell you that life is too short and too darned hard to waste time procrastinating."

I took a huge breath as the truth of her words hit me straight in the gut.

"And what if she doesn't want what I want?" I asked, realizing how ridiculous it was taking romance advice from two sixty-four-year-old women who'd never been married—never had a man as far as I knew.

"Ah phooey," Auntie L said, her eyes still on the TV. "Of course, she does. You just need to learn how to tell her properly, instead of all that He-Man attitude that you boys today think you need."

"She's right," Auntie J added. "Tell her how she makes you feel, sweetheart. The rest will be easy."

"You're wrong, I promise you. She'd probably kick me in the balls." I winced, imagining it.

"She might," Auntie J said, giving me a soft smile. "But then again, she might not."

Shit, I knew they were right. I just had to tell Ellie that I liked her, more than a friend, but tell her without ogling her tits or commenting on what she sounded like when she orgasmed.

"You want coffee?" I asked, deciding that I'd think better after caffeine.

"Don't change the subject sweetheart," Auntie L replied. "Because you know, you shouldn't take too long deciding what to do about Ellie. I hear Delphine's sister's boy is coming back to town next week.

Fucking Thor, he was a damn pain in my backside. There was no way he was getting his hands on Ellie.

It was decided – I needed to sort my love life but definitely coffee first.

About to turn for the kitchen the door opened, and Pop walked in, shrugged off his jacked and hung it on the hook by the door, next to mine.

"I think that cow will calf in the next couple of days," he said as he stooped down to kiss the tops of my aunt's heads. "It's not her first rodeo though, so don't think there'll be a problem."

"That's good." I scratched at the stubble on my cheek and nodded my head toward the kitchen. "You got a minute, Pop?"

"Yeah, sure."

He followed me and went straight to the basin and ran the hot water and began washing up.

"What's on your mind."

"I need to ask you something?" I winced not sure what his reaction would be.

"Okay." He frowned and pulled the towel from the side and set about drying his hands.

I cleared my throat. "Do you have a thing, or would you ever have a thing for Bronte?"

His mouth dropped along with the towel. "Bronte as little Bronte Jackson? Jim and Darcy's Bronte?"

I hung my hands off the back of my neck and frowned. I could tell by Pop's face Ellie had got things *so* wrong.

"Bronte who used to have braces on her teeth and wore pink ribbons in her hair? That Bronte?"

"Yes, sir."

Pop hesitated for a moment and then dropped his head back and gave the loudest belly laugh I'd heard from him in a long time.

"I take it that's a no then," I muttered.

When he finally stopped, Pop shook his head. "Where the hell you get that idea from."

I drew in a breath and then exhaled it real slow. "Bronte's got a thing for you. A crush."

"Bronte has?" His eyebrows almost disappeared into his hairline. "Really?"

"Yeah, and well Ellie's kind of worried you might be flattered and do something about it."

"She does?" He pushed his hands on his hips and moved his upper body closer to mine. "Why the fuck would she think that?"

I shrugged. "I don't know, but that's what she thinks."

"Well, I promise you, I don't. I never would. She's a pretty girl, but that's exactly what she is, a girl. Beside the fact that Jim and Darcy are two of my closest friends. I would never risk that."

"And that's what I told Ellie," I replied. "But she's got this damn idea that we need to stop it happening. She's doing everything she can to get Carter and Bronte together, so that she'll stop crushing on you."

"Shit," Pop groaned. "Bronte and Carter. Damn son, that's like fire and gasoline. Only one way that's going to go and that's *boom*."

"That's what I told her, but she's adamant that nothing is going to spoil all the friendships you guys have."

"You can tell her to stop fretting about it," Pop said as he placed a hand on my shoulder. "It's not and will not ever happen. Too damn weird. I think I changed that girl's butt once when she was a baby. So why you asking me about this? Do *you* think I might do something about it?"

I'd thought about it a lot over the last few weeks and was dubious about Ellie's claims. Now seeing Pop's face and hearing what he had to say I was sure. "No, Pop. No, I don't, but you know Ellie."

He gave a quiet laugh and shook his head. "Yeah, I do. Seems you maybe need to explain a few things to her."

"I think I do."

Images of her came into my head and I felt weird in my stomach. Like I'd just been on a Ferris Wheel that had gone twice the speed it should've.

"It explains a lot though," Pop added, stooping to pick up the towel he'd dropped.

"Like what?" I asked.

"Why she keeps shutting you down. She's got a happy life. Everything in her garden is rosy. She's never lost anyone, her folks are still together, we're all one big happy family. She likes everyone to be happy—hence her getting Melinda to invite us all for Thanksgiving. Ellie thought we could all be happy again."

"That doesn't explain why she says no to me," I said, thrusting my hands into my pockets like a sulky little kid.

"She's scared, son." Pop cupped my cheek with his big, rough hand. "Ellie's scared that she says yes and you two don't work out, we'll all suffer. No more, big happy group of friends meeting up for Thanksgiving."

I thought about what he said and knew that there was an element of truth in what he was saying; all the exact same reasons Ellie had given. Getting Bronte and Carter together didn't matter because if they didn't work out, no one would be surprised. They hated each other, had for years, so it wouldn't change the order of things.

"You know, it could also mean that she's scared of totally losing you. You and she are friends at the moment, but what happens if you become more and it doesn't work out. What then?"

"No one can predict the future. Ellie certainly can't. I could be the best damn thing to happen to her, and she to me." I threw my hands in the air, frustrated by it all, even if I did see her point of view.

"That damn stubbornness we talked about." Pop smiled and slapped me on the back. "I guess you need to persuade her of that."

I grimaced and hung my head. "To be truthful, she may actually not be talking to me right now."

Pop rolled his eyes. "What you do, son?"

"Well, last night she gave Bronte's cat laxative so that she had to take it to Carter. Ellie told me what she'd done, so I made her go and clean the shit up from the surgery and sit with the cat so Carter could come and have a beer with me."

"And he allowed that? His sister in the surgery while he was in Stars & Stripes?"

I raised my brows and shrugged.

"Fuck," Pop muttered. "No wonder Lance isn't ready to hand over the reins to him. Well, I guess you'll only find out how big a grudge she holds when you go around there, and there's no better time than now." He slapped a hand on my shoulder and when I opened my mouth to protest, he continued. "I didn't raise you to be a coward, son. So, seeing as we already got a lot done this morning, I suggest you go wash up and I'll put the coffee on. Oh, and Hunter."

"Yep."

"When you tell her how you feel, maybe be the gentleman your mom raised you to be."

I opened my mouth to protest, but knew Pop was right, asking Ellie Maples to give me a chance was one thing that I needed to do right.

CHAPTER 32

Ellie

Waking up, my nightmare of the night before suddenly came back to me.

Me, gagging, while I cleaned up the diarrhea that Rodrick, Bronte's cat kept squirting out of its ass. The smell was horrendous – a mixture of fish and…well, shit. Plus, Carter lied when he'd told Hunter that Rodrick had shat for the last time. That little bastard shat another three times while I was watching him and giving him sips of water from a syringe. You'd have thought I'd have coped, what with me being a children's nurse, but no my eyes were watering, and I was gagging with each squirt.

Hunter must have thought he was so funny setting me up, but I'd get him back one day. I pulled my handkerchief from under my pillow and sniffed it. I'd doused it with some perfume the night before as sniffing it took away the cat poop smell, for a few seconds at least. I didn't want to waste any more though, so wondered whether Mom had some essential oils left from her yoga and meditation phase.

Throwing my legs out of bed, I padded out of my room and down the hall. It was almost ten, so I knew my parents would be awake. Probably reading the papers like they normally liked to do on a Sunday morning.

"*Mom*," I shouted as I rubbed sleep from my eyes, walking toward their room. "*Mom.*"

Pushing open their bedroom door, I yawned loudly. "Hey, Momma do you have—"

"Ellie, get out," Mom yelled.

I looked over as a slipper came flying past my ear and Dad looked up from between Mom's legs with a grin and a shiny chin.

"Oh my God, no." I squealed and slapped my hands over my eyes. "Oh shit."

"Ellie get out, *now*." Mom's cry was pretty desperate.

"I can't, I'm paralyzed."

My legs just wouldn't move. No matter how much I knew I needed to get out of there, my instinct to run was sadly lacking.

"Sweetheart," Dad soothed. "Just move your legs, turn around, leave and close the door behind you. Mom will be down in a few."

"You are *not* going to carry on?" I screeched. "Oh my God, you're disgusting."

"It's only natural," he replied. "Plus, your mom got hers and I didn't so—"

"No! Not another word, I'm going. I think I'm going to be sick." I made a gagging noise and exited, pretty swiftly considering my legs hadn't been working moments earlier.

"Close the door," Dad yelled.

I slammed it closed and before I'd even made it halfway back to my room, all I could hear was my mom shouting out how incredible my dad was.

There was only one thing that would take away the hideous vision and that was pancakes. Mom usually made Sunday breakfast, but I wasn't sure

I wanted her touching my food, knowing the sausage she'd already been holding.

Still shuddering I walked into the kitchen to find Carter sitting at the island.

"What are you doing here?" I asked, practically snarling at him. "I thought you'd have the hangover from hell, considering I left you and Hunter in Stars & Stripes well after midnight last night."

"Some of us can hold our liquor," my brother replied. "Unlike others."

I rolled my eyes. "Yeah, and some of us can sit in the sun for longer than twenty minutes and not look like raw, skinned flesh."

He gave me a sarcastic smile and I giggled. Where I took after my mom's side of the family and their Native American heritage, Carter was most definitely a Maples. His hair was a dark auburn just like my Grandpa Jeremiah and he had the same fair skin, with a scattering of freckles. That meant it took him a lot longer to get a tan than it took me. He got there eventually, it just took a while and a whole lot of looking like a boiled lobster.

"You're so damn childish," he said as he opened up the refrigerator and pulled out the juice. "What's got you this morning?"

I pointed up to the ceiling. "I just walked in on them doing the nasty."

Carter shuddered. "Ugh, no wonder you're in a pissy mood. When do you figure they stop doing that sort of thing? What age?"

He looked genuinely interested as he pulled two glasses from the cupboard and set about pouring juice into them.

"No idea." I took one of the glasses from him. "Thanks. To be fair, I hope I'm still having sex when I'm their age."

"Yeah, but I definitely won't have any kids to walk in on me. It's a wonder we're not scarred, the number of times I've seen Dad's bare ass with Mom's legs wrapped around it."

"How do you know your kids won't bust in on you servicing your wife; whichever damn stupid woman that might be who marries you."

Carter rolled his eyes. "Because I'm not getting married and I certainly don't want kids." He shuddered. "Definitely not in my plan."

"Yeah well." I sighed. "Someone would want to have sex with you first and that in itself would be a miracle."

Carter looked at me disdainfully and flicked my ear. "I get plenty, thanks very much. And no woman leaves my bed dissatisfied."

I shuddered at the thought and decided to change the subject of my brother getting his rocks off.

"You think that maybe we would get taken away from them if the authorities knew?" I asked.

Carter sighed. "We are twenty-four and twenty-six, so no. Anyway, they were always pretty careful when we were young." He started to laugh. "You remember when they locked themselves in the bathroom and I thought they were stuck, and Mom was making that noise because she was upset?"

"Oh my God, yes," I exclaimed and slapped my hand on the cool granite top. "You called the Sheriff and the Fire Chief to come get them out."

"Dad was just pulling his pants back on when that firefighter smashed the window." Carter grinned. "Mom was fucking mortified."

"The firefighters thought it was me and you locked in there. And the Sheriff, what was his name?"

"Sheriff Dixon."

"Yeah, Sheriff Dixon was convinced they'd locked us in while they went into town drinking. He'd even brought a lady from Child Protection with him."

We both laughed hard, neither of us noticing that our parents had walked in.

"What's so funny?" Dad asked as he dropped a kiss to my head, while Mom hugged Carter.

"Nothing," I sighed and turned to give him a tight squeeze. "We love you is all."

"Aww, my babies."

Mom moved to grab my brother's face to kiss him, but he quickly dodged her.

"No kissing," he cried. "Ellie told me what she just caught you doing."

"I have showered," Mom protested.

"Don't care," Carter ground out as Mom made another dive for him. "It's too vivid in my head."

"You here for breakfast?" Dad asked.

"Yep. I have no food at home, so…" Carter shrugged and smiled at Mom whose eyes went all glassy.

"Of course, you can eat here, sweetheart," she replied. "Go sit down and I'll get it started.

Pushing away from my position at the island, I shook my head, wondering how Carter always managed to wrap Mom around his little finger.

"I'm going to get dressed," I said. "How long will breakfast be, Mom?"

"Twenty minutes, sweetheart."

I then got exactly the same soft smile and it hit me, as it did most days, how lucky I was to have the parents I had, despite their need to fornicate almost every hour of the day. Hunter didn't have that complete family that we had, and I realized how much he must miss his mom every single minute of every single day.

Contemplating life without either Mom or Dad, I was almost to the stairs when I heard a knock at the door. We didn't usually get visitors on a Sunday morning, so I was a little surprised.

When I opened the door, I was even more surprised to see it was Hunter standing there.

"Hey," I said, noticing how hot he looked.

He was wearing faded jeans and a dark green, long-sleeved Henley, which clung to his muscles.

"Cute PJs." He grinned at me and tugged on the bottom of my pajama top.

I looked down at the white cotton with pink sheep all over it and smiled.

"They're the sexiest thing I own," I replied, stepping aside to let Hunter in.

As he passed me, he stooped to speak close to my ear. "I recall a little black dress that was much sexier."

His words were said quietly, and when his breath whispered against my skin, I felt goosebumps erupt all over it. The sensation was incredible, and I had to stop myself from climbing Hunter like he was a tree and I was a damn monkey.

Swallowing I looked up at him and let out a slow breath. "You're here early."

"Yeah," he replied, his eyes looking over every inch of my face. "I wanted to do something and knew if I didn't do it now, I'd probably chicken out."

"You do? Okay."

My breathing got heavy as Hunter moved closer, his nearness sending every nerve ending in my body on high alert. While I was aware that I was mad with him about getting me to sit with Rodrick, I suddenly didn't have it in me to care. My hormones certainly didn't give a damn that he'd set me up.

"What is it then?" I asked.

"I want to ask you something."

As soon as the words left his mouth, I noticed his confident smile slip. He thrust his hands into his jeans pockets and took a step back.

"What?" I felt a surge in my stomach, hesitant about his question. "What do you want to ask?"

Somehow, I knew it wasn't some stupid little favor. It was going to be big. My thudding heart and breathlessness told me so. Hunter had said about us needing to talk, but this didn't feel like it was him wanting to ask me that.

"I know you keep avoiding talking about it, but what's been happening between us…" Hunter tailed off and looked over at the side table where a vase of yellow roses stood. "Are they for my mom?"

I turned and looked at them and it suddenly hit what the date was. It was Sondra's birthday and just as she did every birthday and anniversary of her passing, Mom put out a vase of yellow roses.

"Yeah," I replied, taking a deep breath. "Mom puts them out on her birthday and anniversary."

"I remember." Hunter let out a shaky breath. "Pop always puts red ones out."

Taking his hand, I smiled up at him. "Red is love and yellow is friendship."

"Yeah?"

"Hmm hmm." I nodded and gave his hand a squeeze

"So does every color have a meaning?" Hunter rubbed his thumb up and down my hand, drawing patterns on my skin and sending thrills over my body.

"I think so, yeah," I replied, barely a whisper.

Hunter nodded, looked at the roses and then back to me. "Which color says, 'will you come on a date with me'?"

My breath pulled in sharply and my heart picked up a pace I looked into his brown eyes which felt like they were drawing me deeper and deeper into his soul.

"I don't know," I whispered, while in my head trying to work out what to do if this was Hunter asking me on a date, but also processing the regret of knowing it was.

Going on a date itself wasn't a huge thing but going on one with Hunter was. If it all went to hell in a handbasket so many other people would be affected. Jefferson relied on my parents and Bronte's parent's friendship, but if Hunter and I suddenly started to hate each other, would Jim and Darcy feel they needed to take sides? Would my mom and dad still welcome the Delaney's around, would Carter, would *I* if Hunter broke my heart?

"Well, that's what I'm asking, Ellie," Hunter said breaking into my inner turmoil. "If you'll go on a date with me."

His hand came up and with his forefinger, he pushed a lock of my hair behind my ear and then trailed the same finger down my cheek. We inhaled simultaneously and something more than sexual chemistry passed between us. I didn't know what had changed, why my feelings toward him had moved on, but they had.

"I know you're scared, El, but you must realize that we have something here," Hunter said, his eyes narrowed on me. "Maybe this has been brewing for a while, and maybe we've gone about it all the wrong way, but I'd like it if we could go on a date. I want to take you to the pre-Christmas Dance at the Memorial Buildings on Saturday."

My eyes widened. "You want to take me to the dance?"

Hunter shrugged. "Well, I think we're way past a drink in a bar, don't you?"

His smile was bright and made his eyes twinkle and I felt a traitorous little whoosh in my stomach.

"I guess. But absolutely everyone will be there, my parents, your dad, Mayor Garrison. Everyone."

"I know," Hunter replied, the reverberation of his deep voice filling me with unwanted excitement. "Which surely proves I'm serious. If I thought it was going to be a one off, or doomed for failure do you really think I'd take you to the most important night in the town's social calendar?"

He was right, it surely did, but I still couldn't help thinking that this was not the Hunter I knew. The Hunter Delaney I knew loved them and left them and had done so many times.

"You know that if we did and, and well things didn't work out, it'd cause one hell of a ruckus."

"Who says it won't work out?" Hunter asked, exasperation in his tone.

Watching him carefully, the words he wanted to hear almost spilled from my mouth, but I just couldn't. I cared too much for him to lose him as a friend, or to make life uncomfortable for everyone.

Noticing my hesitancy, Hunter sighed. "You do, don't you? You don't think it'll work."

"I'm sorry, Hunter. But you know, maybe a little bit of this is you wanting what you can't have."

"Seriously, you think I'm that shallow?"

I stalled again and this time his nostrils flared, and fire lit up his eyes.

"Well, you do seem to like my girls a little too much."

As soon as I said it, Hunter's eyes dropped to my boobs which were pushing against the thin top of my PJs.

"*See.*"

"You were the one who pointed them out," he argued, pointing at them. "I'm a guy, of course I'm going to look at them if you mention them."

"You could have fought the urge." I put my hands on my hips and narrowed my eyes at him.

"Ah, now you're just doing that on purpose." He groaned and scrubbed a hand down his face. "You can't mention titties and then push them out like that, Ellie. It's just not damn fair."

"Well tell me I'm wrong. Tell me you don't think about them more than you think about me."

"Of course, I don't," Hunter affirmed, shaking his head. "Anyway, it's impossible. It's like thinking of peanut butter and not jelly or thinking about

Kelly Ripa and not Ryan Seacrest; you just don't do it."

"Well," I said, leaning closer and dropping my voice. "I don't automatically think of your huge whang when I think of you."

Of course, it was a lie. Any mention of Hunter and memories of his beautiful big dick were at the forefront of my mind.

Hunter grinned and put his hands to hips.

"You don't need to frame it," I sneered. "I know it's there."

"Oh, I know you do, and now I know you think of it often. Well, I kind of like that."

I rolled my eyes and waved him away. "You're missing the point, Hunt. I know if you and I start dating you'll soon realize that it isn't what you want. You'll miss your hook-ups and being the town's most eligible bachelor, and I don't want to go through the pain that'd cause me."

"For fuck's sake, Ellie, how many times? I wouldn't hurt you."

"You might not want to, but I honestly don't think I'll be enough for you."

I chewed on my lip as Hunter watched me, his dark gaze burning into me. After a few uncomfortable minutes of silence, he nodded his head.

"Okay, if you really think that's how little I feel about you, Ellie, then so be it. I guess we'll never know now though, will we."

He ran a hand over his head and exhaled heavily as he gave me one last look before turning to leave.

"You know it makes sense," I called after him, having a good look at his ass as he strode away.

"Nope, it doesn't Ellie," he said without looking back. "And stop perving on my butt."

The only sound then was that of his boots stomping on the wood flooring and then the slam of the front door.

"Shit," I cursed as I dragged my hands through my hair. "Shit, shit and crap."

"You okay, sweetheart," Mom asked, coming up behind me.

I glanced over my shoulder at her and then back to the door, which Hunter had just exited from.

"Yeah."

"Okay then. Oh, and by the way."

I turned to face her. "Yeah."

"Dad bought us all tickets to the pre-Christmas dance on Saturday. Won't that be great, all of us going together."

My heart sank as Mom's beautiful face lit up with excitement.

"When you say *all*, who'd you mean?"

"All of us. You, Carter, me and your dad. In fact, the whole gang is going." She winced. "Well maybe except Jim, he's in Lubbock for a few days, but we hope he'll be back. Thanksgiving was such good fun, your dad thought it'd be good to pay for a whole table. His treat."

She clapped her hands and then with a quick kiss to my forehead, raced up the stairs singing to herself.

All of us, on one table. After I'd already told Hunter I wouldn't go with him. Well, wouldn't that be fun. I just had to think of a way of getting out of it, or hope he didn't go, otherwise it could turn out to be the worst Christmas party ever.

CHAPTER 33

Ellie

S hopping alone for a dress at Middleton Ridge Mall was not what I thought of as fun. My dad, feeling all warm and generous, had offered to buy me something for the dance and Bronte had agreed to come with. Then, on the eleventh hour she'd backed out with a headache of all things. Personally, I thought she had a date with a man. Bronte never gave up a day of shopping, unless there was a possibility of sex.

At least I knew it wasn't with Jefferson. He was at the ranch and I knew that because my dad and Jim, Bronte's dad who was back from Lubbock, were helping him to clear out some old barn he'd been storing an ancient old tractor in and had now disposed of.

Mom had also offered, but then got a call from Darcy asking if she'd go for lunch with her. Seeing as Darcy and Jim were having problems, I insisted

Mom go and spend the day with her friend.

That was why I was flicking through the racks of dresses having no idea what on earth to buy. I wasn't a girly girl like Bronte. Yeah, I liked nice clothes and makeup and liked to dress up from time to time, but the Pre-Christmas dance was a pretty fancy affair that most of Dayton Valley attended, so I needed something special.

"Can I help you, miss?"

I turned to see an assistant, probably my age, with her hair in a French braid and wearing the standard black skirt and white blouse that all the staff of Hemmingway's Department Store wore.

"Oh hi," I replied, giving her a warm smile. "I'm looking for an evening dress for a dance but have no idea what to get."

She looked me up and down and then walked around me, until she was right back in front of me. One more glance and then she nodded.

"Size eight, but you need a ten for your top half, right?"

"Woah, yes." I was surprised as I looked down at my jean and t-shirt clad body.

"If you'd like to take a seat, I'll go and find you something suitable."

She nodded to a brown leather sofa that was positioned right next to the dressing rooms. Without another word, she wandered off leaving me to go and sit and wait.

Having checked my phone, I knew I'd only been waiting for ten minutes when she appeared, pushing a rail with four or five dresses on it.

"Here you go. These should all suit your figure. I've gone for the size ten to accommodate your larger top section. But because of the style, the skirts won't look too big."

That was a first, having my boobs called a top section, but I didn't care if the dresses fitted and suited me. There were a mixture of fabrics and colors, so I was pretty sure one of them would.

"That's great, thanks so much."

"No problem," she replied. "Now, I have to go and help out another customer, but just ring the bell in the dressing room if you need me."

She pushed the rail into a dressing room and indicated for me to follow. Once the rail was in place, she smiled and left. Quick, no nonsense, efficiency.

I liked it.

I looked at each dress in turn, wondering which one to try first and decided on a red one which was my least favorite of her choices. It wasn't long, which I'd really wanted, and it looked like it might be real tight and uncomfortable, particularly as there was going to be a four course dinner.

Not sure about the dress, but feeling I ought to try it anyway, I took off my jeans and t-shirt and threw them onto a stool in the corner.

Taking the dress from the hanger, I checked it for a zipper or buttons but when I couldn't find either, figured it must just pull on. I lifted my arms and pulled it over my head. It was *real* tight, as I'd guessed, and troublesome to get on; the stretchy fabric wasn't exactly, well, stretchy. The skirt part wouldn't go over my boobs, which meant my head was stuck in the bodice and no matter how much I wiggled the dress wouldn't move. I could barely move my arms which were pretty much trapped in the armholes by the fabric that had bunched around my head. I felt like damn sausage meat being piped into the skin.,

"Shit," I hissed as I tried once more to wriggle free, without success.

I couldn't even get a hold of a tiny bit of fabric to yank it off, and I was beginning to panic. I was literally trapped and if I didn't get out of it soon, I knew I'd probably pass out through lack of air. The only thing to do was to call for the assistant, but I hadn't taken note of where the bell was to call her. So, my only hope was to feel around the room to find it.

Staggering to what I thought was the wall, I waved my hands around and prayed that the bell was at the right height. Twisting and wiggling in the dress, must have disoriented me though because instead of a wall, I found myself patting at the drape.

"God damnit," I cursed.

Taking small sideways steps, I moved along trying to get back to the wall. Things couldn't get any worse. I kept on patting and groping, I didn't find the wall, but I did find a gap in the drape and stumbled through it.

Staggering forward I tried to keep my balance, but top-heavy from the weight of my arms above my head, and unable to put my hands out to regain my balance, the momentum took me forward and I careered out into the store.

I ricocheted off the side of something, a counter or display cabinet possibly judging by the wobble, and spun around, banging into what I thought was the leather sofa and then bouncing back into another spin. The sight that met the other shoppers must have been both hilarious and scary; a pair of hands attached to a headless body and showing a practically bare ass – why the hell had I chosen to wear a thong - batting around like pinball.

"What the…"

A hard body stopped my path and it was a voice I recognized. I had never been gladder to hear it than I was then.

"Hunter? Is that you?"

My voice was muffled and when he didn't answer immediately, I panicked that he hadn't heard me and had carried on walking, or maybe it wasn't even him. Who would blame whomever it was for passing on talking to some weird red body? They were probably scared to death.

"*Hunter*." His name was a desperate plea.

For a few seconds there was no reply, but then finally.

"El?"

"Oh my God," I gasped, my relief almost making me burst into tears. "You have to help me."

The moment two big hands landed on my hips, my knees buckled, and I whimpered.

"What the hell are you doing?" Hunter asked, his voice cracking.

"Are you laughing at me?" I asked.

"Well, it is kind of funny. Do you know you're standing in the middle of the dress section with your butt on show?"

He started a low chuckle from deep within his chest and I almost wished he'd disappear, but… yeah, my ass was on display, and I was trussed up like a half-made Christmas cracker.

"Just get me back to the dressing room and get this damn dress off me."

"And what's the magic word," he whispered somewhere around the vicinity of my ear.

I let out a long and frustrated breath. "Please."

His thumb swept along my skin and his voice softened, all laughter gone from it.

"Of course, I will, baby."

Immediately my body tingled, and I felt myself get wet, just from his voice, which had to prove I really was gone for him. I looked like an idiot and undoubtedly every eye in the store was on me, but all I could think about was how sexy Hunter's voice was.

There was no hope left for me. Maybe it was time I pushed my stupid insecurities to one side and let myself have what I really wanted – Hunter Delaney.

CHAPTER 34

Hunter

"**S**eriously, El," I groaned as I guided her into the dressing room. "How the hell did you get in this thing."

"I pulled it over my head." Her reply was muffled and came with a little stamp of her foot. "The stupid thing has no fasteners."

"Stand still, let me size up the situation."

"If by that you mean you'll size up my ass, then you can forget it."

I rolled my eyes, though she couldn't see me, and let out a sigh. "You want me to help or not? Because if you do, I suggest you quit moaning and stand still, like I asked."

"Fine."

With my hands resting on my hips, I did a slow walk around Ellie to see if there was any easy way to get the dress off. Problem was, there didn't look to be any other way than taking it back the way it came.

"I'm gonna have to pull it back over your head," I said as I grabbed a hold of some of the material around her arms. "You ready?"

"Yes, and hurry. I'm losing oxygen here."

"I doubt that because—"

"Hunter, I do not want some science lecture on the breathability of elastane fabric. Just damn well get me out of it, please."

I took a step back and crossed my arms over my chest. "If you're going to be a spoilt princess about it."

"I'm not," Ellie said, her voice cracking. "I'm really starting to panic that I might have to live in this dress forever. I might have to get married in it, give birth in it and then fucking die in it."

Laughing, I moved back and took a hold of the dress again. "Dramatic some."

I heard Ellie take a sharp breath, but she didn't speak, evidently thinking better of it.

"Right, I'm gonna pull as hard as I can, okay?"

"Okay." Her voice was a little timid, and I couldn't help but feel bad for her. "Here we go. One, two…"

I pulled as hard as I could, but the dress must have moved about an inch.

"Ahhh, no stop," Ellie squealed. "My nose, my nose."

"What?" I asked and pulled again.

"No, you've got my nose. Shit, damn and hell fire." She stamped her foot and wiggled around, squealing like a little girl. "Oh no, I think I got boogers on it."

Stooping down to look, I couldn't help the belly laugh when I saw that the dress was wet right where Ellie's nose was. Also, if I wasn't mistaken, I could see the slight outline of her nostrils.

"Shit, you're right."

"This isn't funny, Hunter. I'm going to have to pay for it now and it doesn't even fit."

There was that stamp again, only this time it was double footed.

Trying to dampen down my laughter, I bent over and slapped a hand to my mouth. Aside from the fact that she was starting to panic, she looked fucking hilarious. Just two arms sticking straight in the air with her hands waving around, and a bare ass. At least her pussy was covered with the pink lace of her thong, imagine how much worse it could have been, her wandering around the store with most of what she had to offer on show.

"I'm going to have to cut it," I thought out loud.

"*No!*"

"I have no damn clue how else to get you out of it," I groaned.

"What does the price tag say?"

"Why the fuck does that matter?" I asked.

Ellie gave a muted sigh. "Because if you cut the damn dress, Hunter, that's what I'm going to have to pay for it."

"Where the hell is the price tag, anyway?" I looked up and down and then walked around. "Nope, can't see it."

"Oh God, I want to die," Ellie groaned and sagged a little.

"Well, you stay in there much longer and the lack of oxygen will grant you your wish."

"You said I couldn't lose oxygen."

She sounded a little panic stricken and I felt a little bit of a douche, but damn it was as funny as fuck. Definitely worth a picture.

Click.

"Hunter Delaney, you did not just take a picture of me. Tell me you didn't."

I grimaced and cleared my throat.

"Once this is over, you'll think it's hilarious," I offered, laughing to myself as I looked down at the picture. "You kind of look like a red tree with just two branches."

"I hate you."

"Maybe, but I'm the only one who can help you, so…"

She whimpered and turned a half-pace to the right, did a little wiggle and then turned back again.

"What are you doing?" I watched her curiously as she repeated it.

"I figured some movement might make it loose," Ellie replied as she wiggled.

"That dress is stuck fast, El. The only way you're getting out of that is if I cut you out."

"Oh God, this is awful." She was silent for a few beats and then sighed. "Okay but try and make it as neat as you can, that way one of your aunts can sew it back up."

Pulling my pocket knife out, I tilted my head to one side to examine where best to cut the dress. And yeah, I may have spent a little extra time also checking out her butt.

"Okay, I think I can cut the seam around the armhole and down the side a little, then you should have room to get out."

"Thank you," Ellie replied, her voice quiet, and a little defeated.

"Hey, what's wrong?" I asked. "Apart from being stuck in a dress that I doubt even Houdini could escape."

"I just wanted to buy something nice for the dance and now I'll have to get this. Something that I wasn't even that keen on and won't even fit."

I looked over at the other dresses on the rack, and even with my limited knowledge of women's clothing I could see all of them were longer and much classier than the red one.

"You won't have to buy it," I said, taking a step closer to Ellie. "Now, stay still. I don't want to cut you."

My knife was real sharp, seeing as I needed it on the ranch most days, so it sliced down the seam easily. With each inch I cut it started to get looser, until I heard Ellie let out a huge sigh of relief.

"I can breathe. Thank you, God."

Clearing my throat, I stepped back and slipped my knife back into my pocket.

"Okay not just God," she sighed. "Thank you, *Hunter*."

Grinning at her sass, I took hold of the material and pulled it up and off Ellie's body. As soon as it cleared her, she let out a long breath and sagged against the wall.

"You okay?" I asked.

She rubbed her nose and groaned. "Yeah, although is it possible to pull a muscle in your nostrils?"

"No, baby," I laughed "I don't think so."

Ellie's eyes shot up to mine and her face was a little pink. I figured it was from all the exertion and being trapped, but when she gave me a shy smile, it made my heart wonder and wish for other things.

After watching each other in silence for a few seconds, Ellie had a sudden realization that she was standing in her underwear. Her eyes and mine both shot to her tits at exactly the same moment and when I saw a see-through pink lace bra, the image did things to my dick.

"I didn't realize it was that cold in here." My lip twitched as Ellie's mouth dropped open.

"Hunter."

When I gave her a smile, I was glad to see she gave me a beautiful one back and I couldn't help but take a step closer. My body was aching for her. I didn't care whether she didn't want to talk about what we could have. I didn't give two shits if she thought we were a bad idea; I just wanted to kiss her.

I was almost upon her, when the drapes were pulled back and a store assistant stepped inside.

"You rang for assistance," she said, looking between Ellie and me. "Is everything okay."

Ellie gasped and snatched up her tee and plastered it to her body.

"N-no," she replied. "I didn't."

Her wide eyes looked at me and she gave a slight nod to the red dress still in my hand.

"Yes, you rang the bell." The assistant pointed to a button on the wall. The wall which Ellie had flopped against.

Ellie's head turned to look. "Oh God, no I'm so sorry. It was an accident. I'm good. All fine here," she babbled.

"Any of the dresses suitable?" she asked.

Before Ellie had a chance to say anything, I grabbed the hanger from the rail and smiled widely at the assistant.

"Yeah, my fiancée is going to take the red one."

Fiancée? What the fuck had gotten into me?

"Hunter?"

I winked at Ellie and moved toward the drape. "I'll go pay, sweetheart."

"Hunter?"

"Ellie, please, my treat. Just a little gift from me."

"Well, what a kind fiancé you have," the assistant said, giving both Ellie and I a smile. "So, can I help you with shoes, or anything?'

"No, she's good," I replied quickly. "But didn't you want to ask about one of the other dresses, sweetheart?" I nodded at the rail, and hoped my eyes were telling Ellie to keep the assistant talking.

There was a moment where she didn't understand, but then I saw the light dawn and Ellie turned and pulled a long pink gown from the rail.

"Yes, I really loved this one, but wondered if you had it purple? It's my favorite color."

Taking my chance, I slipped out and did what I needed to do.

***

"Oh my God, Hunter," Ellie said as she met me outside the store after I'd sent her a text. "I'm so sorry, how much do I owe you?"

Laughing, I shook my head. "Nothing."

"I do." Ellie looked down and around my body. "So, where's the bag?"

"I didn't get the dress," I replied, taking Ellie's hand and leading her away.

She pulled to a halt and turned to go back. "I have to get it. I can't leave it there. There's at least four inches of seam that needs repairing."

"Don't worry about it." I moved away not letting Ellie go. "It's back on a rack, on a hanger of a different size in the middle of some men's dress pants."

Ellie gasped. "Hunter, they'll know."

"How will they and how could they ever prove it was you. I'm guessing that dress has been tried on by more than just you. It's not like you come and shop here often."

"I guess, but—"

"Seriously, El, it's done and it's all good."

"How come you were there anyway?" she asked.

"They sell the soaps that my aunts like. I was getting them as part of their Christmas gift, but didn't quite get around to it."

Ellie dropped her head into her hands and groaned. "Oh God, I'm so sorry. I've ruined your morning."

I shook my head and laughed. "Forget it, I can get them from the internet. Now how about I treat you to some lunch?" I pointed to a diner all decked out in red and green.

Looking a little unsure, Ellie looked back toward the store and then at the diner. Finally, she nodded her head.

"Yeah, she sighed. That'd be great."

"Good and then afterward, I'll help you find another dress. One that fits this time."

The most gorgeous smile was afforded to me as Ellie nodded. I knew then that whatever happened, one day, maybe not today, maybe not tomorrow, but one day I'd prove to her we were meant to be together.

CHAPTER 35

Ellie

"**H**ey, honey," Mom said as I walked into the kitchen. "You get something nice?"

I sighed and shook my head, before flopping down onto a bar stool and reaching for an apple from the fruit bowl.

"Nope. Although I did nearly have to buy a dress I *didn't* want." I took a huge bite and shrugged.

"What do you mean?"

"Well, long story short, I got stuck in it and then had to cut myself out." I watched Mom from the corner of my eye and then added the important information. "Actually, Hunter cut me out."

"*Hunter*." Mom paused cutting the potatoes and stared at me. "I didn't know Hunter was going with you."

There was a little sparkle in her eye, and I knew exactly what was going on in her head. It was obvious by the fact the twinkling was accompanied by a huge smile.

"He didn't, I literally bumped into him when I was trying to get free from the dress."

I explained what had happened and couldn't help but join in when she dropped her head back and laughed like a hyena.

"Oh, honey, that's hilarious. And you say your ass was on show too?"

"Yeah," I groaned, throwing my finished apple into the trash. "I'm just glad my face was covered and that no one other than Hunter recognized me. Well, at least I hope they didn't."

"But what happened to the dress? Did they try and make you pay for it?"

I shook my head and winced. "Hunter told the assistant he was going to pay for it while I kept her talking. He then slipped it back on a rack. In the middle of men's pants apparently."

Mom gasped. "No way."

"Yeah, he did."

"Wow, that boy is smart."

I rolled my eyes. "Well, he's not that smart."

"Oh dear." Mom laughed. "What did he do?"

I contemplated what to say and whether I actually had any cause to complain. My predicament was all my own doing; I had no one to blame but myself.

"Ellie?"

"After he rescued me from the dress from hell, we went and got a bite to eat. After that he trailed around every ladies shop in the mall with me and didn't complain once."

When I stopped speaking, Mom shrugged. "And?"

"And," I replied, dropping my head to the countertop. "He didn't ask me to the dance."

Mom was so quiet, I thought maybe she'd left the room, but when I lifted my head and looked at her, she was smiling down at me with shining eyes.

"What?" I asked.

She rubbed cool fingertips over my brow and shook her head. "Don't frown baby, you'll regret it in later life."

"Okay, but what?" I repeated my question with a little shake of my head. "Why are you looking at me like that?"

She swallowed and placed a hand on her heart, and I had no idea why she was getting all dramatic about it.

"Mom, are you auditioning for a Hallmark film or something?"

"No," she scoffed. "But just hearing you say you want to go to the dance with Hunter, well… it reminds me of Sondra is all."

My heart clenched a little as a shadow crossed Mom's face, and I thought of Hunter and his sorrow.

"She always wanted you two to be together. Always knew that Hunter would eventually realize you were his one."

"Mom," I cried. "We haven't even been on a date, so how can you say I'm his one? Besides, did I not just tell you that he didn't ask me to the dance?"

Okay, so I omitted to tell her that I was personally acquainted with his huge dick. There were some things your mom didn't need to know, even if she was envisaging the rest of your life in a two-minute show reel.

"A mom knows these things, and Sondra and I knew that you two were made for each other. *And*, he took you to the singles night, so you have had a date."

I felt my face burn up as I thought about singles night.

"It wasn't a date." I cleared my throat. "We went as friends is all."

Friend with amazing benefits maybe, but still friends.

"Oh hush." She waved a dismissive hand at me. "Daddy saw you together in Hunter's truck and said you were practically climbing the boy."

"I slipped while I was trying to get Dad to go back into the house," I remonstrated. "It was an accident."

Mom gave me a secretive smile and turned back to her potatoes. "Well, whatever way you look at it, you like him. If you didn't you wouldn't want him to ask you to the dance. If I have to be honest sweetheart, I'm surprised that you didn't just bat those eyelashes and put some more swing into your ass. Your great-grandma gave us those assets for a purpose, ergo getting Hunter Delaney to ask you to the dance."

Exhaling, I pushed the heels of my hands against my eyes and groaned. "He did ask me," I admitted. "He called on Sunday morning while you were making breakfast, but I turned him down."

Mom dropped the knife into the sink and gasped. "He did?"

"Yes, Mom, he did."

"Why the hell did you turn him down then?" she asked, throwing her hands into the air.

"I don't know." I shrugged. "I just don't want to be one of his hit and run victims."

"Who says you would be?" She moved over to me and combed gentle fingers down my hair. "We Maples women have amazing honeypots that get those worker bees coming back for more."

"*Mom.*"

She grinned and kissed the end of my nose. "You ask your dad."

I closed my eyes and groaned. "Did I not see enough when I walked in on you? I don't need to know anything else."

"Okay," she said going back to chopping. "But I think you do that boy a disservice, and yourself for that matter. You're a beautiful, clever young woman and Hunter would be lucky to have you, but I get the feeling that he'd know that and would treat you like a queen. Just like his dad treated his mom."

Resting my head on my hand, I watched her as she carried on with her chores and realized that there wasn't a day that went by where she didn't do her hair and make-up. She was beautiful and even though she might complain about the extra pounds Carter and I had put on her butt and thighs, she had a great figure. It was no wonder my dad worshiped her.

"When you met Dad, were you scared he might break your heart?" I asked. "Or did you always know he'd be your baby daddy?"

"Oh my God," she said around a laugh. "I thought he was a typical cocky jock who thought his shit didn't stink."

"He had to woo you with flowers, didn't he?"

"Woo was hardly the word, sweetheart. The first lot he presented me with he said, you fancy a date or not?" Mom raised her brows. "I kid you not."

"Wow," I replied. "Dad really had the moves of a douche didn't he."

"Yeah, but he improved as the week went on." Mom smiled and let out a little sigh of satisfaction, the memories evidently warming her heart. "When I gave in, a little part of me felt sorry for him, but the biggest part thought he was hot."

"You two are weird." I laughed and moved from the stool. "I'm going to take a shower, all that shopping and getting trapped inside dresses has made me feel sweaty."

"You mean you need a cold shower after spending an afternoon with Hunter." Mom nudged me and winked.

"Yep," I sighed. "Real weird."

"Maybe, but I still think you should be brave and ask him."

"And therein lies my problem," I replied. "I'm too much of a coward to get my heart broken by him. Plus, can you imagine how it would affect everyone if we had a thing and then broke up?"

Mum shrugged. "We're all sensible adults, we'd cope. If things don't work out between Jim and Darcy, then we'll still be friends with both. Yes, it'll make some get-togethers difficult, but we'll figure it out."

My thoughts went to Bronte and her brothers and how devastated they'd be.

"You don't think they'll work it out?" I asked.

"I think they will. They just need to remember why they love each other. I'm hoping the dance will relax them and give them an opportunity to reconnect."

"You see," I replied. "If Jim and Darcy can't make it, how the hell do I have a chance with Dayton Valley's most eligible manwhore, well except for his dad."

Mom gave me a sideways glance and tsked. "You're being too harsh, on both of them. Hunter isn't nearly as bad as you make out. Jefferson maybe," she said with a laugh, "but not Hunter, he's a good boy."

"Oh my God, if we got together, you'd love him way more than me, wouldn't you?"

Mom laughed and dropped the potatoes into a pan of water. "You know it, sweetheart. But if you're not going to ask him then it won't happen will it?"

"No, I guess not." I quirked a brow at her.

"Listen," Mom said, wiping her hands on a towel. "How about we go into the city? Even if you're not going to ask Hunter to the dance, doesn't mean you can't look hot and show him what he's missing."

I leaned against the door jamb and thought about it. "Yeah, that would be good. I'm off again tomorrow, so we could go then."

"Yeah sure, sweetheart. I'm off too, so tomorrow can be, 'Get a hot dress to make Ellie look smoking for Hunter' day."

She then gave me a shit eating grin and winked, and I knew then that I'd probably made the biggest mistake ever telling her about my crush on Hunter Delaney.

CHAPTER 36

Hunter

My week had been the one from hell. First off, we'd lost a breeding heifer that we were planning on selling. She'd got bloat and by the time Carter got to us, it was too late. She'd gone down with it in the night, so when Pop and I went to the herd in the morning, she was already laying down. It was one of those things, and would probably happen again at some time, but it was still a knock.

My mood then hadn't been improved by the thoughts of the little brunette vixen who filled my head. She'd looked so fucking hot in her pink underwear, even though the whole situation had been hilarious. Problem was, she was an ungrateful little Princess at times. I'd only tried to help her. I kinda understood how she felt about me cutting the dress though. If the store assistant had seen it, she'd have definitely made Ellie pay, or I would have paid at least. At least we got away with it, though I wasn't sure I'd risk visiting Hemmingway's again in the near future.

My other big problem was afterward, when we'd had a bite to eat and then carried on shopping; *then* she'd been all cute and funny. She'd looked stunning in every one of the twelve dresses that she tried on—yeah that's right, *twelve*. It had taken all my time not to say, damn it to my pride and ask her to the dance again, but there are only so many times a man can be rejected. That was why I kept it PG and didn't jump on her every time she came out of a dressing room looking good enough to eat. Ellie didn't quite see things the way that I did though, her heart wasn't in it and every single dress was rejected.

Unfortunately, no matter what my feelings about Ellie were, it was evident they weren't reciprocated unless it came down to sex. I should have just accepted it and looked forward to the next time she needed an itch scratching. Problem was my head was telling me that, but my heart and my hormones were telling me something entirely different.

Knowing we were all going to be sitting at the same table and playing happy extended families at the dance, and that I'd have to watch Ellie all night, I'd tried to cry off from going. I'd even cited the fact that we had another cow due to give birth. Pop had other ideas though and had made it clear we were going to the dance; me, him and my aunts. Tom and Sam were going to stay the night on the ranch, and we were going to go, drink and be damn merry.

Without the possibility of getting out of it, I wasn't sure whether I hoped Ellie would fail to get a dress and so bail, or whether I hoped she'd be there. My feelings fluctuated between what the best possible option could be.

Now the time for wondering was over because we were walking up the steps to the Memorial Hall.

"Ooh this is going to be so good," Auntie L practically squealed as she clung to my arm. "I haven't been to the pre-Christmas dance for years. Not since Ethan Monroe asked me when I was twenty-three and I turned him down."

I pulled us to a stop. "You haven't been since *then*? And, how come you turned him down?"

A shadow fell over Lynn-Ann's face as she glanced over to where my pop was leading Auntie J inside.

"Well, I liked him fine enough. He was handsome and strong and was real respectful to the ladies." She sighed and went a little glassy eyed. "Problem was your Auntie J thought so too. Fact was, she was probably more stuck on him than I was."

"Woah," I replied, taking a half step back. "That's pretty sad, Auntie L. Surely she'd have understood if you wanted to go with him?"

Auntie L shrugged and gave me a soft smile. "Who knows, honey. All I do know is I didn't want to break her heart."

"And what happened to Ethan Monroe?" I asked, not recognizing the name around town.

She swallowed and took a deep breath. "He left town a year later. Met a girl at his cousin Marlena's wedding in Pasadena. I do believe they have four kids and twelve grand-babies."

I watched her carefully, noting the sadness in her eyes. Sadness and regret.

"You wish you'd said yes? Thinking maybe they could have been your kids and grand-babies, Auntie L?"

She smiled. "No point in wishing, honey. It didn't happen and nothing I wish or hope for will change that. All I'll say is make sure you aren't Ethan Monroe in forty years' time, honey."

I frowned unsure of what she meant. "What, be married with a ton of kids and grandkids?"

"No, honey." She reached up and placed a cool soft palm against my cheek. "Regret that you didn't work harder to get the girl. The girl who you really wanted to take to the dance."

My stomach bottomed out and I felt my face heat up. "Not sure I get you," I lied.

Auntie L winked and laughed. "Hunter, you get me just fine. Before he left town, your Grandpa had a drink with Ethan at Stars & Stripes, and they got a little inebriated it seems." Pausing she straightened the lapel of my suit jacket. "He told my daddy, in his drunken state, that while he loved his fiancée and was looking forward to their new life together, he'd always wonder what we might have been, if he'd just tried that little bit harder to get me to go to the dance with him."

"You think I should find myself a girl?" I asked, being intentionally dumb.

"I think you should get yourself *the* girl," she replied. "And you shouldn't take no for an answer. Don't be the man who grows old wondering what if."

Before I could respond, my aunt patted my cheek and reached up on her tippy toes to kiss it.

"Now, come on before your pop and my sister drink the place dry."

Nodding I held my arm out for her and proudly let her into the hall, all the time thinking about what she'd said.

***

The scene inside the ballroom of the Memorial building, was like something from a Christmas movie. Tall, white pine trees lined the edges of the room and strung across the ceiling were hundreds of fairy lights. On the stage, at the end of the Grand Ballroom was a snow scene with more white pines and fake snow with a real gingerbread house center stage. Miss Anderson owned the local cake shop, Cake Heaven, and she and Jennifer, my friend Alaska's girl, had made the house themselves.

"Wow," Auntie J gasped. "Jennifer and Miss Anderson sure did themselves proud with that."

"I know," Pop replied. "And I believe we all get a piece at the end of the night."

That made my thoughts immediately go to Ellie, because I knew how much she loved gingerbread. Then as if I'd summoned her, my eyes caught sight of the beautiful brunette who invaded my head, day and night.

She looked stunning. More beautiful than any other woman I'd ever seen. Fucking spectacular in fact. She'd obviously found the perfect dress. It was floor length, deep violet in color, and the top half had a real deep v which I was pretty sure finished just above her navel. The silky fabric skimmed her hips into a full, flouncy skirt and with each step she made toward her mom, a long, tanned, leg was revealed with sparkly silver sandals on her feet.

"Shit," I groaned and scrubbed a hand down my face.

"What's up, son?" Pop asked as he snagged two glasses of champagne from a passing waitress and gave them to my aunts. "You seem a little concerned there."

He was grinning at me as my eyes moved back to fixate on Ellie.

"She doesn't make things easy for me, Pop," I sighed.

"No one said the best things in life were easy. I take it she's still being stubborn as a pack mule about going on a date with you."

I nodded and ripped my gaze from her. "Yeah. She still says if it goes wrong then it'll be awful for everyone and she doesn't want to risk that."

"You think it'll go wrong?" he asked, now taking two bottles of beer from a young kid who looked like he might choke in his shirt and tie. "Or are you serious about her."

I hesitated, but for no other reason than I was surprised that my response was right there on the tip of my tongue.

"I'm serious about her," I replied, looking him direct in the eye. "I can't think about anything else but her. I don't just want to date her, Pop. I want to be something to her. Only so many times I can ask though, without coming across as a fool."

He passed me a bottle of beer and then nodded over to where Ellie was talking to… damn Thor.

"I suggest you go and make sure that the sun-bleached surfing look doesn't suddenly become appealing to her.

"Pop, she's not interested. She'll say no, *again.*"

"Come on, son," he replied, looking at me with fire in his eyes. "Since when did a Delaney give up on something they really wanted?"

I didn't need telling twice and started to make my way over to the girl of my dreams, but before I had even walked a couple of steps, damn Dylan had taken her hand and pulled her onto the empty dance floor. What a dick! Didn't he know that she'd hate dancing when no one else was?

I was right. Ellie's body was tense and her feet barely moving, as Dylan held her close and whispered something into her ear. I felt my blood start to boil, especially when she threw her head back and let out one of her deep belly laughs.

"You see," Pop said, coming up beside me. "What did your mom always tell you about tardiness and never catching the first worm."

"Ellie isn't a worm, Pop." I sighed. "But the douche holding her is."

Pop let out a laugh and slapped a hand on my shoulder. "Question is, what you going to do about it?"

As Ellie let out another laugh, my insides bristled with annoyance once more. "Go and get her," I growled.

"That's my boy."

CHAPTER 37

Ellie

As I laughed at his 'not so funny' joke, Dylan's hand squeezed my waist and he gave me a smile that I guessed most girls would fall at his feet for. Problem was, I wasn't most girls. I was a stupid girl who, the minute she'd seen Hunter Delaney walk in wearing a navy-blue suit with a white open necked shirt, looking more delicious than one of Miss Anderson's chocolate cream pies, knew she'd made a huge mistake in saying no in the first place, and then not asking him herself. I was also the stupid girl who was too cowardly to go over to him and tell him so.

"Maybe you could come and visit," Dylan said close to my ear. "We could go kayaking."

I nodded but what I really wanted to say was, 'not a hope in hell'. I wasn't sporty at all, and certainly wasn't in any mind to take up a sport that involved water. An ice-cold Topo-Chico was about as close to water as I got, unless it was a paddle in the ocean on vacation.

As the music to Kane Brown's *'Good as You'* kicked in, Dylan pulled me closer, but over his shoulder I saw Hunter walking toward us. His steely gaze was on us and his hand was raking through his hair. He looked amazing, like he was on a modelling shoot and pulling out all his best poses. When he had almost reached us, there was no doubt what he wanted, and I knew I was going to say yes.

He must have been only three paces away when I was being pulled from Dylan's arms and turned around to face Bronte. Bronte, who had dyed her hair into strands of blue, lilac and purple. It looked beautiful, she looked beautiful, as the long, silky waves fell over her shoulders and down her back.

"Oh my God, when did you do that?"

"Today. I wanted a change. I need a change." She grinned and glanced over to where I knew Jefferson was standing talking to Carter and my dad.

"It's so pretty." I turned back to Dylan. "Sorry, you remember Dylan, right?"

"Of course, I do," she replied with a gleam in her eye. "Hi again, Dylan. Sorry, but I kind of need to steal Ellie for a few."

Dylan took a step back. "No problem. I'll go and find my aunt and uncle and I'll see you in a while, Ellie."

As he moved away, Bronte nudged me. "Dylan, hey?"

"He asked me to dance is all. Although it was highly embarrassing with just us on the floor."

I looked over my shoulder to see Hunter had also disappeared, and my heart sank.

"So, what did you want me for?" I asked taking one of her blue tendrils between my fingers.

"I need you to know I'm moving on from Jefferson." Bronte beamed at me and straightened her back.

"You want me to tell you I'm proud of you?" I asked, barely stopping the smile that twitched at my lips.

"Well, I thought you'd be pleased," she protested. "You've been on at me for weeks to forget him, so I have."

Her silver-sequined dress clung to the curve of her boobs as she thrust her hands to her hips.

"I'm glad you've come to your senses," I replied. "But it was kind of stupid in the first place."

Bronte's eyes went wide as saucers and her pouty, pink glossed lips parted into a perfect 'O'.

"I'm not stupid," she finally gasped.

"I didn't say you were," I responded. "I said the idea of you and Jefferson was stupid. Because it was."

"Says you."

"Yes, says me," I replied with a sigh. "Listen, Bronte, I don't want to argue with you. I'm just glad you're not going after Jefferson. I just think it would have caused too many ructions around the place."

As a waitress passed by me, I took a bottle of beer from the tray and downed a large swig. I had to speak to Hunter, I knew that in my heart of hearts, but I also needed a little bit of courage to admit to him that I'd been wrong.

"So," I said, my gaze back on Bronte. "Who'd you have your heart set on now, if it's not Jefferson?"

She wiggled her eyebrows. "Now, that's a secret." She put a finger to her lips and sashayed away.

***

Every time I'd plucked up the courage to speak to Hunter, someone had beaten me to it; either Alaska or Carter had monopolized his time. Even Jason Miller, the deputy sheriff, who Hunter thought was as dull as a mash potato sandwich, had been talking his ear off. I couldn't get near him. It was almost time to sit down for dinner and I really wanted to speak to him before we did, but now he was talking to Belinda Jennings and she was getting much too close for my liking. What was worse, Hunter was damn well lapping it up.

"You okay, honey?" Darcy asked, clutching a glass of champagne and swaying a little.

"Yes, thanks, Darcy," I replied, sweeping a quick gaze over to Hunter and Belinda. "How are you doing?"

"Oh okay, I guess." She sounded wistful, and I wondered whether her and Jim were still at outs, even though they'd seemed okay since they'd arrived.

"You look lovely by the way." And she did. She looked real pretty in a peach colored beaded gown.

"Oh, thank you, honey," Darcy paused to take a sip of her drink. "Can I ask you a question?"

"Sure," I replied, not entirely certain it was wise. She was a little tight on champagne and I was worried what on earth she'd want to ask me that she couldn't ask my mom.

"Do you think I should have a butt lift?" She laid a soft hand on my arm. "Only my surgeon and Jim said it's fine as it is, but I'm not sure. I wonder if it's too saggy, you know."

Before I could do anything, Darcy had grabbed my hands and slapped them onto her ass.

"Squeeze," she commanded. "Go on give it a real good squeeze."

Wincing and feeling more than a little nauseous, I flexed my fingers.

"No," she yelled, making me jump. "Do it properly. Squeeze it hard."

I did as I was commanded and had to agree for a woman in her late forties, she had a pretty tight ass.

"I think they're right, Darcy. There's nothing wrong with your butt."

That brought a huge sigh from her as she dropped her head.

"Your mom said the same."

"So, maybe if we all said it then there really is nothing wrong with your butt."

Darcy contemplated my words and then finished off her champagne. "Maybe you're right, sweetheart."

"I really don't know why you thought otherwise," I replied.

She gave me a sad smile and patted my arm. "Because I thought maybe it would make Jim attracted to me again."

Darcy then walked away and as she did, I caught Jim watching her. The way his eyes followed her; he certainly didn't look like a man who wasn't attracted to his wife. Then, what did I know? I'd pretty much ruined any chance I had with the man I wanted, just because I was stubborn.

Talking of, Hunter was finally alone, and I knew it was my chance. So, with a deep breath and pushing my shoulders back, I walked toward him with purpose. When he started to walk toward me, my heart jumped. He still wanted this, and we were going to meet in the middle of the room, and it was going to be like a scene from a Nicholas Sparks book and we were going to... *damn it.*

Hunter stopped in front of Belinda and then took her onto the dancefloor.

My heart stopped for one, two, three beats, with a bang, bang, bang in the pit of my stomach taking up its rhythm. And, as Hunter pulled her close and placed one hand on the small of her back, I thought I might puke.

They danced close to each other, moving around the floor and when they had almost reached me, Hunter's gaze drifted my way. A small smile tugged at his lips and he dropped his head to whisper something in Belinda's ear, causing her to laugh.

I recognized the move from when Dylan had danced with me earlier, only that time I'd been the one laughing. My merriment had been false and forced, but Belinda's was perky like her tits, and real, unlike her tits. Hunter's grin in my direction though, was not. I knew it wasn't because it didn't reach his eyes, eyes which kept skimming back to me.

"Yeah, well two can play at that game, mister," I muttered under my breath as I sought out Dylan.

He was sitting at a table, talking animatedly to Delphine and Garth. I felt bad for using him, but in every war, there were casualties, and battle was about to commence.

"Hey, Dylan," I said as I went alongside him. "You want to dance?"

He looked surprised, and I guessed it was because I hadn't sought him out after Bronte had whisked me away. Nevertheless, he placed his glass down and stood up.

"I'd love to. I think we have time for maybe a couple of dances, before dinner is served."

Smiling widely, I held out my hand for him. "I guess we do."

As soon as we got onto the dancefloor, I tried to lead us in the direction of Hunter and Belinda, but Dylan was pretty strong and resisted so that we moved away from then.

"So," he said. "You had any more thoughts about coming to visit me?"

"Oh, I don't know about that." I noticed Hunter watching me, so laughed real loud. *"Hahahaha*, I'm so busy."

Dylan looked a little taken aback by it, but resolutely carried on dancing and by some stroke of luck changed direction.

"Well, maybe next time I come visit Aunt Delphine and Uncle Garth, I can take you on a date."

Only Janice-Ann and Lynn-Ann, dancing together, were between us and Hunter and Belinda. I dropped my head right back and laughed uproariously. Dylan let out a shriek and jerked.

"Are you okay?' he asked, frowning at me.

Hahahaha

"I'm perfectly fine. Tell me more about where you live."

"It's my turn to lead," Janice-Ann protested above Florida Georgia Line's *Sittin' Pretty*.

"Ladies," I said as we danced past them.

"Hey, honey," Janice-Ann replied. "Lynn-Ann I'm leading, I told you."

"You always lead. And I'm the eldest by ten whole minutes and you know that."

When we danced past the sisters, Dylan looked over his shoulder at them. His momentary distraction gave me the opportunity to maneuver us next to Hunter and Belinda. As we did, Hunter's eyes narrowed on me, so I felt behind me and moved Dylan's hand closer to my butt.

"Okay," Dylan exclaimed and arched both his brows in surprise.

I smiled and pushed closer to him but kept my eyes on Hunter and let out another laugh.

Hahahaha

As the song changed, Hunter dropped his hand actually *onto* Belinda's butt and I couldn't help but gasp. Belinda said something and it was Hunter's turn to laugh. His was deep and loud and just a tad too long.

"Oh, Belinda," I heard him say, a little too loudly. "You're so funny."

Funny! There was nothing funny about Belinda Jennings! Now me, I was damn hilarious.

"Dylan," I said, leaning closer into him. "Did I tell you the joke about the horse who walked into a bar? The bartender says, hey and the horse replies, you read my mind."

Dylan's laugh was loud, not quite as loud as Hunter's but good enough to make the guy I wanted to whip his head around.

"Oh, Dylan," I sighed loudly. "Your laugh is so lovely."

"Belinda, I have to say you're looking beautiful tonight." Hunter counteracted.

"Your hair looks lovely tonight, Dylan."

I reached up and ran a hand down his shoulder length hair, which was far too girly for my liking.

"Huh." Hunter scoffed and raked a hand through his silky dark hair, which was swept back from his handsome face.

"You okay?" Dylan asked, tilting his head back to study me.

"Me, oh I'm fine."

A quick glance at Hunter. *Hahahaha.*

He stared back at me, his brown eyes piercing as he dragged his teeth across his bottom lip and then slowly sweeping his tongue across it. It shouldn't have been, but it was as sexy as hell move, and when his gaze then raked up and down my body, I felt my panties getting wet.

"Wow," I whispered feeling my nipples harden.

Damn those nipples, they had a mind of their own.

"Hey," Dylan said softly in my ear. "How about we go somewhere quiet after dinner."

My head shot up to see him looking down on me, lust evident in his gaze.

"Dylan, I—"

"Ladies and gentlemen," Mayor Garrison's voice boomed out. "Please take your places as dinner is about to be served."

"I guess we should go," I said to Dylan.

"But before we do."

I didn't see it coming, but his mouth was on mine and his tongue was pushing against my lips, urging me to open up. It felt wrong. They weren't the lips I wanted on me. He just didn't taste right.

"Dylan!"

I pushed against his chest and as I did, I felt a hand on my shoulder, and I was pulled away from Dylan.

"Get your hands off my fucking woman," Hunter growled.

Dylan took a step back, his mouth open as he stared between us. "What's going on?"

"You heard," Hunter replied. "Dancing with her is one thing but kissing her is a damn point of no return. Now, I repeat, get your hands off my fucking woman."

My heart beat rapidly as I looked up at Hunter and marveled at how hot he looked angry. And then, the idiot in me just had to go and do it. She had to say something, instead of basking in the sexiness and manliness that shot ripples of excitement through my body.

"Who says I'm your woman?" I growled as I poked Hunter in the chest. "Not me, that's for sure."

Hunter reared back and looked at me for a few seconds and then threw his arms into the air.

"You know what, El, I give up. I just can't win. No matter what I do or say to you, you're not going to change that stubborn mind or yours."

He moved to walk away, and panic washed over me. I knew if I let him go, I wouldn't ever get him back.

Before I had time to think about my next move, he turned and strode away.

"Hunter, wait!"

"Ellie, what's going on?" Dylan asked, taking my hand.

"I'm sorry, Dylan," I said as I pulled away from him. "I need to go."

Without any further hesitation, I ran from the dancefloor and went in search of Hunter wishing I wasn't so stubborn and didn't have a big mouth.

As people milled around, moving toward their tables, I cut through them with my eyes constantly searching for the big cowboy who had my damn heart. I finally spotted him heading out of the ballroom toward the lobby, with Belinda not far behind him. My pulse spiked and my breathing got faster and faster as I moved through the crowds. I was almost sent toppling over by an angry looking Jacob Crowne as he pushed in front of me to follow his wife out. Wondering what had bitten his ass, I was just about to reach the lobby when Declan O'Reilly and his eldest son Eamon, stepped in front of me.

"Ellie," Declan said, his face impassive and his jaw tight. "Where's your brother?"

"Is he with my sister." Eamon's nostrils flared as he towered over me.

"I have no idea," I snapped. "And I'll thank you not to take that tone with me."

I thrust my hands to my hips and jutted out my chin. The two big men didn't scare me and if they tried anything, I'd be more than happy to throw one of my best punches.

"Listen." Declan held his hands up in a conciliatory manner. "We haven't seen her for over thirty minutes and my guess is she's with your brother."

"Well, she isn't," I replied, pointing over in the direction of the huge doors at the end of the room, which led to the Mayor's chambers. "Because my brother is over there."

They followed my gaze and Declan positively slumped when he saw Carter walking up and down with his phone to his ear.

"Doesn't mean he hasn't been with her," Eamon growled. "And if he's done anything with her that he shouldn't, believe me he's gonna be ending up in that hospital you work at."

I poked him in the chest. "Don't you threaten my brother, Eamon O'Reilly."

"I mean it, Ellie," he replied. "He'd better not have put a hand on her."

Declan pushed in front of Eamon and sighed. "I'm sorry, Ellie, it's just she's easily led, and well she's got a fire in her belly that girl."

"No doubt a kid too," Eamon muttered.

"Eamon. That's enough." Declan smiled at me. "I'm sorry, Ellie, I just know she has a thing for Carter, and she's been staying out late and disappeared pretty much as soon as we got here. Her mom is frantic with worry about what she's going to end up doing."

It was then that I spotted Marie sneaking back into the room and Jim Wickerson's grandson, Evan was close behind, tucking his shirt back into his pants. I really didn't want to get him into any bother, but I also didn't want my brother to get the blame. Plus, I really needed to talk to Hunter.

"Marie is, twenty, a grown woman and you should realize that," I replied, skirting around the two men. "But if you really want to know where she is, she's over there."

I nodded to where I saw Marie and Evan staring lovingly at each other.

"Is that Evan Wickerson?" Eamon asked. "I'll kill him."

As Eamon turned to go, Declan pulled on his arm. "Eamon leave her be. Ellie's right, she's twenty years of age, and Evan's a good kid."

"Oh, and Carter isn't?" I asked indignantly.

Declan gave me a look as if to ask if I was for real, and I had to agree, Carter was a douche where girls were concerned.

"He's also her age," Declan added as he slapped a hand on Eamon's shoulder. "Sorry to have troubled you, Ellie. Come on son, let's go tell your mom we found her and she's fine."

They walked away with Eamon still muttering about ripping Evan's teeth out but giving me the opportunity to continue out to the lobby.

As soon as I stepped into the brighter lights, my heart dropped like a stone and bile rose to my throat. Standing in front of me was Hunter, another woman in his arms, and the other woman wasn't Belinda, but Bronte.

CHAPTER 38

Hunter

"**O**h my God."

The voice I heard was Ellie's and she sounded upset. Letting go of Bronte, I turned to see her watching us. Her hand was at her chest and she looked as though she'd seen a ghost.

"Ellie?" Bronte said moving away from me. "What's wrong?"

With a wild-eyed look, Ellie took a step back, her face shrouded with hurt and anger. She looked devastated and I was scared at what could have upset her so much.

"Baby, what is it?" I moved alongside Bronte, but Ellie stepped away shaking her head. "Did that dickwad do something to you?"

Even though I'd told her I'd give up trying, it didn't mean that I didn't care about her. I'd punch the prick if he'd hurt her in any way.

"No, he's done nothing," she cried. "This is all on you. How could you, Hunter? I know I was stupid out there on the dancefloor, but to get back at me with this. *And don't call me baby.*"

Frowning I looked from her to Bronte and then back again. "Bronte? We were just hugging is all."

Bronte took another step closer to Ellie. "You think me and Hunter?"

"You were the one who said you had your eye on someone else, so why not Hunter?" Leaning forward with a scowl, Ellie gave me a good glimpse of her cleavage.

I cleared my throat and forcibly removed my gaze from the goods. *I would not be the man she thought I was.* Ah shit, one quick look wouldn't hurt.

"Hunter," Ellie snapped her eyes still on Bronte. "I know you're thinking about my tits right now, so don't. Not if you want to leave this dance with your big penis intact."

Bronte gasped. "How do you know he has a big penis?"

Ellie made a gurgling sound, like she was choking on her own blood, and shot her gaze to me. Her eyes were pleading for me to help, but enough was enough.

"She knows because we've had sex," I replied, turning my head to Bronte, who looked like she might be getting ready to catch flies with her open mouth.

"*Hunter.*" Ellie gasped and stepping forward, poked me in the chest. "You did not just out us to Bronte?"

"Yeah, I did." I poked her shoulder. "And what does it matter anyway, you're with *Dylan* now?"

"Well," she replied, with another poke to my chest. "For one, we were supposed to be keeping it a secret, and for two I'm *not* with Dylan. For damn three, I just saw you with your arms around her. No doubt trying to entice her with that beautiful, big thing between your legs."

I took a step closer so that we were only inches apart. "For someone who doesn't want to date me, you talk about my dick an awful lot, *baby.*"

Her mouth gaped like a fish, but no words came out.

"You had sex," Bronte said, sounding more shocked than a nun on a bachelor party.

"Yes." Ellie and I both replied.

"With each other?"

"Of course, with each other," Ellie replied. "How the hell do you think I know about that." She pointed toward my junk. "I'm sorry, Bronte, but I had no idea you had feelings for him. At the time you were all about Jefferson. I wasn't to know you'd swap your affections to his son."

"Me and Hunter," Bronte said and laughed. "Ick, no way."

"What's wrong with me?"

"What's wrong with him?"

I turned back to Ellie and when I saw the hurt on her face, I knew I had her. No matter what she said. Whether she was going to start dating that damn Thor wannabe or not, she wanted me as much as I wanted her.

"He's a great catch," Ellie continued, making me grin like a Cheshire cat. "You should be honored to be his girl."

My heart thumped wildly in my chest and all I wanted to do was kiss the life out of my beautiful Belle look-alike. Fuck I was so gone for her.

"What's going on?"

We all turned to see Carter, his eyes moving across the three of us.

"Did you know Hunter and Ellie had sex?" Bronte asked.

"Bronte," Ellie gasped and swung around to her brother. "Don't you dare punch him."

Carter shrugged. "Why the hell would I punch him?"

"Because I'm your little sister and he defiled me."

"I did not defile you," I growled. "You were all in and damn well loved it."

Ellie waved me away, keeping her eyes on her brother.

"Ellie," Carter sighed. "I hate to tell you this, but I don't give a shit whether he defiled you or not. As long as he didn't hurt you or give you some nasty disease. I can't sit down to Thursday night dinner with someone who has crabs." He held up a hand. "I'm sorry, call me unsympathetic, but I saw with Erik Mackenzie at college what those little critters can do."

"I do not have crabs," Ellie huffed out. "How dare you."

"I did not give her crabs. I'm clean as clean can be."

Carter threw his hands in the air. "Seriously, how you two haven't got together before now, I have no fucking idea. I didn't say you'd given her anything. I pointed out that would be the only reason I'd punch you."

"Yes, well," Ellie said, narrowing her eyes at me. "It might just be Bronte he's given them to now."

"I don't have fucking crabs, or any other disease of the dick."

"What do you mean?" Carter's tone stopped me in my tracks. It was low and pretty murderous.

"What the hell's wrong with you?" I asked, turning to him. "What do you think I mean. I'm fucking clean, man."

"Not that. What did Ellie mean about you giving Bronte crabs?"

"Carter," Bronte sighed. "Don't be an idiot."

He swung his gaze to Bronte and the look he gave her almost knocked me on my ass. It was soft and gentle, and it was just like the ones that I found myself giving Ellie.

"Carter?" Ellie said his name so softly it made me wonder if she'd seen it too. "I was only joking. Well, kind of, I did find Hunter with his arms wrapped around her."

Boom!

The punch landed right on my chin and it did actually land me on my ass.

"*Carter.*"

Ellie ran to me and dropped to her knees, her dress gaping open, and even as I saw stars, I couldn't help but think how amazing her legs looked.

"Are you okay?" she asked, cupping a hand around my face and gently rubbing her thumb along my jaw. She looked over her shoulder to Carter who had taken a step toward me. "You're a damn idiot."

"You said he was kissing Bronte," Carter exclaimed, looking at Bronte.

I pushed myself up into a sitting position.

"Just lie back down," Ellie said pushing a hand against my forehead. "You might be hurt."

Shaking my head, I sat up and rubbed my chin. "I'm fine. Like he could hurt me."

"I totally could," Carter scoffed.

"You could not," I replied, getting to my feet and then holding out a hand for Ellie. "You caught me unawares is all."

"Even I could lay Carter out," Ellie said, scowling at her brother.

Grinning down at her, I helped Ellie up. "She could too." Once she was standing, I didn't let her go but pulled her closer.

"Hunter," she said softly as she collided with my chest.

I bent my head so that my mouth was close to her ear. "Ellie, where in the hell would you get the idea that I was kissing Bronte?" I whispered, ignoring Carter's voice whining on in the background.

"You had her in your arms," Ellie replied, glancing over my shoulder.

"I was hugging her."

"Before we get back to whether you can take me in a punch up or not," Carter said. "Tell me why the fuck you were hugging her."

"Carter, don't be an idiot," Bronte added. "He was just hugging me because he saw I was upset."

"Why were you upset?" Carter asked and moved over to Bronte and placed his hands on her shoulders. "What upset you? Tell me."

"She was upset about her mom and dad. Why the hell would I kiss *her*?"

"What the fuck is wrong with kissing Bronte?" Carter snapped.

I rolled my eyes. "Nothing if that's what you want to do, but I don't. You're as bad as your sister for getting the damn wrong end of the stick."

"I saw you," Ellie cried.

"I was a little tearful, because I know my parents are going through a rough patch," Bronte offered. "Hunter found me crying."

"Why didn't you come find me?" Carter crooned. "I was only taking a call about a pig with mastitis."

"You left the main room with Belinda," Ellie said to me, her bottom lip trembling. "Are you going to start dating her?"

Letting out a sigh, I shook my head. "No, I'm not. Dancing with her was a stupid thing to do. It was a dick move to both her and you. So, I told her, I'm only interested in one person and it's not her."

"Bronte?" she asked.

"Damn it, Ellie. Are you being obtuse on purpose? Who the hell do you think I mean? Who is it I've been trying to persuade to date me for the last few weeks?"

She took a deep breath. "Not Bronte."

"No, you idiot, *not* Bronte."

I placed my hands upon Ellie's arms and turned her around to face her brother and best friend. Carter was gently stroking Bronte's face and whispering softly to her.

Maneuvering Ellie in front of me, I wrapped an arm around her chest and leaned in to whisper in her ear.

"Look at them, baby. Does it look like she's in love with anyone else other than your brother?"

Ellie gasped and turned her head to look at me. "How long have you known?"

I shrugged. "About a minute longer than you. Why else would he punch me? Not because I had sex with you, but because he thought I'd kissed Bronte."

"But they hate each other," Ellie said, still looking at me.

"I guess not." I nodded to where Bronte and Carter were standing. "Take a look."

Carter was kissing the life out of Bronte, and she was kissing him back just as enthusiastically without any hesitancy.

"Oh my." Ellie sighed and grabbed a hold of my arm wrapped around her. "That's definitely not a new thing is it?"

"Nuh uh, I don't think so."

After a lot of kissing and heavy breathing, Carter pulled away from Bronte but grabbed her hand as he turned to us.

"Stay away from my girl, Delaney."

His tone was low, but there was a smile on his lips.

"How long?" Ellie asked.

Bronte winced and bit her lip. "Three months."

"But what about… oh my God, you told me that you wanted to be with… you little liar."

Carter rolled his eyes. "We knew that if you knew about us, you'd interfere. The whole damn lot of you would interfere," he said. "Mom and Darcy more than anyone, and there's no way you'd be able to keep it from them."

"So," Bronte added. "We decided to put you off the scent." She paused and glanced down at the floor. "I'm sorry for tricking you. I really am, Ellie. You're my best friend, but we didn't want anything to spoil it. No offence, Hunter, I love your dad and all, but he's just way too old."

"No offence taken," I replied with a smile.

"If you'd asked me not to say anything, I wouldn't have," Ellie said, her voice cracking.

"We couldn't take that chance, sis. We've known each other all our lives, so we just wanted to check this was real and not just something we'd fallen into before we told everyone."

"And?" I asked.

Bronte gazed at Carter and I had my answer.

"So, at the party when you put your knee to his balls, you didn't mean it?" Ellie asked.

"Oh God yeah, I meant it." Bronte nudged Carter with her elbow. "You're my best friend and he was a dick."

Ellie and I both laughed as Carter cupped his junk, evidently reliving the moment that Bronte's knee collided with his dick and balls.

"What about my pop's shirt you stole from the laundry hamper?"

Bronte grinned. "Mom wanted to know what size he was as she wanted to buy him a shirt for his birthday gift. It was fun messing with you though."

"Yeah, that's kinda what gave us the idea," Carter offered, not even looking guilty.

"And all the times she's reamed you out over the last few months?" Ellie asked

Bronte giggled. "All for show. I *always* made it up to him."

"Oh, and that little prank of yours, to text us from each other's phones," Carter said with a sigh. "Totally pointless. We guessed it was just you trying to get me back for something or other."

"Yeah," Bronte added with a secretive smile. "Our texts to each other are so much dirtier, so we knew straight away. I knew it was you getting him back for Belinda's party."

Ellie cleared her throat and shuffled her feet.

"I guess we don't need to mention the plan," I whispered close to her ear, allowing my lips to brush against them.

She shivered in my arms and I knew it was time for us to talk and for Carter and Bronte to go and... well leave us alone.

"Okay," I said moving from behind Ellie and taking her hand. "I need to speak to Ellie, so..." I nodded toward the entrance of the grand ballroom.

Carter looked at the door and then back to me. "Oh, right, yeah. Come on, sweetheart, I think it's time we came out of the closet to the family. Oh, but just a minute, I need to tell Ellie something."

He took Ellie's hand and pulled her away from me, talking quietly to her. Whatever it was made her giggle and if I wasn't so worried about what he was saying, I'd have thought she was cuter than a kitten with a bow on.

Once he'd finished, Carter grabbed a hold of Bronte and led her back to the party, leaving Ellie and I alone. We waited in silence as they left and once the door closed behind them, I dragged Ellie over to one of the huge leather couches that was tucked in a quiet corner of the lobby.

"What was he saying to you?" I asked as I guided her to sit down.

"Oh, nothing," she replied with a quirk of her eyebrow. "Just something about Bronte's Christmas present."

I didn't believe her but had more important things I wanted to discuss than whatever shit Carter had been saying. I lowered myself next to her. "Okay. You and me, need to sort this out once and for all. You with me?"

Biting her lip, Ellie nodded. "Yes, I know."

"First off, don't ever dance with that douche Dylan ever again. And you most certainly never let him put his lips on you *ever*."

Ellie opened her mouth to speak, but I silenced her with a kiss. Quick and hard.

"Second off, I don't want to date you, Ellie. I—"

"I knew it." She tried to get up, but with a hand on her shoulder and the other at the back of her head, I guided her mouth back to mine.

"I don't want to date you because that won't ever be enough for me," I said, once I'd thoroughly kissed her.

"It won't?" she asked, her voice quiet and hesitant.

"Nope. I want you to be my girlfriend. My girl. My woman, my *only* woman."

"You do?"

"Yes, baby, I do." I blew out a breath, knowing that what I said to her next could scare her away. I had to though, because any other words wouldn't be enough and would be a huge damn lie.

"You are all I think about, every single minute of every single day. I see you, Ellie. I see the woman you've become, the woman that I would be proud to call my partner. You're so damn beautiful and sexy, but you're strong and brave—well apart from when it comes to cows." I paused for thought. "Oh, and yeah, maybe you can't sing a note, but I can put up with that."

She threw her head back and laughed and it just made what I was about to say to be more of a truth than any words I'd ever said before.

"You have a big heart, and an honesty I'd never tire of. In fact, I can't imagine having to spend a day without you." I took a deep breath. "I want you in my life, Ellie. I want to *share* my life with you, and I swear down, I'll do everything I can to make sure I never hurt you. I'll do everything I can to always make you happy because the truth is, baby, it sneaked up on me, but I've fallen real hard for you. So hard, I can't stand the idea of you not being mine."

Ellie gasped and flattened a palm against her chest. She didn't speak for what felt like hours but just stared at me, her eyes sparkling.

"Ellie, baby, please say something."

My heart was racing, and adrenaline was pumping hard through my veins. I watched and waited. Finally, she took a deep breath.

"How the hell is your proposal going to beat that, Hunter Meredith Delaney?"

Before I spoke, she threw herself onto me and tugging at my hair, she poured every single ounce of her energy into kissing me. Hands, teeth, tongues and heavy breathing were all parts of the jigsaw that made up the perfect kiss. A kiss that sealed the deal. In fact, it was a triple threat of a kiss. It was long, it was hot, and it was fucking delicious.

"Does that mean you finally agree with me about us being together?" I asked when she pulled away to catch her breath.

Nipping at my bottom lip, she nodded. "Oh yeah," she said breathily.

"Wholeheartedly. I wanted you to ask me at the mall, but you didn't."

My mouth dropped open and I stared at her for a few. "You damn well drive me crazy, you know that?"

She grinned and nodded. "I know, but it's a good crazy right?"

"Yeah," I replied, gently brushing her bangs from her forehead. "It's a good crazy."

Sagging against me, she then gave a satisfied mewling sound. "Okay, what next?"

"Now we just have to give the family their second shock of the night."

Ellie pulled away and looked at me with a frown. "We could stay a secret," she offered.

I shook my head. "Nope. You're mine. I want to make sure everybody knows it."

Two hours later, once dinner was over, I made true my promise and showed the whole damn town who Ellie Maples belonged to.

As Luke Combs' *'Beautiful Crazy'* played, I danced with my girl and kissed her with everything I had. The best part about it – we were the only ones on the dancefloor and Dylan watched on as Ellie loved every damn minute of the love and attention that I gave to her.

CHAPTER 39

Ellie

The breeze blew the drapes at the open window, and as I cranked up the volume on Shawn Mendes and Camila Cabello's *'Senorita'* I giggled to myself.

"Baby, what the hell are you up to?"

Hunter was on his bed, his back against the headboard with his eyes tightly closed. At least that's what I'd asked him to do for his surprise.

"One minute," I replied and checked myself once more in the full-length mirror on his wall.

Turning my head, I looked at the gorgeous cowboy and felt my heart rate rise. God, he was so damn amazing, and for the last two months he'd been all mine. Something which I knew made a lot of the girls in Dayton Valley jealous. Not just the girls, the women too. Davis had been right; Mrs. Callahan was most disappointed it wasn't Hunter dressed as Santa making me swoon in the calendar. It had also been made clear to me many times that March was indeed by far the most popular month. It didn't worry me though, because Hunter was my man and boy, had he gone a long way to prove to me that in turn I was his. The sex had continued to be awesome and had been even better just from knowing that I was getting orgasms from my *boyfriend*.

Whenever I thought about the fact that I was Hunter's girlfriend, I got a stupid smile on my face. Bronte called it my sex smile, but it wasn't just about that, we were so much more than I'd ever expected.

We talked a hella lot, we laughed even more and yeah, we had lots and lots of sex, but the best thing he'd done; accompany me to my therapy sessions about my fear of his cows. Hunter had been real supportive and had actually been the one to find the therapist for me. I'd only had three sessions, but they were going well. I could actually go to the ranch in daylight without breaking out in a sweat and had even stood six feet away from one. Which was why I was currently about to fulfil what I hoped was a little fantasy for my man. A little thank you for all his help.

"Okay," I whispered close to his ear. "Open your eyes."

I glanced down his body and could see the anticipation of what I might be about to do already made him hard in his grey sweats. Although, he'd been hard pretty much all weekend, seeing as his dad had taken his aunts to meet up with their brother Miller and his wife, who were on a business trip in Houston. Jefferson had employed the Williams brothers full-time, so Hunter had taken the weekend off too and apart from a trip to Middleton Ridge on Friday night for dinner and a movie, we'd spent most of it in the bedroom.

"Fuck," Hunter groaned out as he rubbed a hand down his face. "You look... fuck, El."

I gave him a little twirl and was happy to hear him give another moan of satisfaction.

"Is that your original Belle dress?" he asked as he moved to the edge of the bed.

"Yep, with a few alterations, with the help of your aunts."

Hunter's eyes widened as he silently mouthed, 'fuck' his discomfort causing me to laugh.

"Don't worry, they thought it was for a costume party."

Hunter's hand reached out and touched the bottom of the short yellow dress I was wearing, before slipping beneath it to land on my butt.

My old Belle from Beauty and The Beast, dress, was now much, much shorter than I was sure Mr. Disney would have thought proper. Not to mention how low the neckline was, which had Hunter's full attention.

"Baby," he said hoarsely. "I think I can see your nipples."

I gave him a little wink and lifted my leg, placing my foot next to him on the mattress.

"You like the thigh highs too?" I asked as I ran a finger along the edge of the white nylons and then up the garter attached to it, giving it a little snap. "I can sing you Belle's song as well if you like."

"No, baby it's fine," he replied a little too quickly.

He still hated my singing, but who cared.

"I guess we just need to concentrate on other things then," I said as I trailed a finger down hard, ripped, ab muscles and pulled at the waistband of his sweats.

Hunter swallowed hard. "You have to be the sexiest thing I have ever seen in my whole damn life. Shit, El, I'm as hard as steel."

He reached up and took a tendril of my dark hair and twirled it around his fingers. His eyes swept over me, full of lust and maybe even some reverence.

"You even did your hair the same."

I leaned forward and nipped at his lip, before dropping a soft kiss to it. "Anything for my man. I'm just glad you like it."

As my tongue licked down his neck, he dropped his head back and grabbed a hold of my butt with both his hands.

"Where's your panties?" he asked.

I shrugged. "Must have forgotten them."

Hunter's eyes closed momentarily as he let out a quiet groan. "Damn it, Ellie."

Feeling more turned on than I thought possible dressed as a Disney Princess, I moved forward to straddle him, reveling in the feel of his hardness pulsing beneath me.

"You really do like it don't you?"

"I love it," he breathed out, his chest rising and falling rapidly. "So damn much."

"Good." I pushed him, forcing him to lie back on the bed. "Now, I'm going to show you how much I appreciate you, my Mr. Triple Threat."

Hunter stilled beneath me. "W-what?"

I started to laugh and poked him in his side. "Triple threat, isn't that what you say about yourself?"

"In my fucking head maybe," he groaned. "How the hell do you know about it?"

I tapped his forehead and winked.

"You cannot read my damn mind, Ellie. How did you know?" he asked, looking pained.

"Carter told me." My giggle was bubbling into full blown laughter as Hunter's face blanched.

"I never told him," he said, rolling us over so he was now on top of me. "Tell me the truth."

"Hey, watch the dress cowboy," I laughed as he crushed me beneath his beautiful, hard body.

He stole a kiss and then nipped at my earlobe. "Don't stress it, because this dress is going to be ruined anyway when I've finished with you. Now, tell me the truth."

I smiled as the music turned to Sam Outlaw and reached up to kiss Hunter. He, however, had other ideas and tickled my side.

"The truth, cutie pie," he said, insistently.

"That is the truth. Apparently, you were shouting it *real* loud one night, when you were drunk on my dad's peach wine. Carter felt he should tell me. In fact," I said reaching up to kiss his neck, "that was what he whispered to me in the lobby at the Christmas dance. He said it was collateral in case you ever pissed me off, but it's much more fun using it this way."

Hunter shook his head and groaned. "Bastard. I'll get him back somehow for that. I didn't even know I'd said it to him. And just so you know, I still have the picture of you trapped in the red dress."

"You threatening to use it against me, Mr. Triple Threat?" I nipped his jaw, making a mental note to erase the picture from his phone someday.

"If you keep Triple Threat our secret, then I won't need to will I?" he said seductively.

"But you do agree? You do think you are a triple threat?"

His eyes grew dark and it was pretty clear by the way he licked his lips and ran his hand up my leg that he was thinking about his theory.

"You want me to prove it to you, don't you?" he asked.

"Yeah, I think I might."

"Okay," he said, grinning. "Brace yourself, honey."

Soft lips dropped to mine as his hands threaded through my hair. Instinctively I parted my legs and when his rock-hard dick pushed against my stomach, I knew he was going to prove himself right.

He was long.

He had a good girth.

He had the technique.

And he was all mine.

EPILOGUE

Carter

"Seriously, Carter, if they're having sex around the back I'm going to barf." Bronte took a sip of her wine and then pushed it away, curling her lip as she did.

"Of course, they are," I replied and picked up her glass. "Want me to change this sweetheart? Something wrong with it?"

I sniffed at the drink, and while I wasn't a wine connoisseur, neither was Bronte, so didn't get why she was turning her nose up at it.

"What's wrong with it, you never turn down a glass of wine?"

Wrong thing to say.

Bronte gave me a glare that could have iced over the Atlantic Ocean and crossed her arms firmly over her tits – tits which were looking amazing by the way.

"Do you have a new bra?" I asked, licking my lips.

"OMG you did not just say that."

"And you did not just say OMG." I laughed and took a drink of my beer.

"What's wrong with that?" my beautiful girlfriend asked.

Damn, and wasn't that a shocker—*Bronte, my girlfriend*. Couldn't imagine not being with her though. Admittedly, it had gotten a little harder since we'd gone public. Not in our relationship, but rather the fact that my mom was nosey and interfering, and my sister was an even bigger pain in the ass than usual. She and Bronte liked it when we *double-dated*, me not so much. I liked it when me and Hunter went out on our own for a few beers. I enjoyed our once a week at Stars & Stripes, or when we went into Jennings Bridge, to a club. Not any longer though. It wasn't Bronte or Ellie who'd put a stop to it, but fucking Hunter. He wanted to spend every damn moment he could sticking it to my sister.

The thought of that should have grossed me out, but I wasn't that precious about Ellie; she was my annoying little sister that was all. I knew he'd thought I might be, but only because I'd known what *had* happened, *would* happen. I knew she'd entice him with whatever it was women enticed us men with and he'd become too addicted to want to hang out with me – and I was right. Call me Nostra-fucking-damus.

As for me and my little Lollipop, Bronte. Well, she was damn amazing and if being with her meant not so many boy's nights, I'd probably live.

"Carter, I asked you a question." Bronte leaned across the table with her eyes full of fire. "What's wrong with me saying OMG?"

"What's wrong is that you're not seventeen." I grinned, using my regular get out of jail one that I knew made her panties wet.

"And that's not going to work," she replied, scowling at my smile.

"Why not? It usually does."

I gave her another one, just in case she hadn't been watching properly.

"I got it the first time," she snapped. "And it was just as shit then."

"Woah," I said leaning back into my chair. "Who the hell stole your pickle this morning."

Her eyes narrowed on me. "You. You're the one who stole my pickle, you huge big ass hair."

"What the fuck have I done?" I threw my hands into the air.

"What have you done, you stupid pickle stealer? What have you done? Well, if you don't know Carter, I'm not going to tell you."

She pushed her chair back, and pushed out of it, almost sending it toppling over.

"I'm going home, and I don't want you to follow me."

Tears were welling in her eyes and I didn't think I'd ever seen her look so angry. We'd fought hundreds of times, but she'd never ever cried before.

"Hey, sweetheart, what's wrong?" I asked, getting out of my own chair.

"Don't," Bronte barked. "I told you I'm going home."

"How you going to get home? Ellie is DD and she's currently humping Hunter somewhere."

My sister and my best friend had disappeared over a half hour before. Apparently, both needed the bathroom and hadn't been seen since. So, unless they'd both eaten some dodgy shrimp, my guess was they'd found a quiet corner to fuck in.

"I'll call my dad, or Shaw, he's home for the weekend."

I reached out to her, but she batted my hand away. "Leave me alone, you douche."

"Bronte, what the fuck is your problem?" Frowning I shook my head. "I didn't realize it was the time of the month."

Bronte's eyes went wide and her mouth dropped open. "You did not just say that to me," she gasped.

"Well, yeah I did, because you're being a little bitch."

"Oh, God," Ellie groaned coming up behind Bronte. "What now?"

"He," Bronte ground out and pointed at me, "is a pickle stealer and I hate him."

"What the hell is a pickle stealer?" Hunter asked, coming around to my side of the table while he tightened the belt on his jeans.

"Have you just been fucking my sister?" I growled not sure who else to take my frustration out on.

The bastard grinned and gave Ellie some damn adoring look that he'd suddenly perfected whenever she was around.

Where the fuck had my best friend gone?

I scratched the back of my neck and looked over to Bronte. Tears were now rolling down her cheeks and the sight of them cracked my heart open.

"Sweetheart, what's wrong?" I asked softly.

Her bottom lip trembled, and her chin wobbled as she took a deep breath.

"Us is what's wrong, Carter. Us. And that's why I'm ending it, as of now. We are over."

My heart stuttered and my dinner was in danger of making a reappearance as her words sunk in. It couldn't be over. We'd been great together, I felt we were going somewhere. It'd been only two days ago that we'd talked about her maybe moving in with me.

"Bronte, no," Ellie said. "Why?"

"Come on guys, just sit down, forget that Carter is a douche for an hour or so and everything will be fine," Hunter offered.

Bronte shook her head. "Nope. I'm sorry, but that's it. We're over."

She then turned and ran across the bar. I moved quickly to go after her, but Hunter grabbed my hand.

"Let Ellie go. Go baby, go after her."

Ellie nodded. "I'll be back. She'll be fine."

"What the hell was that?" Hunter asked. "You argue tons, but she never breaks up with you."

I stared over to where Ellie was chasing after Bronte and shrugged.

"I have no idea." I turned to Hunter and felt a swell in my stomach. "I think she means it," I said. "I think she's really breaking up with me."

Hunter grimaced and shook his head. "Nah, no way. It'll be golden, you'll see."

As the door to the Stars & Stripes banged shut behind Ellie and Bronte, I had to wonder if he was just talking horse shit, because it certainly seemed real to my heart.

To be continued in The Jackpot Screwer, coming in 2021

THE TRIPLE THREAT PLAYLIST ON SPOTIFY

Link - shorturl.at/dtzP0

Body Like A Back Road	Sam Hunt
Look What God Gave Her	Thomas Rett
How Will I Know	Whitney Houston
Cowboy	Kid Rock
Tenderheart	Sam Outlaw
Good As You	Kane Brown
Sittin' Pretty	Florida Georgia Line
Beautiful Crazy	Luke Combs
Speechless (feat. Tori Kelly)	Dan+Shay, Tori Kelly
Senorita	Shawn Mendes, Camilla Cabello

NIKKI'S LINKS

If you'd like to know more about me or my books,
then all my links are listed below.

Website:
www.nikkiashtonbooks.co.uk

Instagram
www.instagram.com/nikkiashtonauthor

Facebook
www.facebook.com/nikki.ashton.982
Ashton's Amorous Angels Facebook Group
www.facebook.com/groups/1039480929500429

Amazon
viewAuthor.at/NAPage

Audio Books
preview.tinyurl.com/NikkiAshtonAudio

EXCERPT FROM
THE *Jackpot* SCREWER
COMING EARLY 2021

Carter

"**L**ollipop, open the damn door."

"Go away you pickle stealer."

I swung around to face my best friend. "What the hell is she talking about? Why is she going on about me stealing some damn non-existent pickle?"

Hunter shrugged but had a huge, teeth showing grin, which was totally unwanted. We were outside my girlfriend's house because only an hour ago she'd ended our relationship. In the local bar of all places. I had no idea why, just that she'd accused me of being a pickle stealer and said we were over – *she doesn't even eat damn pickles!*

What made it worse was that it all happened in front of my sister and best friend, who had recently started going out. They were sickeningly loved up and had just returned from a quick sex session. Where they'd had sex, who the hell knew, but while they both had satisfied grins I was shrouded in misery, trying to reason with Bronte.

"This is not funny dick head," I hissed at Hunter. "If my sister ended things with you because you'd stolen her invisible pickle, I doubt you'd be smiling like that."

"One I would never steal Ellie's pickle and two what the fuck; *Lollipop?*"

"And?" I asked, frowning at him. "You don't have a cute nickname for Ellie?"

He colored a little and moved to bang on the Jackson's door. "Bronte, just come out and speak to him."

"What is it?" I asked, giving him a nudge, my misery momentarily forgotten. "Tell me, I won't repeat it."

Hunter rolled his eyes. "Yeah right. It's marginal who is the biggest gossip in this town, you or Mrs. Callahan at the gas station. Anyway, if I have a nickname for Ellie, and that's a big if, it's between me and her."

At that moment, my sister walked out of the house. She looked a little mystified and was shaking her head.

"She won't come out and she won't tell me what you did."

"I didn't do anything," I protested. "Not a damn thing. I even told her how good her tits were looking."

"Well, it's a little bit caveman and not the most romantic of compliments," Ellie sighed. "But even for Bronte, it's a little harsh to dump you on your ass for praising her assets."

"Exactly." I threw my hands into the air. "She's definitely hormonal, like I said."

Ellie's eyes hardened as she widened her stance. "You did not?"

"Yeah, she was being bitchy, so I said I didn't realize it was that time of the month."

Hunter winced. "Shit man, that was totally the wrong thing to say."

"No wonder she dumped you." Ellie glared at me before turning to Hunter. "Let's go. I can't deal with his stupidity any longer, plus Dad took Mom away for the weekend, so we have the house to ourselves, remember."

My best friend grinned like he was the fox who'd stolen the fattest chicken from the coop. "Okay, let's go."

"So, you're not going to help me?" I asked as they both turned and practically ran for Hunter's truck.

"Sorry, but your sister needs my full attention." He took Ellie's hand and brought it to his mouth, kissing the back of it.

"You disgust me," I called. "You know that, right?"

Hunter flipped me over his shoulder without even looking back.

"Hey, Ellie," I shouted.

"What?" she sighed, pulling up short and turning toward me.

"What's Hunt's cute little nickname for you?"

She shrugged her shoulders and answered. "Cutie pie, why?" at the same time as Hunter shouted, "Don't tell him."

"Why'd you tell him?" Hunter asked as he dragged her away.

"He asked," Ellie replied, sounding a little frustrated.

"Yeah, well now he's going to give me shit about it."

"But I am your cutie pie."

I rolled my eyes as my sister stretched up on her toes and kissed the life out of my best friend.

"Please, just go," I called to them. "Leave me to my damn misery."

Laughing and tangled in each other, they stumbled to the truck. When it finally rumbled away down the quiet street where the Jacksons lived, I turned back to the door. It felt impenetrable like the drawbridge of some damn castle and there was no way I was going to get through to the damsel.

However, I was never one to give up, and fisting my hand banged on it again.

.... *To be continued*

nikki ashton

Printed in Dunstable, United Kingdom

65230134R00167